Where Loyalty Lies

Rosemary Chapple

First published by Busybird Publishing 2022

Copyright © 2022 Rosemary Chapple

ISBN
Print: 978-1-922691-77-4
Ebook: 978-1-922691-78-1

Cover design: Busybird Publishing

Layout and typesetting: Busybird Publishing

Busybird Publishing
2/118 Para Road
Montmorency, Victoria
Australia 3094

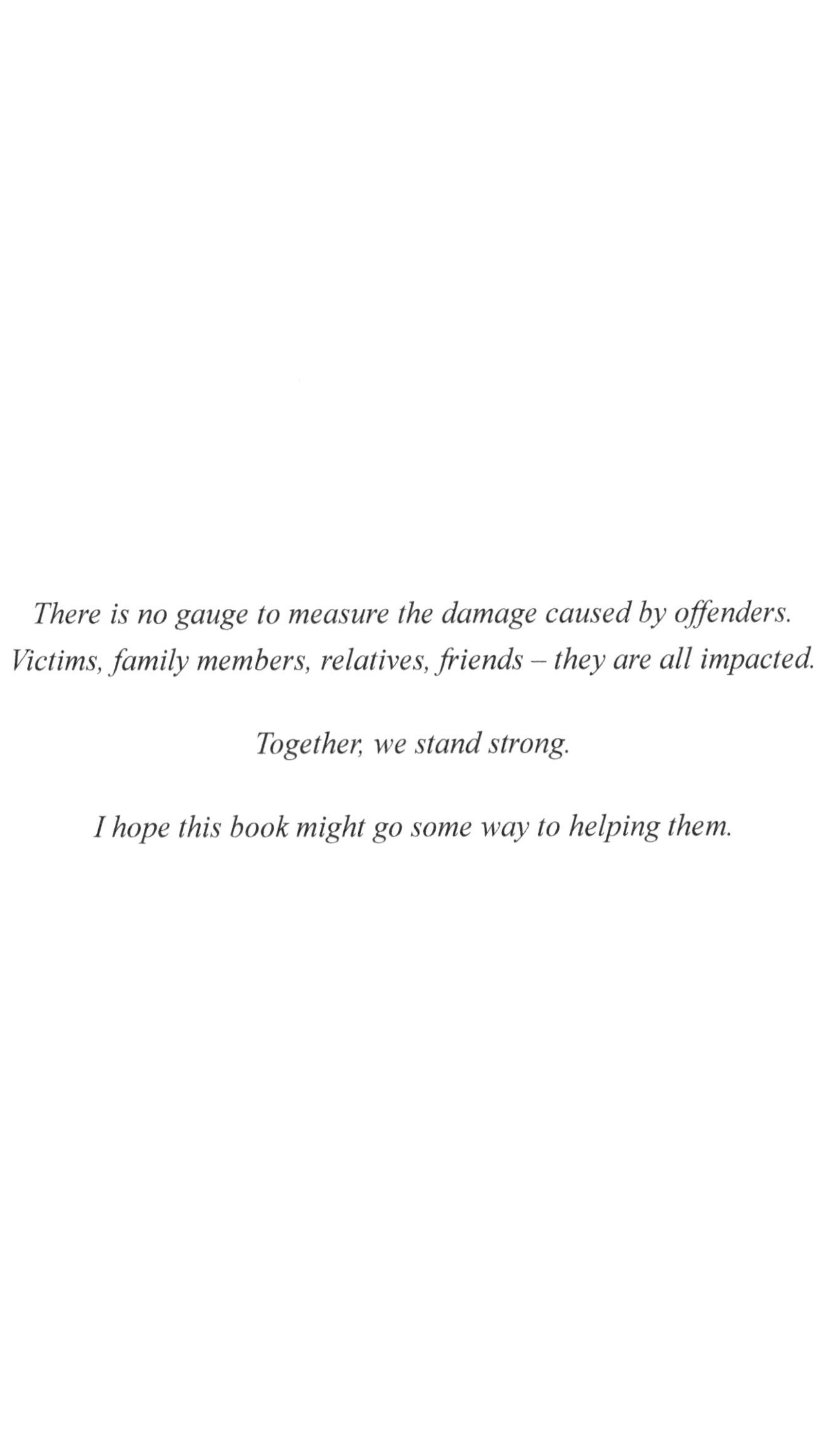

There is no gauge to measure the damage caused by offenders. Victims, family members, relatives, friends – they are all impacted.

Together, we stand strong.

I hope this book might go some way to helping them.

Chapter 1

Until the day they arrested my husband, my life had been normal – some might even say boring. I had passed Year 12, gone to TAFE, got a job, then met and married Anthony. No-one in my family had died, I had never been in a car accident. I was naïve, unequipped to deal with trauma.

He was my first real love, and I was his. When we met, it seemed it was meant to be. We courted, got engaged and had a wedding at our local Catholic church. Dad gave me away with a big smile across his broad Hungarian face. He'd probably thought he'd never get me off his hands, though he never said as much. Our family priest, Father Nick, conducted the ceremony, his kindly eyes resting on us as we made our vows.

After the reception, the guests saw us off, and we spent the night at a city hotel before we journeyed down the Peninsula to Sorrento for our honeymoon. Not exotic, but highly romantic. We walked on the beach hand in hand, slept late, and discovered each other's bodies.

I guess most girls dream at some time in their life of a white wedding, of romance, flowers, of a walk down the aisle and rose petals. And of course, they make the assumption that they'll have a happy future. We did.

Our first house was rented – tiny and dirty, but ours. I didn't unpack everything as I was waiting for Our House, so we could set up permanently. We lived out of boxes and loved it. A card table and two folding chairs made up our dining suite. Everything was exciting.

We talked, we played, we even worked together delivering pizzas for a while, trying to get some extra cash for the mortgage. We sat for hours after dinner (usually leftover pizza from our delivery rounds), figuring out how paying an extra twenty dollars this week could save us hundreds in the future. It didn't matter that we had few material possessions – we didn't need them. We always had each other.

About six months after the wedding, we moved into our own house (well, technically it was the bank's) in a quiet street. Most of the houses, like ours, were older and in need of a makeover. That was how we could afford to buy there. It was our nest, and I made everything just the way I wanted it – choosing drapes and matching bed linen, buying flowers we couldn't afford and arranging them in wedding present crystal vases, finding the right place for everything. For me, it was the start of my independence from my parents and a new direction. I loved to open my kitchen cupboards and see rows of matching jars, spices, flours, sugars, and to make sure the storage tubs were arranged in sizes. It annoyed the heck out of Anthony sometimes – he was a bit more of a slob – but the kitchen was my domain.

It was strange at first, changing all the documents and answering to a different name – but I loved playing wife. Every morning I was first out of bed to put the kettle on, unload the dishwasher, and make sure everything was neat and tidy for when he got up.

Before church on Sundays, I sometimes allowed him into the kitchen to make pancakes. I sat at the table and watched him. He always smiled when he caught me looking. He made a big fuss about getting the pan temperature just right, then a great drama about successfully flipping the pancakes. I took some photos of pancakes mid-air, and one of the photos sat proudly in a frame on the bench.

Life wasn't complicated. We were a simple couple with simple tastes, a little garden and a big mortgage. We worked, visited our families and tried for a baby. We went to the movies and walked on the beach. Friends and family visited for home-cooked meals. Our cousins gave us a rather complicated coffee machine as a wedding gift. Anthony was the only one who could make the coffee just right in it.

We didn't want pets to tie us down, so we got some goldfish. I decided the rude things people said about them were nonsense. Our fish knew us and always had a friendly wave of the tail when we greeted them.

On the balcony, I planted a container of Tom Thumb tomatoes. I grew parsley and chives in big ceramic pots. A roster on the fridge showed whose turn it was to move the pots each day to get the sun as the fence overshadowed the garden. I loved to pick my herbs and tomatoes fresh for a salad while he grilled steak on the barbeque. We ate outside when the weather was nice.

After dinner we sat at our respective computers to chat online, check Facebook, blog or Twitter. Sometimes we even chatted online with each other while sitting in different rooms.

"Hi Hon!"

"What's up Big Bear?"

"Cup of tea?"

"Are you offering?"

"Meet you in the kitchen in five minutes. Hope there's some chocolate biscuits left."

I never told my parents this. The idea of conducting any part of a relationship electronically was like something out of Star Trek for them – let alone when you were both in the same house! He was a real tech-nerd, always up with the latest. He tried to show me, but I found it boring.

I was usually in bed first while he kept working. When I was tucked up in bed I called out to him, and eventually he joined me, leaning over to kiss me, his moustache bristling. Sometimes I sent him for a shower before bed – he sweated heavily, and body odour was occasionally a problem. He claimed I snored, I claimed he did, and we often teased each other about it.

On weekday breakfast duty, I lined the cutlery up neatly for cereal and toast. Blue striped mugs stood next to the mats; the coffee plunger was ready for freshly boiled water. Bread and cheese were sliced and laid on a plate – my Hungarian parents had instilled in me this breakfast tradition.

I opened the curtains and checked the rapid progress of the house being built over the road. Each day I looked at it carefully, assessing the impact the two-storey building might have on our modest house. The one over the road had been a simple one storey dwelling being turned into a monster which threatened to cut the sun from our tiny front garden, planted with lavender bushes and daisies, carefully nurtured by me through drought and hail. One neighbour was a single man who came and went at strange hours of the night. We never spoke to him. The other side was an empty house.

For over eighteen months, we lived as a happy, newly-wed couple, in love with each other and life.

The day it all started was no different than normal. I slipped out of bed just before six. He knew I had gone because he grunted. I leaned over and kissed him. "Don't get up just yet. I'll call when the coffee's ready."

He smiled. "OK, honey."

We didn't need to leave for work till half past seven – he to manage the Recreation Centre and me to the brokers in the city, where I had worked as a clerk since I finished my TAFE course. Still in my pjs, I unhooked my dressing robe from the back of the bedroom door, pulled it on and padded into the kitchen. I filled the kettle, flicked the radio on, then slid the curtains open. Through the window, I could see our quiet little street was alive with action.

"Hon, something's up. Come and look. The cops are here! It looks like a raid!"

He joined me, wearing only his Donald Duck boxers, hairy chest showing erect nipples, face badly needing a shave. We peered into the street. Three police cars had pulled up, slewed halfway across the street, one with its lights flashing.

I turned to Anthony. "Hey, I bet it's the man next door! I always suspected him of drug dealing!" We giggled at the thought of the surly man getting his just desserts.

Six policemen and one woman, all in uniform, wearing flak jackets, guns in holsters at their hips, hauled themselves from the cars. Synchronised, they put their hats on and had a brief pow-wow in the street, then headed off purposefully. But they didn't go to the neighbour's. Instead, they came to our front door. Four of them trooped up the path; the other two disappeared down the side. The doorbell rang, sounding harsh and aggressive. I think the police officer just kept his finger on it. We looked at each other, my raised eyebrows mirroring his. Anthony gestured to answer the door and went to drag on jeans and t-shirt.

I opened the front door part way, ready to redirect them to the correct address, but they piled in, having already pulled the screen door open. The first one thrust a paper into my hands.

"Mrs Grey? Search warrant for this address. Please sit at the table. Now."

Anthony joined me in the kitchen, still buckling the belt on his jeans. The police woman sat with us, and I raised my hands at my husband, asking in mime, "What's going on?" He shook his head, brow furrowed.

"What's going on? Why are you here?" I expected at any moment that they would realise they were in the wrong house and apologise. "What are you looking for?"

"It's all in the warrant, ma'am. We're looking for electronics." The woman sitting with us pointed at the paper, but I couldn't concentrate on reading. I wanted answers. I watched in horror as they invaded our privacy and our lives.

"Do something!" I hissed to Anthony.

"What do you expect me to do?" He looked as confused as I felt.

Breakfast dishes were pushed aside as policemen came and went, showing each other pieces of paper, putting piles of our letters and bills on the table, sorting through them and returning them to the drawer.

One of them brought out two black zip-packs containing our laptops. "We'll be taking these. I'll give you a receipt for them." I went to speak, but the policewoman raised her hand to stop me.

I heard the ping of the computer as they turned on the power, then someone yelled, "What's the password?"

I called out, "Why?" but no answer was forthcoming, just another request – more a demand this time. Anthony remained silent, so I gave it. Four or five of the big men crowded into the kitchen and I could hear murmuring. I made a face at my husband, and he just kept shrugging his shoulders, mouthing, "No idea, hon."

One of the police staggered out with the desktop computer, which had been wrapped in plastic. They took it outside. The man nodded at us as he went past. "You'll get a receipt for this, too." Next went the photo albums, pulled from the bottom shelf of the bookcase. They took our wedding album, too, and the digital photo frame. I went numb. None of this made sense. I wanted to make coffee, but I thought I wasn't allowed to move. My heart was racing, and I noticed my fists were clenched in front of me.

Books were rifled through, then the magazines on the table. The DVDs and videos were boxed up, likewise our mobile phones. They played the answering machine, but there were no messages. I would have told them that if they had asked.

"Have you any more computers in the house? Phones?" On the verge of saying no, I remembered the old Atari in the garage, the one we used to play games on. They made their way outside and returned with the plastic-wrapped machine. Anthony still said nothing.

I don't know how long the search lasted. It seemed like hours. I gave a fleeting thought to phoning my workplace, but the policewoman stared at me and I couldn't move from the chair. This misunderstanding, this invasion, it would all go away and things would be back to normal. Maybe I hadn't actually woken up and this was a dream. We must have done something really bad. I thought frantically about last year's tax return, trying to remember if I had submitted it. That was the most likely explanation – *the Tax Department on a witch-hunt* I thought with a smile, but kept it to myself. But then it didn't seem funny at all.

Finally, they finished. They brought in more boxes and loaded things into them, then took the boxes out. They put papers in front of Anthony and he signed them without reading – I think it was a list of the things they were taking. Two of the men and our woman left, leaving the plain clothes Sergeant and two other policemen. The Sergeant sat down at the table with us.

"My name is Alex Price. I'm the Sergeant in charge of this investigation."

The two other policemen loomed behind.

"At last!" I breathed an inward sigh of relief. "He's come to admit the mistake and talk about how it happened." I almost smiled at him. He seemed to be our saviour, the man who would make sense of things. Despite the procession of boxes and computers they took, I was sure he would now apologise and arrange to fix the mistake.

He spoke, his voice low and calm. "Thank you for your patience, Mr and Mrs Grey. Anthony Grey, I am arresting you for possession of child pornography. You are not obliged to say anything, but anything you do or say will be taken down and may be used in evidence. Do you understand?"

As the words left his mouth, the two policemen almost lifted Anthony to his feet, pulled his hands behind his back. I saw the glint of handcuffs and heard the clicking as they closed. It sounded so loud, echoing through the room.

I looked at the Sergeant, speechless and disbelieving. "What? What did you say?"

The policeman raised his eyebrows and nodded in Anthony's direction. I know Anthony. I could see he was stunned. The bristle on his cheeks and chin stood out against the sudden paleness of his face. His eyes were wide and his mouth had dropped open.

"Anthony! Tell them you didn't do this! It's ridiculous."

"You'll need to come with us, Sir." (How ridiculous to call someone you've just arrested for child porn 'Sir'!) "Mrs Grey, you might wish to follow us, and I advise you to call a solicitor. We are going to St Kilda Rd Police Headquarters. I can give you a moment to dress if you wish."

I heard the words, but they had no meaning. I knew I had to be there with Anthony, to help him sort this out and bring him home. I went straight into Coping Mode. Reality had been suspended. I blinked to clear my vision and took a deep breath.

"Please wait a moment." I ran into the bedroom and grabbed the clothes I had been wearing the previous day. I was back within a minute. My hands were shaking, and I was sweating.

They were waiting by the front door. Anthony was wriggling his shoulders, trying to get a degree of comfort with his hands tightly cuffed. One of the policemen had his hand on Anthony's shoulder. Anthony's face was still white under his slightly tanned skin and whiskers.

My car keys hung on a rack, and I almost pulled the whole thing off the wall.

"I can call a solicitor from the police station?" The words sounded unreal even as they left my mouth. Solicitor? We didn't have one. Police station? Never go there. How then, could I have got up this morning to make coffee and now be talking about ringing a lawyer – and for Anthony, my husband?

The Sergeant nodded. "We can give you a list of lawyers if you don't have one."

We left the house, the police ahead of me, marching Anthony between them with the Sergeant bringing up the rear. I watched as they opened the back door of one of the police cars and protected Anthony's head as he sat, then swivelled his legs in. The car door slammed. One of the police sat in the back seat next to Anthony, while the other got in the driver's side. I could see Anthony looking at me, eyes wide.

The Sergeant touched my arm. "I understand that this is a shock," he said. "They'll need to take your husband through some processes before you can see him. Follow my car, and I'll get you into the police car park. You might be there for a while and there's no parking in the street. Are you OK to drive?" He was so nice. I felt he understood. "If you get lost, just go to the St Kilda Rd Police Station – do you know where it is?" I nodded. We had driven past the complex several times. "Park at the front and come in and ask for me. I will make sure your car isn't towed away."

He handed me a business card, which I held numbly in shaking fingers. He gently took it out of my hand and dropped it into my handbag, which was hanging open on my arm by just one handle. "Are you sure you're OK to drive?"

I was watching the other car pull away, carrying my husband. "Oh yes. I'm fine," I lied. He knew I lied, but he was probably thinking of all he had to do. I was thinking of the breakfast we hadn't had, the life we had lost.

I hopped in the car and followed them to the station. St Kilda Rd Police Station was just out of the Melbourne CBD, about 16 kilometres from where we lived in Highett. I was grateful that the police car was not flashing its lights and playing the siren. That would have been embarrassing, even though no-one knew I was following the car.

As we neared the city and traffic got heavier, cars pulled in between us, but I saw the police vehicle as it bobbed and weaved ahead of me.

By the time I turned into the police complex, the Sergeant had the entrance gate open for me. He motioned me through and I parked, terrified of hitting a police car (as if a traffic violation is worse than child pornography). As I clicked the central locking, I noticed the time – half past seven. We should both be leaving for work. Today was not turning out to be a normal day.

Chapter 2

I dropped the car keys twice before I managed to get them into my bag. The policeman waited patiently, then walked me to the back entrance. I had to remember that he was the enemy, and his niceness might be a cloak covering insincerity – but at the moment I held on to him for sanity.

He used a card on a lanyard around his neck to wave at some security machine, which buzzed the door open. There were long corridors, 'Do Not Enter' signs and interview rooms with lights over the top of them.

Eventually we reached a busy foyer. I saw people in uniform and thought they were staring at me. Maybe they were. The Sergeant opened a door off the main reception. "I'll get our receptionist to bring you a coffee. How do you take it?"

I sat on one of the hard plastic chairs. "Milk and I think two sugars, please." Actually, I don't have sugar at all in my coffee. I stared blankly at the wall opposite, expecting at any moment to find myself back home, waking from a nightmare. The girl brought in a pale brown liquid in a plastic cup and gave me a weak smile as she placed it on the table with a napkin and a biscuit.

Half the wall was a mirror, and I amused myself by thinking this was a TV show, with the occupant of the room observed from behind a one-way mirror. I smiled, but in the reflection it looked more like a grimace. Inspiration hit me. Maybe this was a new 'reality' show! (Although I had never thought there was anything remotely real about them.) Maybe it was a psychological test, only valid if the participants knew nothing! Maybe Anthony had set it up as a joke! Maybe right now there was a cameraman behind the screen, and some big name star poised outside the door to come in and catch my expression of total amazement as he revealed the surprise. But as quickly as the excitement of the possibility gripped me, it left, leaving me in despair. Bile rose in my throat. A gripping pain in my stomach squeezed my body as my head pounded. The room became blurry, and instinctively I put my head down, but that just increased the hammering.

I stood up, but too quickly. The cup still full of coffee went flying to the floor, soaking the sugar-covered biscuit which rested on the napkin. I looked up. The walls were closing in on me and I felt nauseous.

The Sergeant rescued me. Maybe he had been watching. He brought a young uniformed female constable with him. "Let's get some fresh air."

The constable helped me stand, her arm half way round my waist. It was the only way I could walk. The automatic doors hissed open, and we were facing St Kilda Road. The air felt cleaner, less contaminated despite the peak hour traffic, and I gulped it in.

"Steady." They walked me to a smoker's bench. The stench of dead cigarettes rose from the disposal bin next to the chair and added to my bilious feeling. The Sergeant sat next to me and the woman stood behind the bench.

"Do you smoke?" I shook my head. "Sit down, anyway."

The normality of the traffic calmed me. A tram trundled past, dinging its bell to hurry cars out of the way. Traffic roared as the lights changed. It amazed me that people were going about their lives as if nothing had happened. Ordinary people wearing suits and carrying briefcases walked past, talking into their mobiles and sipping take away coffee. They had got up this morning, just like me.

A tram bell clanged violently. Car horns tooted and brakes screeched. There was a tinny sound of metal on metal. The Sergeant looked up. "Another collision. Well, that's a problem for Traffic Branch to solve."

After a while, I could relax my shoulders, and felt more under control. It seemed perfectly normal to be sitting there with police officers surrounding me.

He nodded. "OK. Feeling better? Shall we go back? Have you rung for a solicitor? Mr Grey wants one, so we can't interview him yet."

I shook my head. "Sorry. I was busy knocking the coffee over." Somehow I found a fragment of my customary humour.

The doors hissed open, and he used his magic card to get back into my waiting chamber. "I'll get some fresh coffee." He nodded to the woman, who disappeared. "Here's the list of solicitors people often use. Just press any of the green lights on this phone. You'll get a line, then dial the number." I nodded. Simple instructions were good. He picked up the fallen cup, shoved the napkin and its soggy contents into it, then quietly left the room.

I scanned the plastic-covered list, wondering how many greasy fingers had handled it before me – maybe criminals, maybe relatives like me, all in a state of shock. One name on the list – Szili – sprang out at me. It was a Hungarian name. I felt disproportionally comforted by the familiar name and felt that this solicitor might understand. I dialled the number.

"Hello, this is Mr Szili speaking. Can I help you?" I was surprised that Mr Szili himself answered and glad I didn't have to wait for a list of options. I imagined the recorded message for this situation.

"Press 1 if your husband has committed murder. Press 2 if your husband has raped someone. Press 3 if he is a pedophile."

"I need a lawyer. My husband has…" It was so hard to say. "My husband has… been arrested."

He must get many calls like this, and he replied readily, "Of course. I can come now. Please tell me your names, what he has been charged with and which police station you are at." He was easy to talk to, and I managed to say the words "child pornography" without too much difficulty, although it still wasn't real.

The Sergeant appeared with another cup and fished my mobile out of his pocket. "Here's your phone. We've finished with it. We still have the rest of your property though." My phone felt vaguely slimy, as though it had been brushed with something.

"Thank you. The solicitor is on his way. It's Mr Szili." Suddenly I remembered work. I hadn't let them know. They would be expecting me. "Can I make some other calls?"

He nodded. "As many as you want. I'll come back in a few minutes and let you know what's happening."

I rang my work and left a message, though probably no-one had missed me yet, anyway. They would have seen my empty desk and assumed I was away. At the Recreation Centre where Anthony worked, I spoke to a receptionist who didn't seem to care whether or not he was coming in. I didn't know any of the people at his work – they were constantly changing. He was one of the few who had stayed over two years. He'd worked in recreation management for as long as I had known him.

It was only half-past eight, less than three hours since the raid. How long do life-changing experiences take? How long before my life reverted to what it had been? There was nothing to do but wait. I was grateful that my mind was blank. In my head, I knew there had been a raid and Anthony had been arrested. I knew the charges were to do with child pornography. But in my heart, I was in no way accepting the turn of events.

I considered getting up and peering through the mirror window, but before I could move the door opened and the Sergeant Price came in. He sat down and gave me a sympathetic smile.

"We are ready to interview Mr Grey when the solicitor arrives. I'm afraid you can't be present, but you are welcome to wait here. It could be some time. Or we can ring you when we are finished and tell you what's happening."

As he spoke, the panic started up again. This didn't sound as though they were admitting to a mistake. But they must! Thoughts crowded my mind. Should I ask him what all this was about? I didn't really want to know, but I had to. Should I ask if it is possible there was a mistake? What if he said no, no mistake? Should I stay or go? Maybe I could just go to work and pretend it hasn't happened? I shook my head as if that might clear the thoughts.

Sergeant Price leaned forward. "Mrs Grey." I pulled my wits together and focused on his face, giving a grunt in assent. "Mrs Grey. We are investigating your husband's part in a child pornography ring, which was conducted through the internet. These are Commonwealth offences, so that's why the Federal Police and myself are involved. We have arrested him because he was accessing a site we have been monitoring. We have been waiting for the service provider to give us your details. That is how we got your address and why we raided your home this morning."

He sat back. I don't think I moved – I didn't think I could. But I recall seeing his tie, and thinking how brightly it was coloured. Maybe my eyes fell from his face. Maybe I couldn't meet his gaze.

"I should also tell you, Mrs Grey, that we have found some photographic images of children at your house. My officers will need to interview you as well, though you are not a person of interest at this stage."

I do know I reacted to that. "I should think not! I'm not a 'person of interest' to anyone! And what do you mean, photographs? I am sure there's a mistake somewhere. This will be cleared up, and the sooner the better." It sounded hollow, even to me.

"You are entitled to speak to a lawyer before the interview. Do you wish to? If not, then we could run your interview while the solicitor is speaking with your husband."

"Do I need a lawyer?"

"You don't. You are free to go, to stop the interview at any time. You are not under arrest. The officers who interview you will make that clear."

"Then let's get it over with. But I'd better wait for the lawyer first. He'll need to see Anthony."

Sergeant Price stood up. "Of course. He should be here…" As he spoke, the door opened and a portly man, shorter than the Sergeant by about six inches, was shown in to the room.

"Mrs Grey? I am Mr Szili from Szili, Szili and Kiss."

Sergeant Price nodded at the solicitor and left the room. The ridiculous name of the law firm struck me at the time, but only as an incidental. Our discussion didn't take long. I knew nothing. I gave him our details, and told him what had happened, and asked whether he thought I should do the interview.

"It's up to you, Mrs Grey, but sooner or later they will want to talk to you. They will want to check all sorts of things that have gone on in your lives. It doesn't seem such a silly idea to get it over with now."

I realised later that I should have asked about money.

Chapter 3

Mr Szili left to speak with Anthony, and I followed Sergeant Price down the corridor to an interview room. I was alarmed when he turned to leave and two strange policemen came in. The Sergeant must have seen my face, and he came back into the room.

"Mrs Grey, this is Sergeant Porter and Constable Nguyen. They will interview you. It's OK." Then he turned to them. "I'll be in Room 2."

As the heavy door swung shut, I felt the tiny room closing in. Constable Nguyen escorted me to a chair behind the desk, furthest away from the door. I gave a little gulp and told myself not to be stupid. The constable asked if I was alright, while the sergeant called to someone in the main office to bring some water.

I wasn't used to being looked at by two huge uniformed men. The sergeant was especially tall and had quite a stomach on him. He seemed to block the doorway. The constable was much shorter, but with the flak jacket on he seemed bulky.

I hadn't been in a police interview room before. It was grotty and hot and smelt of sweat and disinfectant. The table had carved into the top the word "PIGS", which I assumed referred to the police. The letters were all smudged and unclear. The policemen didn't seem to notice the smell – they were used to it, I guess.

They wheeled in a trolley and started plugging in a recording machine. The trolley blocked the tiny aisle between the desk and the door. I asked them why they were recording me. They said they always recorded interviews, that I wasn't under suspicion, and that I could leave at any time. It didn't make me feel any better.

There seemed to be a lot to do before we started. There were three DVDs, all different colours and wrapped in plastic. The police busily wrote something on each and inserted them into the machine. To my horror, a picture of me appeared in a little window on the machine. I looked dreadful, and didn't want to be on camera.

"Don't worry, Mrs Grey. The picture disappears after about ten seconds, but the discs will still be recording. At the end, the machine will play back a few seconds, just to ensure it recorded correctly. And you will get a copy of the DVD recording before you leave."

At the start of the interview, the police stated their names and I had to state mine. They informed me of my rights and said I could call someone or ring a lawyer. Finally, they showed me a watch and asked me if I agreed with them on the time. I couldn't imagine why this was necessary and what would happen if I said I didn't agree, but I wasn't feeling strong enough to make even a little joke of this sort.

Sergeant Porter asked most of the questions. He started by summarising what had happened, and I winced as he outlined the raid, the arrest and bringing Anthony to the police station. Then he looked directly at me.

"I would now like to ask you some questions about your husband. Did you have any knowledge of Mr Grey's involvement in child pornography?"

"No," I spoke firmly, indignant that they could even think such a thing. "I still believe you've made a mistake."

"Did he ever bring young boys to your home?"

"No." I pulled a face and spoke more definitely. "No!"

"Have you ever had boys stay at your house?"

"No." My answer was instinctive, but then I thought of how we had hosted some homestay students from an international exchange group. Anthony said he wanted boys because he didn't understand girls. He only had a brother. We had joked about what he would do if we had a baby girl. Should I tell the police about the boys? No, not relevant. But they must have been alerted by something I did.

"You hesitated, Mrs Grey. Have you remembered something? It's better to tell us now." (Better for whom? Them or us?)

I didn't answer, and that confirmed for them that there was something. They just kept picking away. Finally, I gave in. "We had two boys, at different times last year, for a foreign exchange program. We had an interview and a police check. The coordinator visited our home. They said we were an ideal family, just what they were looking for. The boys were with us for three weeks. One was in June and the other in October."

"And what happened? Why did you not want to tell us this, if you had no concerns?"

"It's just that…" Oh God, this was hard. "Anthony was often alone with the boys. He took them out to the footy, to the beach, to the swimming group he ran through work…" I stopped again. Swimming group! My God. Was it possible? I felt a bubble in my throat and bile rose in my mouth. I clamped it tight shut. The taste was horrible.

They saw something was wrong and asked if I needed a break. I nodded without speaking.

"Interview suspended." They pressed the pause button and opened the door. A ladies' toilet was directly opposite, and I was able to spit out the vomit and wash my mouth out. The taste remained. I scrambled in my handbag for some mints. The paper wrapping had got all fuzzy, and bits of fluff had attached themselves to the mint, but I didn't care. I crammed the chewy tablet into my mouth and swished it round. My tongue kept finding little half-digested pieces of food lodged between my teeth and gums, and pieces of vomit I hadn't got rid of.

When we resumed the interview, they started just where we had left off. They hadn't forgotten. "You were telling us about the overseas boys?"

"Look, they were fine. They never said anything. They still email and send… send us… photos."

"What age were they?"

"Eleven and twelve."

"And the swimming group?"

"What about it?"

"Are you aware of anything that might have happened there?'

I shook my head, but they said I had to speak out loud for the tape. "No. Nothing."

"What about your husband's workplace?"

"I don't know anything about it."

"Have you ever seen images on your husband's computer that you have felt uncomfortable about?"

"No."

"Have you got any images of children on your computer?"

"No!" I was indignant. "Of course not! You can look!"

"Thank you. We will."

The questions went on and on. Was he ever late home from work? Did he ever go out without saying where he was going? Was he ever late home unexpectedly? If so, did he give you an explanation? Did you believe the explanation? Where else had he worked? What relatives did he have? Did he ever turn the computer screen off when you came into the room? Did he get angry if you looked in his drawers? Did he have a lot of backup discs or hard drives? Did he make overseas phone calls?

I answered them all, despite wanting to say how impertinent they were, but realising that if I hesitated or refused to answer it was worse than being straightforward.

Finally, they said they were nearly done. "Just a few more questions, then we're finished. Can I get you a cup of coffee?" I nodded wearily, and asked for the toilet as well.

"Interview suspended at 12.05." He stopped the tape.

Twelve? Midday? Was it only six hours since our home had been invaded and the nightmare had started?

When I returned, my coffee was waiting with a sandwich. The filling was indistinguishable, but it was food and I ate quickly, regretting it immediately as nausea returned. I shut my eyes and waited for relative calm to help me settle.

The police came back and restarted the tape. I felt more used to the process now. Someone had brought in a portable fan and the air was cooler, though the odour was now circulated to every corner instead of lingering around the sweaty armpits of the policemen.

"Thank you, Mrs Grey. I am going to ask you some questions which are quite personal. Remember, you are still free to leave at any time, although we do appreciate your co-operation. Do you understand?"

I think I nodded, because they told me again to speak up for the tape. "Yes, I understand." My voice sounded loud in the tiny room.

"Do you sleep together?"

"What do you mean? Of course we sleep together! We're husband and wife. We've only been married two years. We want a family."

"Thank you. And would you consider your sexual relations normal?"

"Normal? In what way? What do you mean?"

"Does your husband ask you to engage in any practices which make you feel uncomfortable? Any bondage, fantasy play? Anything unusual?"

I grimaced. "No. And I don't want to answer those sorts of questions. We just have a straightforward love life. OK? We have sex

– just normal, everyday common sex! Will that do?"

"Just one more thing. Did your husband ever want to film you having sex? Or ask you to watch erotic movies before, during or after sex?"

I turned my head away. My good intentions about answering questions honestly disappeared.

"I don't want to answer any more questions."

There was a pause. It was long enough to make me want to say something. But I didn't.

"Then thank you very much for your co-operation. Interview terminated at 12.23." They stopped the machine. "I'll take you back to the waiting room and find out what's happening with your husband."

"Can I see him?"

"Not until the interview has finished. I'll go and check. Steven will take you back to reception."

Steven was young and probably shocked by hearing about sex, though maybe he was more shocked that we didn't do anything kinky. Young people probably knew more than we had when I was at school – and that was only about twelve years ago.

He scanned his card to get entry to my old reception room and left me with just a nod.

I sat at the desk and looked blankly at the mirror window. How odd it was to be in this room when I should have been at work. I remember looking at the mirror, aware of nothing until a teardrop fell on my hand, followed by another, and yet another brought my mind back to the room.

The tears kept coming. My eyes felt hot. I sat still and let them fall. I had a vision of the tears gathering under my hands then dripping away onto the floor, damming up like a swimming pool, until the police opened the door to get me, then being washed away like a flood.

With another wave of pain, I realised that no-one else knew what had happened. My God! How am I going to tell people? My parents, his parents, my relatives, our friends, our workplaces, everyone – what would they say? How would I find the words? What if it hit the papers and TV? Please God, please let this be a mistake, then no-one need ever know.

I took some quick gasps of breath, which made me lightheaded. The door opened and young Steven came in with yet another coffee and a box of tissues. He silently placed them on the table and departed. I pulled out a tissue and held it against my eyes, drying them without rubbing, then placed the tissue on the table where it mopped up the wet patch. As though on cue, Sergeant Price came in.

"We're nearly finished, Mrs Grey. Your husband has made a number of admissions to us, and we will be charging him with several offences. Do you understand what this means?"

I looked at him. Admissions. That meant… I shut my eyes tightly. When I opened them, he was still there, sitting opposite me, calm, relaxed and waiting.

"No, I don't understand. I mean, I know what the words mean, but what does it mean for Anthony? Can we go home now?" Even as I spoke, something inside me was aware that Anthony was in big trouble. However unreal, this was actually happening, and I couldn't control it.

"It means that your husband has admitted he has acquired and used child pornography, among other things. We are charging him with several offences. We have more investigation to do and other charges may follow. He will go to court this afternoon, and a magistrate will set bail."

I don't remember how I got from the reception area to the interview room to see Anthony. I don't know what was in my head except that I still believed firmly, honestly, that he couldn't have done this. He wouldn't have. Together we would work it out, whatever the cost, with Mr Szili's help.

We were left alone. The room was beige, tiny and, like every room I had been in that day, it stank of body odour. As they closed the door, I saw a policeman standing outside. Was it to keep Anthony in? Surely not. This was my husband. No need to guard him! The idea seemed ludicrous.

I looked at him. He started speaking. "I'm sorry, hon. Really sorry. I just didn't think. It's been so long…" He tailed off, frowning. Something on my face must have told him my mind was elsewhere.

"Anthony, it's OK. I know you didn't do this. I know there's been an awful mistake somewhere and we have to get it fixed up. You have to be patient, and Mr Szili and I will do all the hard work to get this finished with." I smiled at him – a calm, confident smile to help him relax and smile back at me, like he had so often before.

"I don't think you understand, hon." He pushed his hair back from his forehead impatiently. "I had these pictures on my computer, from years back. I'd forgotten they were there. It was ages ago, before we even met. You know what computers are like – you just file things, and they hang around. I thought it was all deleted, anyway. It's stuff from when I was a kid."

"That's what I mean! Don't worry! They said they are going to court for bail, and then we can go home and start to work out what to do, OK?"

But he didn't relax. He pressed his lips tightly together and looked down. "Gee, hon, I don't know if they told you. It's quite bad. They explained that there are some really strict laws about this stuff. They said…" he stopped and rested his head in his hands. "They said… I might go to jail."

I felt faint, sick, disbelieving, scared, angry, anxious – you could pick almost any emotion you liked and I probably felt it. We were a law-abiding, normal, happy couple who had never been arrested, never been to a police station, in a police car, to a court – and today we had experienced them all.

"Prison? No way. Just for having some photos? You must have misunderstood them."

He shook his head. "They said that the law is really tough, and that courts take it seriously. They said the maximum I could get is ten years."

The words fell into the silence that lay between us. If jail itself was inconceivable, then how much more inconceivable could ten years of jail be? In ten years we would have a family, and Anthony would have been promoted to manager. I'd be helping in the kids' school canteen. I looked up at Anthony, sitting opposite, now gazing at me.

"Honey? Can you forgive me? I can't ask that you stand by me. I have to do this on my own. We have been so happy together that my old life didn't matter anymore. I just shoved it in a corner of my mind and took every blessed day with you as it came. I believed, and still believe, that God put you there for me. You are my reason for living. I treasure you. And so I have to let you go and see this through by myself. I can do it, honey, I have to. It's right that I should."

He leaned across the table and took my hand. I let it lie limply in his. I heard the words, but they meant nothing. He seemed to be taking this really calmly, though his eyes were fixed on mine. I had lived with this man for nearly two years. We had courted for eighteen months. Before marriage, we had shared physical and intellectual intimacies. Afterwards, we shared sexual intimacy. Never, ever had it crossed my mind that there was something in him I had not seen. There couldn't be. I knew him.

The calmness must be shock. We were both in shock. It does strange things.

I patted his hand. "It'll be OK. I'll make sure of that. I love you. We are married. We stick together on this. Regardless of what they say, we stick together. OK?"

The immediate joy on his face was my reward. Here was the man, my lover, my friend, to whom I had committed my life. "For better, for worse." Those were the words in the marriage ceremony, and that was what we would abide by. God would reward me. I felt strong, triumphant.

The policemen came in and stood by Anthony. "We need to go to court, Mrs Grey. It's the Melbourne Magistrates'. You'll be coming?"

I nodded. "Of course. But I might catch the tram, if it's OK to leave my car."

And so the arrangements were made. Thoughts of informing our relatives flashed across my mind, but I let them go. One thing at a time.

I kissed Anthony, lingering with my arms around him for as long as I dared, until one of the policemen cleared his throat. I drew back. "See you, darling." I watched as they took him out. He looked back over his shoulder and gave me a crooked smile. I felt the warmth of his love and the comfort of our mutual understanding.

I picked up my bag and, feeling better than at any other time since the raid, I went out the main door.

Chapter 4

The lunch hour rush was nearly over, but a tram came along within a minute. The sense of unreality was ever present, but I kept it under control by distracting myself with watching the scenery and the people around me. Most people were wearing earphones or playing on their phones, and I thought how we all had become less social.

I changed trams in the city and got off at the corner where the County and Magistrates' Courts were located. The only other time I had been there was on a City Open Day held last year, and then we just walked past. I don't recall having any sense of anticipation that I would go up those steps in less than twelve months to face an unimaginable situation.

There was a television crew waiting at the wheelchair ramp, eagerly looking up as people came out. Someone famous must have been in court. I never gave a thought that the crews might have been there for Anthony. As it happened, they were waiting for some footballer or other who was charged with assault. What a happy alternative.

I put my bag on the security conveyor belt and walked through the detection door. Nothing went off, so no-one had to wave a wand over my body. Such a lot of procedures to go through – I felt like I was at an airport, which would have been preferable.

Directly ahead of me was a reception desk. A group of young people loitered around a drink machine. Next to them, a woman with a screaming baby in a pram was trying to extract a bottle from a large cloth bag. Her pierced lip and tattooed arms made me think she was here because of something she had done, not to support someone. A young couple sat hand in hand on a bench. They didn't look like master criminals. Two security guards with guns in their belts stood on either side of the reception desk. They glared at people as they entered. One of them moved closer to the youths at the drink machine.

I felt much better now that I was doing something. I was involved in the process and we were going to make it. It was going to be alright. However, it was a challenge to ask the woman at the front desk where to go. I tried to sound as though this was something one did every day. "Bail hearing? Could you tell me which court? Grey, Anthony Grey."

She wasn't interested in why I was there. She didn't ask if I was his wife, if this was a sudden and unexpected thing. She didn't care if our lives had been turned upside down. For her, this was the norm. She consulted the screen in front of her.

"Court 8, third floor. Lift over there, or stairs behind me."

I thanked her and took the stairs. It put off the moment a little longer, and gave me a chance to compose myself. The opening of a lift door and suddenly Being There would be more difficult than seeing ahead up the open staircase.

On each landing I stopped for a breath. As I climbed the last few steps, I saw a foyer, padded seats, a few people sitting looking blankly at walls, and some potted plastic plants.

The three courts were all numbered, and I went to Court 8. On the left, before the main doors, was a little room labelled "Witnesses." The door was partly open. Sergeant Price was there with a woman, who looked to be in her twenties and wearing a tight skirt and coat with high heels. A couple of men in suits hovered, frowning over some papers. They stopped their earnest conversation when they saw me, and Sergeant Price came over.

"Come and sit down, Mrs Grey. I need to talk to you for a moment." Something in his expression made my stomach fall as though I was in a fast lift. "The woman in the room is Julia Obermeyer, from the Office of Public Prosecutions. She tells me they want to remand Mr Grey."

"What does that mean?" He held my gaze, and I felt tears starting. I blinked furiously, and they subsided.

"It means that, if the Magistrate agrees, Mr Grey stays in custody until the trial, which could be months away. Is your solicitor coming to court today?"

Looking back, as I write this I realise how numb I must have been, not to have reacted to the revelation that Anthony might be in prison and not at home with me. So I responded to the question about the solicitor.

"Mr Szili should be on his way. He went to his office first."

"Then please tell him about this. I will try to get the case delayed until he can talk with Ms Obermeyer."

"But can't you do something? You said we would go to court and get bail! Can't you explain to Ms Whatever that he just needs to be at home?"

He shook his head. "That's out of my hands now. I'm sorry."

This was going from worse to even worse. The lift went 'ping' and Mr Szili stepped out, wiping a crumb from his suit jacket. He had stopped for lunch, something I hadn't even considered.

I almost ran towards him. "You have to talk to someone called Julia – they want to put him in prison. The sergeant came and told me you have to talk to them. Please, just get him out!" I continued to babble, and Mr Szili gently detached my arm from his.

"Where is she?" Before I could answer he saw her, and left me standing, crying. People were looking at me, but I didn't care. My mobile rang, but I ignored it.

I watched their animated conversation through the tears. Julia shook her head. Mr Szili used a lot of hand gestures, including pointing at me. He came back to me and asked some questions about the house, our bank balance, loans, cars, passports, etc. I couldn't think to answer most of them. My head was like cotton wool. Then he went back to the woman, but still she shook her head. She was younger than me, but she had so much power. Mr Szili opened his briefcase, took out a volume and opened it to an orange bookmark, pointing out something on the page. Julia refused to look at it, and just opened the courtroom door and marched in, followed by the suits.

Sergeant Price glanced at me, raised his eyebrows, then followed the others into the court.

Mr Szili came back to me. "They are still holding out for remand in custody, but I'll argue for bail. Come on, the court is about to start. Just sit behind me, OK? Anthony will be in the dock, so don't be alarmed. You won't be able to talk to him or sit with him. Understand?" I understood nothing, but I nodded, followed him and sat behind as instructed.

"All rise," the clerk said in a voice that sounded abnormally loud in the silence of the courtroom. We all obediently stood. "Melbourne Magistrates' Court is now open. His Honour Gleason presiding. Please be seated."

Everyone except me bowed. By the time I realised what they were doing, it was too late to join in.

I couldn't see Anthony anywhere and was about to ask Mr Szili about it when the clerk called "Anthony Grey," and a door opened. Anthony appeared in the dock behind a glass barrier with a guard at his side. He looked confused and lost, a slight wrinkle on his forehead. He stared straight ahead, but didn't seem to see anything.

Without being able to shave that morning, his face looked bristly and unkempt. He wore the same clothes he had been wearing when they arrested him, and they were crumpled and untidy. I willed him to see me, but he just kept looking ahead.

"Ms Obermeyer?" The Magistrate had a pleasant, deep voice. My first glance at him showed a man maybe in his fifties, balding, neat, in a grey suit and yellow tie. I expected him to be in a robe and wig. Our fate depended on him, but I could only look at Anthony.

"Your Honour. Mr Grey is charged with two counts of possessing child pornography. The police inform me that other charges are pending. We are requesting remand in custody."

"In custody, Ms Obermeyer?" I was relieved to see a slight frown and hear the disapproval in his voice.

"Yes, Your Honour. The defendant has access to many children through his work at a Recreation Centre, and his involvement in a children's swim group. He has easy access to witnesses and we are afraid he will attempt to discourage them from giving evidence."

"The police are still investigating?" In other circumstances, I might have enjoyed listening to his resonant voice.

"Yes, Your Honour. Pursuant to a search warrant this morning, police seized a computer belonging to the defendant, and at the last count had located 20,000 images of child pornography in a hidden file. They have also located a number of images of children in bondage. It is likely that these will be the source of future charges. It appears they do not come from the same origin as most of the other images. Police have requested time to locate the children in the photographs and interview them. Since at this stage we do not know their identities, we believe that releasing the defendant on bail puts these children at significant risk. I am informed that Mr Grey was not co-operative in identifying any of them."

Like so much that had happened that day, I couldn't believe what I was hearing. Thousands of images? Mr Grey 'not being co-operative?' Anthony would give anyone anything! Children at risk? Not from my man. This was getting bigger by the minute.

The Magistrate looked at Mr Szili, who shot up as though fired from a cannon.

"Your Honour. We strenuously oppose remand in custody. My client has no previous convictions. He has a stable family – his wife is here in court to support him." He indicated to me. I half stood, but my knees felt weak and I couldn't make it all the way up. "He and his wife own a house, and they are both employed full time. There is no risk of him not attending court."

Little Miss Obermeyer bobbed up again. "Your Honour! We are talking about serious offending here. The defendant has made admissions…"

Mr Szili interrupted. "About the computer, Your Honour. Not about the photographs."

"As I was saying, Your Honour, the photographs were found in the defendant's house, in a box in the bottom of the wardrobe under the defendant's shoes. I'm not sure whether Mr Szili is arguing that the photographs did not belong to the defendant, but we feel very strongly that these children will be at substantial risk if the defendant is granted bail."

Mr Szili stood up quickly. "I refer Your Honour to the Bail Act. Bail should not be refused if the defendant can be satisfactorily accommodated and sufficient restrictions are placed on the defendant to make the risk to the public acceptable. In this case, Your Honour, we will accede to fairly limiting restrictions. We understand where the Prosecution is coming from, but this is a man with no prior convictions who has led an exemplary life to date. He is entitled to bail."

"What line of work did you say Mr Grey is in, Ms Obermeyer?"

"He's Media Liaison and Assistant Manager at a Leisure and Recreation Complex, Your Honour, which includes a large swimming pool. Children come for lessons, schools come for sports days, and the pool is open to the general public. Mr Grey ran the swimming classes at this centre, and we believe this is where he met some of the children."

Julia looked back at me, then at Mr Szili. I read contempt in her expression – maybe it was the tilt of her head, or the way she glanced down at me. The Magistrate was silent, and both lawyers stood looking at him. Anthony turned his head and looked in my direction, but it was as though he didn't even see me. There was no recognition, no smile. There was nothing behind his eyes. I was frightened.

"Ms Obermeyer, Mr Szili. I am going to give this some consideration. Does the defendant have a passport?"

"Yes, Sir, the police have it in their possession."

"Very well. We'll return at…" he looked at the clock opposite him, "at 3 pm." That was in fifteen minutes. He stood, and the clerk ordered us to rise while he left.

Mr Szili and Julia talked together and referred to some papers. Then he turned to me.

"Can we surrender the house mortgage? Do you know where it is? The passport will be held by the police. How much cash can you put up? Is there anyone else in the family who can put up money? It's looking like he might grant bail under strict conditions." Mr Szili was speaking quickly, and I had trouble hearing his low tone.

"How much money are we talking about?"

"I just need to know how much we have to bargain with."

I thought about money. Anthony's family had some, but I hadn't even told them about the arrest. We didn't have any savings, not with the mortgage we were paying. When we were married, we rented a flat for a few months, then bought our house. We had a tight budget, but knew we would be better off in the long run. I explained all this to Mr Szili.

He nodded. "I think we can make a good case for bail."

They brought Anthony back into the dock. It was so scary that suddenly he had no power over his own actions. The Magistrate returned, and we all stood again. He cleared his throat.

"I have considered the issue of bail. At this stage, I am satisfied that the Prosecution has sufficient concerns about the safety of members of the public that I should not release the defendant. Mr.

Grey is remanded in custody."

"Thank you, Your Honour." The obsequious Julia Obermeyer cast a look at me and gave me a lop-sided smile of triumph. Anthony just sat there until the guards tapped him on the shoulder. He started, as though he had been asleep, and looked at me as the guard unlocked the door in the back of the dock and took him out. But the look was blank, as if he did not recognise me.

Then he was gone. I caught a glimpse of a corridor before the door shut behind him.

The Magistrate tapped on the computer, then called the next case. It was over, just like that. He says, "No bail," and Anthony is locked up! I can't believe the justice system can work like that and then, having totally disrupted our lives, the Magistrate goes on as though nothing had happened.

Julia waltzed out, leading her suited entourage. Mr Szili was packing up his papers. Sergeant Price motioned to me to go ahead of him. People were already coming in for the next case. We went into the little room outside the court.

"Can I see him? Where do I go?"

Sergeant Price was waiting for me. He pulled out a chair for me, and I was grateful to sit. "He will be taken to the Melbourne Assessment Prison, for tonight at least. You won't be able to see him today. You need to ring them and enquire about the process."

Julia reappeared and summoned the Sergeant. He shook my hand and left, nodding to Mr Szili as he came into the room. Mr Szili sat down next to me.

"Now, Mrs Grey, we will re-apply for bail. Not for a few days, I'm afraid. I wonder if you could come down to my office as soon as possible and we can chat about what sureties you have and how much money you can put up?"

I nodded dumbly. Everything seemed to go in slow motion, and I was hearing things as though I was underwater. Words had to be translated into meaning, one statement at a time. Mr Szili said in a 'few days' we could ask for bail. That must mean that not only would Anthony be locked up today, but also for the next however many days. What would I do? How would I cope?

"Right now, I need to ask you for some money to retain my services. There will be a lot of paperwork to prepare a bail application that has a good chance of success, and I have put cases aside today for Mr Grey." The amount he asked for took my breath away and mopped up most of our liquid funds. We arranged an appointment for the next day, and he walked me to the lift. In the foyer, he turned and shook my hand. "Until tomorrow, Mrs Grey." And he left.

I stood alone. It was quiet now. The youths had gone, as had the woman with the baby and the young couple. Only the receptionist and one of the security guards remained. I felt like a dead fish washed up on the beach, with water ebbing and flowing around. I was utterly alone. My life had turned upside down, and I was by myself, in a court, with a husband in jail. How had this happened?

The physical pain attacked without warning. I started shaking, my heart racing. I became aware of a raging thirst. I ran down the side corridor towards the sign marked 'Toilets' and burst into the women's room. It was empty, and I leant my forehead against the cool wall, then banged it sharply. *Thump, thump, thump.* It made no difference.

My bag dropped from my shoulder to the floor, but I was frozen. If I didn't move, perhaps I could regain control. My hands were clenched tight. I'm not sure how long I stood there. Somewhere in my head, I knew I should go, but the energy just wasn't there. I was frightened.

Eventually, I unclenched my hands and lifted my head from the wall. Picking up my bag, I went into a cubicle. It was not too clean, but I covered the seat with toilet paper and sat, head in my hands. I heard someone else come in, lock a door, use the toilet, wash their hands and leave. I thought it might be getting towards court closing time. I didn't want to stay here overnight, locked in like Anthony.

As though on automatic, I flushed the paper away, opened the door, washed my hands, and looked in the mirror. I knew it was my face because no-one else was there, but I bore more resemblance to my driver's licence than at any other time. I, too, looked like a criminal.

Outside in the freshly polluted city air, people were leaving their offices and heading for the tram and train. The tram was crowded and stuffy, but I was grateful just to be surrounded by people.

Back at the police station, a girl in reception arranged for my car to be brought out of the compound, and I asked them for a contact number for the Custody Centre.

I barely remember the drive home. The last time I had been in the car, I was following the Sergeant. I had been optimistic that the position I found myself in would soon be resolved. Well, it had been resolved, but not in the way I had imagined or hoped.

Chapter 5

When I opened the front door, my first instinct was to run away. The searchers had been reasonably tidy, but they had not kept my high standards. Things were out of place, and books had been pulled from shelves. In the computer room, wires and cords were on the floor, drawers were open and contents had been strewn around. Although there were people to contact and things to do, I had to regain control of this portion of my life. This I could do.

I swept through the house, rapidly restoring it to neatness and cleanliness. There were gaps where things had been taken. I moved other photos to where the digital frame had been and spread the books out to fill the hole left by the removal of the albums. I banged drawers shut and wiped everything down with a clean cloth.

For a moment, I paused by the large photo of our wedding party, which hung on the wall above the television. It had been a happy day. Even my dad, who was not photogenic, looked proud and confident. The photographer had captured me looking up at Anthony with a tiny smile, while he had his arm around me protectively. He couldn't protect me now.

Now I had to start telling people about what had happened. How? Who? When? Procrastinating, but only to keep things structured, I found a notebook and made a list. My family. His family. Our friends. My friends. His friends. No-one else needed to know. Under these headings, I then listed the names of the people. Some I decided to email. Oh, what about work? Too hard.

I would start by calling Mum. Next, I had to decide what to say? Oh God. In my head I walked through several variations.

"There was a dreadful mistake today, Mum. Anthony was arrested for child porn."

"Hi Mum, something dreadful happened. Anthony was arrested."

"Hi Mum, I don't know how to tell you this, but our house was raided this morning."

I thought if I wrote a script out, it might be easier – but when I tried, the tears came and dripped onto the page. I couldn't stop thinking about Anthony, where he was, what they had given him to eat, how they had treated him. Would he be alone, locked up in a tiny cell, with bars facing a long corridor? Or in a big dormitory? Would he be safe there, or attacked by other prisoners? So many things I'd never had to think about before.

What would he be feeling? Would he be crying? Feeling numb? Worrying about me? He had looked so remote in the court – maybe he was ill. Would they have medical assistance there?

I had to ring the Custody Centre. I had to let people know. What should I do first? Even the simplest decisions were difficult.

The phone rang and shocked me out of my lassitude. The effort of reaching out across the table to pick it up was enormous. My voice shook as I answered. "Hello?"

"Darling, what's the matter?" It was Mum. She knew me, and knew something was wrong. "I tried you several times today and there was no answer, and now you sound like someone has died. What's up?"

The tears fell so fast that I gave up wiping them away and became hysterical. I gasped for breath, then hiccupped. My nose ran. I tried to blurt out what had happened, but she kept saying she "couldn't understand me" and "what are you saying?" In the end she just said, "I'm coming over," and hung up the phone. I sat and wailed like a baby.

Mum and Dad lived a couple of streets away. A few minutes later I heard her open the door with her own key. The feeling of her arms around me was immeasurably comforting.

"There, there." She murmured the age-old words, meaningless, but something to break the silence. She rocked me back and forth, smoothing my hair and mopping my streaming eyes with a handkerchief. Mum hated tissues.

It was a sign of her strength that she didn't pester me for the reason. It was enough for her that she could see I was alright – physically at least.

Eventually, when I was calmer, she said, "I'll put the kettle on." At first I held tightly onto her hand, but she gently said, "I have to put the kettle on." I loosened my grip. Physical contact had made me feel stronger. I watched her from the table, knowing that I couldn't put off telling her any longer. While her back was turned, I started.

"Mum, Anthony was arrested. He's in jail. For child porn."

There was the slightest pause in her movements. It was unnoticeable unless you had been looking for it. Then she continued getting the teapot out of the cupboard, spooning in tea from the canister. Two cups were unhooked and put on the bench. There was a hiss as the hot water hit the tea leaves.

She brought the cups over and sat opposite me. "Anthony arrested? Tell me what happened." Her matter-of-fact attitude helped, though I knew that inside she would be raging and boiling. She had always been one to think before she spoke. I hadn't inherited that quality.

"Police raided our house this morning. They just arrived on the doorstep. They took the computers and arrested Anthony. They said he has child porn on his computer. The Magistrate refused to give him bail. He's locked up. Mum – what am I going to do?"

She took my hand, but didn't speak for a moment. Eventually, I looked up at her and saw tears in her eyes. "I have questions, obviously. It's no use to say how shocked I am. That won't help. What happens next?"

"I have to see the solicitor tomorrow. Can you come with me? I need to find out about finances. We can apply for bail again in a few days. And I need to get to the prison to see Anthony. I need to let people know, but I don't know what to say. I need to get time off work…" So much to do. How life had changed since this morning. I felt constantly on the verge of panic. Mum was calm, and it helped me.

"Your dad will need to know. Leave that to me. I'll tell him when he gets home from the club. What about Anthony's family?"

"No-one knows but you. But we'll need some financial help from his mother. How am I going to tell her, Mum? I can't even think about it myself. How do I tell people?"

"I'll ring her. Get her to come over here, but you know Leila – she'll need time to put on her makeup. Why don't you go and have a shower? I'll make you something to eat. I suspect you haven't thought about food today."

She was right. I remember having a sandwich at the police station, but that was all I had eaten. I wondered how it was that I didn't seem to have inherited my mother's flair for calmness, logic and organisation. Maybe, as a child, you observe and copy. Maybe what happened to me was that I observed and just let her do everything. I kissed her and went to our bedroom.

"And I'll call the priest," she added.

Anthony wasn't hugely religious, but my Mum and Dad were, so we went to church reasonably regularly. I'd gone to Sunday school and Bible class. Anthony didn't mind one way or the other, so often I just went with my parents. Mum had a habit of summoning the priest when there was a crisis of any sort. He had learnt over the years it was easier to comply with Mum's requests than to make excuses.

I looked at the bed, rumpled from where Anthony had rolled out of it this morning. On my side, the covers were neatly peeled back, and the pillow lay ready for my head, plump and smooth. On his side, the sheet had got tangled up like a whirlpool. Both were untucked from the end of the bed, and his two pillows lay at right angles to each other. He usually did some flopping around when he first came to bed, but once he had his nest made, that was it for the night.

I smiled at the memory until his absence recalled me to today's events. There was no energy left in me to feel anything. I peeled off my clothes and stood under the shower, just letting the water fall, washing away the smell of the police station and some small part of the tension.

Chapter 6

I t was getting on to nine o'clock. It had been a long day. I thought about putting on my pajamas, then remembered the priest, Father Nick, and Leila, Anthony's mother, should be here soon (my father was out at the Hungarian Club). Our house was halfway between both our families. Sometimes it meant a little too much contact, but mostly it was convenient.

Leila owned several houses in the area – she had picked up one from each husband along the way. Since she was at husband number three, and that relationship was none too secure, I imagined she would soon have another to add to her stable.

Reluctantly, I got dressed. Mum had made an omelette, poured orange juice, coffee and set out fresh fruit. I couldn't face the omelette, though my stomach was growling. I felt better for having Mum there, even though I knew she couldn't always be there to shield me.

The bell rang, and I had an instant flashback to the morning raid. The image that was frozen in my mind was opening the door and seeing gigantic policemen crowded onto the porch. It only lasted a moment, but swept through me like a whirlwind, leaving me feeling weak.

Leila bustled in. "What's the matter? Where's Anthony? Is he alright? Why wouldn't you talk on the phone?"

I picked up a small piece of cantaloupe and allowed it to slip down my throat.

"Sit down Leila." My mother was firm about not being hurried. "I want to wait for Father Nick before we talk. Anthony is OK."

I sat with a tissue to my eyes while Mum peered out the window, the same one from which I had seen the police cars this morning. Was it only this morning? Had it actually happened? Mum must have seen a car pull up, as she went to the door and ushered Father Nick in.

I had mixed feelings about Father Nick. He was very stern in his sermons, but in reconciliation he was quite mild and gentle. I had never been sure which was the real Nick, and after today, I wasn't sure I could ever trust my judgement of people again.

Leila was getting more and more infuriated, but I let it wash over me. Mum was in charge, thank goodness.

"Now, Leila and Father, listen to what my daughter has to say. It is difficult, but she will need your understanding, support and prayers." She nodded to me. I had expected her to tell them, and it took me by surprise. I looked at her, and she smiled and nodded.

I gulped some juice down, then told the story right from the events of the morning. I looked at Mum the whole time. I didn't want to see the expressions on the faces of Leila and Father Nick. When I finished, Leila burst into noisy tears and the Father fingered his rosary and asked us to pray.

My mother led a matter-of-fact discussion, mainly with Leila, about how much money she could contribute for bail. Any time Leila started wailing and weeping, she cut her off and insisted on her being sensible and helpful. Father Nick just shook his head and prayed under his breath. I sat there, staring at the wall. Eventually, it was arranged for Leila to pick me up the next day to go to the lawyer's, and she and Nick departed. I could hear Leila's voice going on and on at Father Nick as they went down the driveway.

Suddenly, I felt ravenous and forked up several large mouthfuls of the cold omelette. Mum extracted a pill from a bottle in her bag and made me swallow it. She led me, unresisting, to the spare room, helped me take off my jeans, along with my shoes and socks, then tucked me in.

"I've rung your dad and told him what's happened and that I'll stay here tonight. Just sleep. That tablet won't take long to work," she whispered.

Mercifully, she was right. The fog in my brain thickened and snuffed out consciousness, and when I woke, it was to sun peering its way through the cracks in the shutters, asking to be let in.

I looked around the room, admiring the gentle green colour of the walls, the dado around the top, with eucalyptus leaves interwoven with wattle flowers, the prints in golden frames hanging on the walls. A glorious sense of wellbeing and rested relaxation suffused my body. I felt strong and capable, and ready to start a long holiday. Then I remembered. Physical pain hit, clawing my stomach, shooting nausea volcanically into my mouth. I pulled my legs up under my chin, trying to send the period-like cramps away, without success.

Then came the mental pain – the memory, the shame, the disbelief, the horror. It felt as if I was tearing my brain apart, and I moaned and writhed. Overlaying them both was the spiritual pain – the grief, the moral horror of actions taken and deceit practiced, of love betrayed.

The groans must have alerted my mother, because she appeared in the doorway. "It's nine o'clock. Time to get up and have breakfast. Leila will be here at ten, and there are things we need to decide." It was right not to give me pity, even though I craved it. Where did she get her tower of strength? Why didn't I have it?

Bending double, I almost fell out of the bed. Hanging onto the dresser, I straightened slowly. Obediently, I showered and dressed, cleaned my teeth, and emerged to a breakfast of assorted foods and drinks. I wasn't hungry, but I ate because my mother told me to.

"Darling, your father and I have discussed what has happened, and we think it is best if you come back and live with us while all this is sorted out. Then you can apply for the divorce, and we can sort out the finances. I know you need time, and Anthony needs to have assistance, but it will be easier to support you if we have you at home. I don't like to think of you living here alone."

The food had cleared my mind a little. I rewound the tape in my brain. She had said something I needed to challenge. Squawking fast forward noises in my head. Ah! Got it! I had to tell her right away.

"I'm not leaving Anthony. He's done wrong, but he needs me. We are married, a couple in the church. You must understand that."

"Darling, I don't think the church ever intended you to stand by a man who was a criminal, and especially when the offences were against children. No, dear, your father and I think it best that we look after you. Then you could rent this house out and get some income to help pay the mortgage."

"Mum, you aren't listening! Twenty-four hours ago, we were a normal married couple. Today we aren't. I have a lot of thinking to do, I know that – but at the moment I am fully intending to do whatever I can to help. Look, we have to talk, we have to discuss this – but first I have to ring the prison." (How easily the word slipped out, yet I couldn't even say it in my mind at the moment.)

There was a pause. "Sweetheart, you were never a normal couple. You thought you were, but we know now that it was all a sham."

"Shut up! Just shut up! You don't understand! You never will!" I didn't anticipate my own reaction, and I frightened myself. I only knew that I couldn't handle the thought of going home as a child again, needing to be looked after by my parents. Slamming my way across the room to my handbag, I rummaged for the phone number.

"I'm sorry, Mum." I couldn't look at her. "I'm a bit on edge. Could you please ring work – the number is in the mobile. And Anthony's work. Say we won't be in for a few days? Thanks."

I rang the prison number and had to listen twice to the recorded messages. I didn't know which department I wanted, so I just waited on the line for a real person. When I got someone, I didn't know what to say. "Um, my husband is in there. Can I visit him?"

Then I had to go through the whole rigmarole about who Anthony was and who I was and how I could be identified (I didn't understand then why they had to check identities so closely before they allowed people to visit.) Mum was listening to my end of the conversation. I scribbled down the website to look up so I could find out all the rules.

"What did they say?" Mum poured herself another cup of tea.

"So much to remember. The guy sounded as though I should know all this already. He said I could bring in a letter for Anthony, but I couldn't see him because I had to book a visit the day before! And Anthony has to put my name on a visit list. That's so unfair! Now I can't see him till tomorrow or even the next day. But today I can bring him in clothing, and take the others for washing, even if I can't see him. And there's a list of things I can and can't bring. It's too much. I can't understand it all."

I thought Mum looked sympathetic, but the vibes I was getting about Anthony were not so kindly. "Darling, can you tell me a little more about what Anthony did? We haven't really had a chance to talk much about what the police said."

I shook my head. "I don't really know anything. They told me he had been on some internet thing and bought photos, and they got our address through that. I think they could see the photos as well. They showed me one or two in the interview. But in court, there was something about other photos. I'm scared, Mum. It was horrible yesterday. I didn't know what to do or say, and I should have been at work. I mean, how could I have got up normally yesterday and ended up in court? And how could Anthony have done this to me?"

Mum raised her eyebrows at me and shrugged. "Not only to you, sweetheart. It's something we will have to talk about over the next few weeks. But Leila will be here any moment. What do you need to say to the lawyer?"

"I haven't even given it a thought. I've got a splitting headache already. How can it be only a day since this all happened? I just can't believe that Anthony did this. Mum, I love him! How could I love him if he did this, and I never knew?" The tears and the shaking started up again.

My mother got up and went to the door. Leila had arrived. "You can't afford to cry. You need to be strong. Cry later," she called over her shoulder.

I felt chastised, and though I kept shaking, the tears stopped.

Chapter 7

Leila drove me into the city. Mum didn't come. Conversation on the way was mostly one-sided from Leila. She had hundreds of questions, practically none of which I could answer.

Did I know? When did this happen? Was it true? How did the police find out? What happened when they came round? Where was Anthony now? Could she visit? When would he be allowed out? What happens in court? She barely drew breath to allow me to answer what I could before the next question fell into the space between us.

Did I believe he was innocent? How could her family be falling apart? Why had Anthony done this when he knew how upset she would be? How could he? Then she got onto the "life wasn't fair" track, and all of this while she was driving. It affected her concentration, but she was totally oblivious to the tooting of horns and screeching of brakes. I shut my eyes for most of the trip.

Parking in the city streets was impossible as usual, and we ended up in a multi-storey car park a short walk away from the lawyer's office.

Mr Szili was prepared with papers, forms and information. "We have a bail hearing on Monday."

I was dismayed. "But I have to see him, to talk to him." I tried to explain how bereft I felt, how incomplete. But he was a lawyer. Things were black and white for him.

He put the cap on his pen and laid it on the old-fashioned blotter in front of him. "It's actually not a bad thing if he stays in custody for a week or so."

"What? How can you say that?" Leila was angry. "He's not your son, or you might work harder to get him out!"

"I don't mean to appear uncaring, but I mentioned to you earlier that the penalties for these offences can be up to ten years in prison. If he has some time in custody now, it will be taken into account when he is sentenced."

"But first he has to be found guilty, doesn't he? I mean, isn't that how it works?" I knew there had to be a jury and a trial and a judge.

Mr Szili stopped fussing with papers and looked at me, a wrinkle in his brow. "Mrs Grey, I thought you knew? He wants to plead guilty, guilty to everything."

Leila and I looked at each other. I could see her swallowing hard. We spoke simultaneously.

"He wants to plead guilty?" Leila squeaked.

"What did you say? Guilty?" My mouth stayed open.

Mr Szili nodded. "They were his instructions when we last met." I learned later that 'instructions' was solicitor for 'That's his story.' Mr Szili paused before continuing. "There is another reason."

I didn't want another reason. I had my mind firmly fixed on how we could fix up this mistake. It didn't involve Anthony admitting to doing anything wrong. But Mr Szili went on, anyway.

"The Prosecution are serious about having him remanded in custody till the trial. That could be months away, possibly a year. They are still investigating. They don't want him on the streets while there are potential witnesses they haven't been able to locate. It's conceivable they may lay more charges later." He made Anthony sound like some sort of predatory monster stalking the highways and byways looking for children. "On the other hand, if the authorities have him in custody, they can observe him and make some sort of judgement about his suitability for bail. We might not get that if we go in too quickly."

Even while I was processing all this, I could see why Mr Szili was making this suggestion. "So, should we wait for longer than Monday?"

"I don't think so. It will have been nearly a week, and though the police might not want it, we may be able to convince the court that Anthony can be looked after by you Mrs Grey, and you, Mrs Knightly – if you are willing to assume that responsibility?" He looked at Leila and then me, and we both nodded. "I imagine there will be some fairly tight bail conditions – that is, there may be restrictions on where he can go, and who he can see. And there will be a hefty financial commitment."

Leila said she was willing to provide her house as bail surety, and while she and Mr Szili discussed it, I borrowed paper from the desk and wrote a note to Anthony. I intended to visit the Custody Centre after the solicitor.

It was hard to know what to write. The prison people had told me on the phone not to be critical or give any bad news in a letter, just to keep it matter of fact. They said he would probably be suffering from shock, because he had never been locked up before. I tried to be encouraging and optimistic.

Dear Big Bear,

I wish I was allowed to see you, but I can't until tomorrow. They tell me they will give you this letter, though. Your mum and I are doing everything we can to get you home.

I know you would never deliberately have done anything to hurt our precious relationship, and I want so much to see you and touch you and talk to you, so we can work out how this happened and how we solve it.

We will get you out on bail as soon as we can, and with our love, and the love of God, we will get through this.

I am thinking of you night and day.

Your Honey Bear.

It was short, but I hoped there was something in it to see him through the dark hours. Picking the words was harder than I had anticipated.

Leila finished talking bank stuff, then we tidied up some final details and left. I was aware that the interview had already cost another chunk of money. I told Leila not to worry about driving me, I could walk the few blocks to the Custody Centre. She wanted to come, but I dissuaded her by explaining all the administration that had to be done first.

Melbourne Assessment Prison was a neat, red brick building just up from the Southern Cross Railway Station. It was not immediately obvious that it was a prison until you looked up and saw the barbed wire coils at the back and the high brick walls. Then you became aware of the huge cameras, pointing up and down Spencer St. People hurried past, as though a dangerous inmate was likely to escape and run unchallenged through the doors. People in Spencer St sometimes looked as though they were escapees – tattooed, dirty, probably smelly if you allowed yourself to get too close to them.

How strange it must be to know that barely a hundred metres away was a train that could carry you to Sydney, Adelaide or beyond, yet you couldn't leave your cell. How ironic that a homeless beggar, who wafted by me in a flurry of assorted dirty clothes, would be refused entry to this place, where the bad people automatically got their human rights looked after meticulously. Some of Melbourne's homeless wouldn't care about being locked up in return for a bath, bed and food.

The concept of liberty was not something I had considered before. It was an assumption of our entitlement to go where we pleased, do what we want at any time. I could liken legal liberty to incapacitation caused by illness or disease – an external force can dictate your movements. I didn't like it.

It was physically difficult to force myself into the building, as though iron weights were attached to my legs. Travelers walked up from Southern Cross Station, chattering, laughing, pulling suitcases – but as they reached the prison, they looked around, lowered their voices and hurried their steps. They didn't want to be associated with such people by walking past. Well, I was associated with such a person. I wondered how they would cope if it was a relative of theirs inside. No-one knows until they are in that position.

An intimidating-looking officer staffed the reception. He turned out to be very understanding. He helped me sort out the clothes I had brought since they were not all permitted. The hoodie wasn't allowed, and I had to cut the cords off the tracksuit pants. The underwear and t-shirts were OK.

He took the letter and promised to deliver it (after it had been read by the prison authorities – as if I was going to discuss escape plans in a letter!) and said if I came back the next day I could take Anthony's soiled clothes home. I booked a visit and provided my identification so I would be allowed to see him. Anthony had already put me and his mother on the visiting list.

I had not seen my husband for over twenty-four hours. Since our marriage, we had never spent a night apart. It was already early afternoon, and I hadn't eaten since Mum forced me to have some breakfast.

I left the prison, feeling marginally more cheerful at the thought of seeing Anthony the next day. I stopped at a café and bought coffee and a donut. At that time, calories didn't count.

Then I had to do something about telling people. For the moment, there was nothing more I could do for Anthony.

Chapter 8

My best friend was Nellie. Her real name was Helen, but I had always called her Nellie or Nell. We had known each other for years, and our lives had been intertwined in various ways. We first met as teenagers at a local council youth group, where we did activities and games, first on the school holiday program and later at an after-school club.

She was a bit wild as an adolescent, and her mum sent her along to the youth group to have some 'guidance' from the leaders. I went because my parents thought I was socially backward. We clicked right away. I responded to her zaniness, and admired her for not caring what people thought. She found in me, I guess, someone who looked up to her.

Our lives took different paths – she studied nursing, and I went to do an admin course, but we always kept in touch. She'd had some experiences with men and with drugs, but she grew up to be a caring, kind person who was still just a bit 'out there'. She no longer took drugs, but enjoyed a glass or two, which was fine, as I drove her home after a night out.

After I met Anthony, we often went out as a threesome – she didn't care about not having a partner, and we never considered her a 'spare wheel'. We never bothered looking for a date for her – she was perfectly capable of bringing someone if she wanted. From time to time there was a man on the scene, but generally she came alone. Our lives had all had ups and downs, but we had always been there to support each other. She was a straight talker, abrupt rather than tactful, and this was sometimes what made people shy away from her.

I texted to tell her I was coming to visit. I expected she would be home because she worked night shift at the local hospital. She said people were much saner at night, except during the full moon.

As I walked up the driveway, I was feeling OK. Perhaps even after one day, I was hardened to trauma. I was sure I could hold it together. Nellie answered the door. Despite my good intentions, my face must have revealed something, because her brow wrinkled and she held out her arms.

"Oh Erica, what on earth has happened? Come in, you poor thing! I'll put the kettle on!"

So much for my acting skills. Tears started again and wouldn't stop. I didn't really want them to. My mother had been matter of fact – helpful, but matter of fact. Leila had needed sympathy, but no-one had given me any. I let Nellie take care of me.

She sat me at the kitchen table, made some tea, and let me cry. Wet soggy balls of tissue mounded until Nellie got a bag to put them in. That made me laugh. Finally, the tears slowed a little.

"Are you OK now to tell me what the problem is?"

I nodded. "Anthony…" I barely got the second syllable out when it was back. The pain and the tears combined.

"Anthony? Did something happen? Is he dead?"

Shake of the head.

"Injured?"

The questions flowed, and I just shook my head to each of them. She went through pregnancy, miscarriage, drugs, separation, and finally ran out of options. I still couldn't speak. There was a huge lump in my throat. She produced a pen and paper.

I wrote, "Arrested. Child porn." I bit my lip and looked at her through hot, swollen eyes. But I couldn't meet her gaze, terrified of what I might see.

"What? Anthony? Child porn? But… did you know?"

My voice was hoarse. "Of course I bloody didn't! What do you take me for?"

"Sorry, I didn't mean it like that. I just thought that there would have been a hint, a call from the cops, something beforehand. You mean they turned up, just like that?"

"Yes. At six yesterday morning. We were still in our pajamas. And they searched the house and then just took him away! In handcuffs." I suddenly realised that was the real indignity.

"Oh Erica, you poor thing! I can't believe it! Tell me about it, from the start."

Despite her first reaction, I found I could. I trusted her. I told her everything. She just listened and held my hand.

"And what now? You said there's a bail application on Monday? What happens for that?"

"I think it's under control. Leila has to take house documents, I get the bank statements. The solicitor said I might have to talk in court and say stuff about our life, our marriage, how he was at home. I hate the thought."

There was a pause. I guess it was a lot to take in. Then she pushed the empty cup away and put her elbows on the table. She started examining her fingernails, which were bitten short.

"Look, I just need to ask you something."

I frowned. "What?" She bit her bottom lip. I started to get worried. "What is it? Tell me, you're making me scared."

"OK." She looked me straight in the eye. "You *do* want him at home? On bail?"

At first I was puzzled. "Of course! I need to talk with him and work out what happened and how we can fix it up. I can't do that if he is locked up, maybe for months."

Nellie considered this. "I guess I am just a bit more removed from it than you are. Two days ago your life was normal – work, relaxing together, trying for a family." (Nellie knew everything.) "Next thing you have a most horrible, inconceivable, unbelievable situation, and you just want him home so you can feel as though life is back to normal."

Thank God she understood. Before I could say anything, she inched her chair closer and lowered her voice.

"But your life won't be back to normal. Even if he gets bail, it won't ever be back to normal." She paused and looked at me for a moment. "I suppose I am actually asking whether you think he did it."

It was like a body blow. I stood up and walked towards the window, where normal people were walking past. How could I not have seen it? How could I have been so blind to the possibility that he had some sort of hang up, even a fetish, about children? Obviously, I believed he hadn't – or at least, if he had photos on the computer, that he could explain them. He would tell me about it, and then we could deal with it. The alternative prospect – that he had actually bought photos, and got a job working with kids just so he could maybe touch them – I couldn't even go there. I couldn't. I wouldn't.

I had a plan to deal with things and not even Nellie could change my mind. It was a comfort having that decision fixed firmly in my head. I sat down again. Nellie looked at me, eyebrows raised.

"Nell, I have known Anthony for nearly six years. I was 24 when we met at a party. You remember, you were there." She nodded. I smiled at the memory. "The moment I walked into the room, I marked him out! And it's been just what I wanted. He's a softy, a teddy bear. He loves me, he loves children, he loves family, he loves life. He would never, ever put that at risk."

"OK then. You trust him. You need to get him home and speak to him. What can I do? Obviously, the focus has been on helping Anthony. I don't mean to be rude, but you really look as though you haven't slept." She patted my hand.

I looked at the table. "I haven't, not much. I had a tablet, and that helped."

"Tablets are fine. What did you take?"

"I don't know. Mum gave it to me."

She nodded. "Can you go to your doctor and tell him what has happened? Ask for sleeping tablets and a medical certificate?"

I thought this over. "Probably. He's known me forever. I suppose he would give me sick leave, even though I'm not sick. But how embarrassing to tell him why I wanted them."

"It's probably going to hit the papers, though. Everyone will know eventually." The thoughts sent cold chills up and down my spine. Nellie went on. "He's a doctor, he has to keep things confidential. How many sick days do you have?"

"No idea. Quite a few, I think."

"Find out and take them all. You won't want to go back to work for as long as possible. Hey, am I am being too pushy?"

I squeezed her hand. "This is exactly what I need. Thank you so much. I can't seem to find my way out of a paper bag."

"That's not surprising. I'm not feeling too good myself. But tell me if I go overboard. I tend to get carried away. Now, what about a counsellor? Do you have one, or know one?"

"Work has one. They've told us about it, there's a scheme. I can try that."

"And what about telling people? Where are you up to with that?"

"Mum, Dad, Leila, and you. That's it. They're the only people who know. I need to tell some others."

"Probably better to do that sooner rather than later. Do you want some help?"

"No, I think I'll email. I don't want to talk to people." I had to get going. I stood up. "Thank you, Nellie. I feel so much better."

"Do you want me to come over and stay the night? So you are not by yourself?"

I thought about it. "I might have to get used to being alone. Can I call you in the middle of the night if I panic?"

She smiled. "Of course. Any time. I'll leave the mobile by my bed."

When I got home, Mum had been and left a salad in the fridge. Her note read, *"Give me a ring when you get home, OK darling?"* I took a deep breath. Knowing I could count on support from people made me hopeful. I rang.

"Hi Mum."

"Have you eaten the salad? How was the day?"

First things first! Mum had always counted on food solving the world's problems.

"I haven't yet, but I will, thanks. And today was OK. Leila is basically going to look after the bail money, and we will have to pay for the lawyer. And I dropped my letter and some clothes off at… the prison. But Mum…" I scrabbled in my handbag for the envelope Leila had dropped into it just before we parted. "Leila gave me a letter to give to Anthony. They told us at the prison to only say cheerful things, but I am afraid she will have given him a piece of her mind. Should I read it?"

There was silence for a moment. Mum was going through the same ethical dilemma as me. "They'll read it at the Custody Centre, anyway." Why didn't I think of that!

"Can I read it out to you?" I tucked the phone under my chin while I opened the letter. "OK, here goes."

Son. I am in shock, as you can imagine. You are my little curly-headed boy, my future, my life. You are the joy of my old age with a beautiful wife, a career, a nice house and soon, God willing, babies.

You are the only one in the family who ever went to university. How proud we were when you graduated! And your step fathers have always been as proud of you, as I have. When your brother was in trouble, you were the rock.

For all these reasons, I love you. These things you have been accused of, they are wrong. My little man, he could never do anything bad with kiddies, I know that. Because it would break my heart if it was true.

I will be standing with you as we fight this. By the Grace of God, your innocence will be proven. If I thought I had born a monster like the one they say you are, I would kill myself, my pet. I have the trust and love in you and I am waiting for the day when we can hug each other again.

Go with God, my child.

Your loving mother.

There was silence at the other end of the phone. I couldn't give this to Anthony – not with that stuff about her killing herself.

"Mum, can I come and spend the night at your place?"

"Eat your dinner, and I'll be there to pick you up."

She hung up abruptly, and I unwrapped the plastic from the plate, and forked up some pasta and a tomato. There was no flavour to the food, but it wasn't Mum's fault. I kept chewing away at the cardboard. The strawberry yoghurt went down more easily. I packed some underwear and waited at the door.

Mum put the car away while I ran into the house. Dad just gave me a hug.

"Hi Pet. Love you heaps."

Mum put me to bed in my old room and made me take another sleeping tablet. It worked until about two o'clock, when I woke alert and in a panic. Sweat poured down my face, and I found myself listening intently for a sound. Sleep deserted me. I threw back the doona, padded into my parent's room, and shook Dad on the shoulder.

"Can I come in, please?"

He woke up, looked puzzled for a moment, then rolled out of bed and opened the covers for me. I crawled in and he pulled the doona back over me and sat at my side, stroking my hair back from my head, like he had when I was little. Then he started rubbing my back, a gentle scratch with his nails.

I must have drifted off, for in the morning, I was alone in the bed, Dad was snoring in my room and Mum was making breakfast. I lay and felt comforted, smelled the coffee brewing, and pretended I was a child again and that other people could solve my problems.

But I couldn't put off starting the day forever. I got up and logged onto the family computer (the police still had ours). I sent emails to our friends, giving the barest information, and one to Nellie to tell her I was OK.

Dad and I didn't talk much. He just hugged me and sat close. Then Mum took me home. I needed some space. It was too hard trying to avoid talking about things.

Chapter 9

Two days after he was arrested, I finally got to see Anthony. It had taken all that time to arrange. I took the train in to the prison and presented my licence at the window. The place smelt of cleaning fluid, and everyone seemed to wear a uniform. They were all very matter of fact, but to me their questions seemed intrusive and unnecessary.

Finally, I was allowed through one heavy door, which slammed behind me before the next door was opened by another guard and they showed me to a row of booths. "Just pick up the phone when you see the person you are visiting, OK? You'll have about 15 minutes."

The man opened the door, and I went in. There was a grey plastic chair facing a scratched glass window, and a phone hooked up to one side. The glass seemed to have a network of fine wires in it, as though it was strengthened mesh. No-one was on the other side, but I picked up the phone. It was cold and felt greasy, and I wished I had brought some cleaning wipes with me, but I'd had to put everything in a locker at reception before I came in.

The door on the other side opened, and Anthony came in. He looked thinner and tired, though he smiled at me in the boyish way I loved. A little dimple formed in his chin. He picked up his phone.

I tried not to cry. "Hi darling. I know it's a silly question, but how are you?"

"Don't worry about me. What about you?" His voice was blurry and metallic as it came through the phone line. The cord attached to the handset was short, and he had to lean forward in what looked like an uncomfortable position in order to hear me.

"We are applying for bail again. Have you been sleeping? And eating?"

He smiled. "Well, the cook here isn't as good as you, but I'm getting used to sleeping. Beds aren't very comfortable, though. Do you miss me?"

I glared at him. "Do you really need to ask that? Come on! I want to make sure you are OK. What do you do all day? Can I bring you in anything?"

"I was just joking, little one. Of course I miss you, horribly. I hope they didn't leave too much mess in our house."

My mind went back to the morning of the raid, and I swallowed hard to stop the tears. "No, they were fine. But when can I visit again?"

"Sweetie, it's a bit hard to visit here. I'm in a separate unit, and I'm not allowed to mix with the others. They have to have someone just to get me to and from the visit area. I know it's hard, but maybe we should just wait till I'm out on bail." I thought he was trying not to cry, so I didn't object. It was almost harder to see him, but not be able to touch, than not to see him at all.

Anthony went on. "I can phone you every day, but they will listen to our conversations. I hate the thought of that. Will you be OK if we just wait till Monday? You can drop a letter in every day, though. I'd like that."

That was some comfort. And hopefully, on Monday, he could be home.

The guard knocked at my door and then came in. "Sorry Ma'am, time to finish." At the same time, an officer came into Anthony's space and gestured to him to hang up.

"Goodbye for now, my love." His voice was soft and strained. I blew him a kiss and left the room without waiting for him to go. That would have been too hard.

His mother's letter was consigned to the bin.

Chapter 10

The days passed slowly while we waited for the bail hearing. There were meetings with the lawyer and visits to the Custody Centre, but I also went to work to see my boss, Kerry. I had given her an outline on the phone of what had happened, and made an appointment to come in and sort out some leave.

It was hard actually going into the building. Harrison Hanover Brokers and Agents was on the top floor of a Collins St building. The entrance was through an intimidating, cold, green foyer and up in a bank of high-speed lifts. I waited out of sight until a lift arrived in case I saw someone I knew. When I had a lift to myself, I pressed the button for the seventeenth floor and hastily pressed the 'close door' button. As the lift rose my stomach fell, along with my mood.

Stepping out into the familiar foyer, I smelt the gentle perfume of the floral display in the reception alcove. They directed clients to the right, but I turned to the left into the open plan office. Desks ran down both sides, with an illusion of privacy given by carpeted partitions about two metres high. Kerry had her office at the end, where she could look out over everyone. That meant a long walk down the centre aisle.

I went in just after ten, when traditionally it was coffee break time in the staffroom. I was surprised that everyone seemed to be working assiduously. At the first desk was Lydia, my morning coffee mate. I smiled at her.

"Hi," she said, and buried her head in a file. On the other side was Jamie, who bought my lunchtime salad sandwich when I remembered to give him the money. He looked up.

"Morning, how's things?" It wasn't a question, though.

I continued on past Jasmine, the Malaysian who never spoke to anyone, and Craig, who gave me a smile. Sylvia, an older lady, ignored me as usual, and the other desk was mine. It looked different somehow.

The meeting itself was not as I had expected. Kerry was on the phone and waved at me to show she knew I was there. I looked back down the aisle, but no-one was showing any signs of wanting to speak to me. They all seemed busy.

I saw Kerry gesturing through the window to come in. She pointed to a chair and rolled her eyes as her phone conversation continued. "Yes, of course. I understand. Naturally. Yes, I'll see to it." Eventually she replaced the receiver and gave me her attention.

"Now, you want to take some leave. I've checked with Personnel, and you have over a month of sick leave, and after that, of course, you can have leave without pay if you wish."

I nodded. "That's great. I really appreciate it. I think my files are up-to-date and self-explanatory. I might spend an hour here now, just getting things tidy."

Kerry smiled without showing her teeth. "No need, my dear. When you told me what had happened, I thought it best to see where you were at, and I have allocated your work out to the others. They can cope in the short term till we see whether you are coming back." She adjusted the diary on her desk.

"Of course I'll be back! I just need to get this situation sorted out first. It might be a few months, but if you give me leave without pay, then I'll come back as soon as I can."

Kerry picked up a pile of papers and tapped them on the desk. She was a bit of a neat freak, something I quite liked about her.

"The thing is…" she stopped.

"The thing is what?" I had a sudden bad feeling.

"Management… they are a bit concerned… if there is publicity… we don't want the firm mentioned."

It hit me like a rocket. They didn't want the firm mentioned because they might be associated with me, and I was married to Anthony, and he might be convicted of child sex offences.

"But that's unfair! I had nothing to do with any of it."

"Of course, I perfectly understand. It's just that the clients… they might think…"

"Think what? Think that if my husband is into child porn that I am? Think that I bring photos to work and everyone drools over them? What the bloody hell has it to do with me?"

Kerry was shocked. She had only seen me at my most polite and I don't think she knew how to react. "Look, let's just let things take their course, shall we? I didn't mean to upset you, I just thought you should know."

"Know what? That you want to sack me?" I had a sudden burst of energy and stood up, walking to the window. From Kerry's office all you could see were rooftops and air conditioners. The clients, in the other half of the building, got the view of a garden and some tall trees.

Kerry cleared her throat. "Not at all, no, of course not. You are an excellent worker. All I am saying is let's just wait and see, alright?"

I deflated as quickly as I had blown up. "Of course, Kerry, you're right. I'm sorry, I'm not myself right now." Tight-lipped, she nodded.

After signing some papers, I held my head high as I left Kerry's office. Everyone was staring at me, and no-one said a word as I strode out of the room. It was obvious that not only had Kerry told them about Anthony before I arrived, but that they had been listening to our conversation through the paper-thin walls of Kerry's office. I went home exhausted.

The bail hearing was scheduled for ten o'clock on the Monday. The weekend dragged. I sat at home, watched TV and cleaned. Mr Szili told me all the cases were listed for the same time, and in fact, ours could be any time that day. It might mean hanging around till the afternoon.

I arrived early and checked the board to see which court we were in, trying to look nonchalant as though I were a mere spectator. Upstairs again.

It was a foreign environment. We didn't belong there. We were employed, married, paying a mortgage. We were normal. We weren't like them.

Mr Szili was right about the timeline. Our case had not been called by lunchtime, and Leila and I were getting on each other's nerves. I had asked Nellie and Mum not to come. I didn't want people hearing the details, not yet – not till I had talked with Anthony. It upset Mum that I planned to go with Leila, but I know she didn't really want to come, anyway. I had brought a book, but I couldn't concentrate on reading. Sometimes I opened it just to make Leila stop talking. I got to know people by sight, those who were waiting all day, like me.

Finally, Mr Szili came up and said we were on next, and we could go into the court. At least I knew what to expect this time.

Anthony was wearing his suit, which I had taken to the Custody Centre. It was a bit rumpled, but better than what he was wearing when they arrested him. He looked pale and confused. His facial hair, which grew prolifically, had made a short beard. He must have been allowed to tidy it up a bit. Sometimes on holidays he didn't shave, and within two days he looked an absolute scarecrow.

Julia flounced in again, seemingly annoyed at having her custody conditions challenged. But this time we were better prepared.

Mr Szili went on the offensive. He had the Bail Act and what he referred to as 'case authorities'. I didn't understand all he said to the Magistrate, but when he glanced at me, I felt my heart change gears. I sat up as he went on firmly.

"Since Mr Grey has strong ties in the community, there is no reason for him to fail to surrender to bail. My client is quite prepared to report daily to police as part of the conditions. Your Honour, he has no prior record and since he is in his thirties, he is not likely to suddenly embark on a crime spree. Ms Obermeyer put it to Your Honour last week that Mr Grey might interfere with witnesses. Your Honour, the police have removed house phones, mobile phones and computers from Mr Grey. He has, in effect, no form of communication other than actually speaking face to face."

"Are you telling me, Mr Szili, that he could not purchase another phone, or use a payphone? Or go to someone's house? Or an internet café?" The Magistrate emphasised the last two words as though they were some foreign language. I tuned in again to Mr Szili.

"No, Your Honour. These options are all theoretically possible, but I argue my client is far less dangerous than many violent people who are granted bail, and that sufficient conditions can be imposed to satisfy the Prosecution that the public are indeed safe. Mrs Grey is here and willing to make herself available to supervise Mr Grey, if you deem that a safer option."

He nodded in my direction. I felt myself going red as the Magistrate looked at me, eyes narrowed. I read dislike in his expression.

"Ms Obermeyer? I'll hear from you."

She stood up and pulled down her tight blue skirt. "Your Worship, we request continued remand in custody. The police are working on identifying the children in the photos and we are still concerned that Mr Grey might try to contact them. He has not been helpful to the police in this respect. We believe, even with strict conditions, that there is an unacceptable risk to the public. These alleged offences are against children, Your Honour, and the community does not tolerate such acts."

I could not believe what she was saying. If Anthony was this sort of person, then why hadn't I seen it? How could he have hidden it? Why was he safe to be around the public one week and not the next? I wanted to jump up and cry out that they were wrong, that they didn't know him. The Magistrate tapped on his computer again, then looked up.

"Before I make a final decision, I want to hear from Mrs Grey." He looked straight at me. "Mrs Grey, would you please take the witness stand?"

His request took me by surprise, even though Mr Szili had said I might have to give evidence. I felt shaky and weak. Putting my hand on the back of the seat in front, I stood up, and slowly, like an old woman, made my way to the box where the clerk was waiting.

She handed me a Bible and a card, then asked me to repeat the Oath. I was grateful that my voice came out in something that wasn't a squeak. I was still clutching the Bible, and the clerk gently took it out of my hands. The Magistrate looked at me and asked if I needed to sit down. My lips were quivering uncontrollably. He asked for a chair to be brought into which I sank.

"Mrs Grey. I understand you are feeling overwhelmed, but I must ask you some questions."

I nodded.

"You work full-time? In administration?"

"Yes, Your Honour, but I have taken leave from my job."

"And how long can you continue to be away?"

Mr Szili had warned me I might be asked these questions. "I have 35 days of sick leave. After that I can take leave without pay."

"And are you prepared to do this, so you can be available for supervising Mr Grey, if that is what I should decide?"

"I am." I was pleased how at firm I sounded.

He continued firing questions at me and I started to feel more in control. They were questions about our life and our relationship. Being able to say that everything between us was normal was a great comfort. I felt our side was being heard at last, even if only in this court.

At last, he had no more questions.

"Thank you, Mrs Grey. Ms Obermeyer, do you have anything you wish to ask?"

I was glad when she shook her head. I didn't like her – nothing personal, just that she was on the 'other side'.

The Magistrate looked out at us in the court. "I am going to take some time to consider what to do in this case. We will resume at two o'clock. Mr Grey is remanded into custody over the lunch break."

Another delay! When could I take Anthony and go home? Mr Szili said it was good sign, though. "The chance of bail is higher if he is giving himself a lunch break to consider imposing conditions. If he was going to refuse it, I think he would have done so on the spot."

This encouraged me, and I was able to go to the café downstairs to eat sushi and drink coffee. Leila went off and did some shopping. I was glad. Normally we might see each other once a week and then she was diluted by Anthony's presence, but the last couple of days we had been joined at the hip.

Finally, the court resumed. I was in the groove now, and shot up the moment the clerk said, "All rise." I wanted this to be over so much. The Magistrate took his seat, put on his glasses, and peered over them into the court.

"Ms Obermeyer. I have considered carefully your arguments. I have looked at the Bail Act, and I don't think I am in a position at this stage to deny Mr Grey bail. I am therefore prepared to grant it under strict conditions. Mr Szili, I will expect you to make these clear to your client." He turned to Anthony. "Mr Grey, you will be released on bail on the following conditions – that you report daily to the police station closest to your home. You will be confined to your home address unless in the company of your wife, who has agreed to take charge of you in public."

He shifted his gaze to me. "Mrs Grey, I have put this condition in based on your evidence. Do you feel you can comply with this? You understand that Mr Grey must not leave the house unless he is in your company at all times?"

I nodded, but remembering that at the police station I had to say things out loud, I also croaked, "Yes, Your Honour."

He nodded and turned back to Anthony. "You must surrender your passport."

Ms Obermeyer stood up. "We have his passport, Your Honour."

The Magistrate tapped something into his computer. "Mr Grey, you will need to provide a surety to the value of $100,000. You must not have any internet connection to your home. You may not use any computer which has an internet connection on it. This includes any phone, mobile phone or other device. You must not contact any victims, families of victims, friends of victims, or anyone associated with the case. And of course you must not commit any other offences. If any of these conditions are breached, you will immediately be taken into custody. Do you understand, Mr Grey?"

Anthony's face had lost colour, and I worried he might faint. But the words came out clearly. "Yes, Your Honour."

The Magistrate looked at Mr Szili, eyebrows raised. "Anything to say Mr Szili, Ms Obermeyer?"

Mr Szili turned to Leila. "Will you look after him as well?" She nodded, and Mr Szili continued. "Your Honour, Mr Grey's mother is also prepared to share the supervision of Mr Grey outside the home. Would Your Honour vary the bail conditions to include her?"

"No objection."

"Very well. With the exception of being in the company of these two people, Mr Grey is not to leave his house. Mr Grey, if you wish to add any other people to the supervision roster, please negotiate that with the police. If they agree, then I will vary conditions."

Mr Szili bowed slightly. "Thank you, Your Honour."

"Does that address your main concerns, Ms Obermeyer?"

"Thank you, Your Honour."

I could tell from her face she was really cheesed off. But I didn't care. Anthony was coming home!

"All rise." The Magistrate was on his way out. I could have hugged him.

Mr Szili gathered Leila and I into the witness room. "We have to get some papers, sort out the financials, then Anthony will have to sign things. It will still be several hours before you can take him home. He will be released from the side of the court, around the corner, where the police cars come in and out. If I get the chance, I'll let you know when he will be there."

I couldn't believe that after the hours of waiting, it was going to be another long delay. I signed whatever he put in front of me – didn't read it, but I knew I had to keep Anthony in my sight when we were out of the house. Mr Szili stressed that I couldn't even let him go to the toilet by himself, say at a shopping centre. It would have been bizarre a week ago. Now, I accepted it without question.

The surety side of things was more complex. I left Leila to do her paperwork and went to the café. Even though we would be short of money with the legal costs and Anthony not being able to work, I bought a large coffee and a cream bun. I actually felt hungry. I called Mum and told her the news. She was pleased for me, if not for Anthony.

The sun was shining, so I went for a walk and sat in the gardens near the Federal Court, watching people. I hadn't missed going to work at all. If I had thought about it, I would expect work to be a large part of my life. At the minute, I didn't care if I never worked again, especially in that place. Just the memory of walking through that intimidating, silent office was enough to make me want to resign, though I couldn't afford to.

After an hour, I wandered back to the court to find Leila had finished and was ready to get the car. We arranged for me to wait just outside roller doors where prisoners were released. When a car park became available, I would stand in it, waiting, while she went to get the car. She would then drive round and round till she could park, and/or until Anthony came out, whichever was first. So many machinations!

Peak hour was in full swing by this time, and traffic was heavy. However, within minutes a car park became free as a businessman flung his briefcase into the backseat and eased out into the traffic. I stood right in the middle of the parking space, watching in both directions. It was in the centre of the road, so cars could pull in from either direction. Luckily, no-one tried because they would have had to run me over. I was not moving!

Once Leila had secured the park, she stayed in the driver's seat and kept the car running, and I waited at the corner. Minutes passed slowly.

A man in jeans and t-shirt was loitering nearby. He kept looking at me, and I suspected he was wishing I wasn't there. I wondered how long it would be until his loved one was getting out. I had a real fellow feeling with people who found themselves in my position, but I thought it was not tactful to look at him.

Finally, I saw the roller door go up. I ran towards it, but I was slower than the man in jeans, who had thrown himself onto the ground and produced a camera, which he poked under the door and started clicking furiously. He was a press photographer – the horrible blood-sucking parasite! He wasn't waiting for anyone except Anthony! I couldn't believe it. I had wasted valuable sympathy on this man. There should be a law against this type of behaviour, I thought. Then the irony of thinking about law-breaking struck me, and I turned my attention to protecting Anthony.

The door was open enough by that stage for Anthony to duck out, and I shielded him from the photographer and hurried him across the road. Leila gunned the car, and we got out while the man started chasing after us, trying to get one of those photos of people in the back of a car which you see in newspapers.

We didn't talk on the way home – well, Leila did, but Anthony and I just sat, with me in the front, him in the back. I think we were both in shock.

Leila took us home, and wanted to come in but I said firmly no, that we needed time by ourselves. She turned her nose up at me, said to expect her in the morning, and drove off.

Chapter 11

I unlocked the front door, and Anthony just stood there, looking inside. "Home! It seems like so long since I was here. It feels like a different life," he said.

I was short with him. "It was. Come on, I'll put the kettle on. And I don't want to talk about anything tonight, OK? Let's just spend time together, drive to the beach and take a walk, have dinner, and get some rest."

"I really need a shower. Do you mind getting tea?"

So we just carried on, almost as though nothing had happened. It was bizarre and a little frightening. I wasn't scared of Anthony, just the situation. Although the undercurrent was there, we skimmed the waves. He shaved and showered, came out and drank tea, savouring it as though it was nectar, and slowly ate a Tim Tam.

We drove to the beach at St Kilda. It was our favourite Melbourne beach. Sometimes we saw the little penguins there, but there was no sign of them today. We walked along the shoreline. The water was really cold, but the pain of the cold at my feet was heaven compared to the pain I had been experiencing. Anthony tried to hold my hand, but I couldn't touch him, not yet. When he reached out, I pulled away. He looked at me, a trace of sadness in his eyes, but he didn't make another attempt.

We bought fish and chips and sat on the beach to eat. They always taste much better when mixed with a light sprinkling of sand. With cold cans of Coke, it was a perfect meal. We didn't talk, except when Anthony said how delicious the fish was compared to the meals he had been having. I didn't comment. No-one was swimming. I watched a cargo ship meander across the bay on its way to Geelong. Seagulls squawked and swooped on our left-over chips.

Anthony sighed. "Simple pleasures. I didn't realise how important they were." He was idly scooping sand into a mound with a half shell he had picked up. "The ability to go where you like, when you like. Being able to choose what to wear and who you talk to. Eating what you like. Going to bed, getting up, watching TV. In… there you had nothing to do and plenty of time to do it in." I nodded but didn't reply. I couldn't imagine what it was like. I wasn't sure that I even wanted to.

On the way home, I raised the subject which had been most on my mind during the day. "Anthony, I'll be in the spare room tonight. It's where I have been sleeping when I haven't been at Mum's. I think we have things to work out before I can feel that we are back to being a couple."

He looked at me for a long moment, then back at the road. "I do understand, hon. I'm sad, but I understand. My mum will be round early tomorrow, but I'll try to get rid of her so we can talk. I think I might go straight to bed. I haven't slept well the last week."

"Join the club – though I guess I had a softer bed!"

We smiled at each other. It was a moment of shared understanding, and I inwardly heaved a sigh of relief. It wasn't just my imagination that our relationship included a meeting of the minds. With Anthony away, I had started to doubt everything that I had previously taken for granted.

Our first night back together was spent apart. I took a tablet and fell asleep. I don't know what Anthony did.

The doorbell woke us in the morning. Just the sound sent me into a frenzy of fear, thinking the police had returned, until I remembered Leila was coming. I let her in, made coffee and left her to talk with Anthony. I heard the door slam about an hour later. True to his word, he cut her visit short. I could see he had been crying, but I didn't comment on it.

"We had better get dressed and report you in to the police station before they come and get you," I said.

It was embarrassing doing the sign-in. We went up to the desk, but I left the talking to Anthony. When he gave his name, everyone looked up and stopped talking, as though they knew him – and as we turned to leave, I worked out why. There was a newspaper lying on the bench. The front page had a huge colour photo of Anthony, half hiding under his jacket, unshaven, crumpled clothes, as he left the court. The reporter had taken a brilliant photo depicting the nastiest, most evil criminal you could imagine. But he wasn't – it was Anthony, my husband. If only people could see that. They all accepted that dreadful photo was the real person. They didn't know him like, well, like I thought I did. I turned the paper face down and almost dragged him out.

Safe in our home, I shut the front door and stood with my back to it. Anthony looked at me.

"I'm sorry. I'm sorry. I never meant to hurt our relationship, or you. I'm so sorry."

I stopped him with a look. "Sorry? Why didn't you tell me? Didn't you trust me enough? How could you do such a thing to us?" He took a step towards me, but I shook my head. "Answer me." He hesitated a moment.

"I don't know. I just… I… It was never a matter of trust. Before I met you, I was stupid, I was a boy, I was confused. Then when you came along, I didn't want to lose you. I thought I'd get to know you, then tell you. Then we got closer and closer, and when you agreed to marry me, I couldn't tell you at all. I was terrified you would dump me. And so I filed the photos in a folder on the computer, and buried that folder in another folder, and I just forgot about them. And that's God's truth."

With that, he lunged at me and fastened his mouth on mine. I pushed him off. His breath and body smelt of stale sweat. "Stop it! Get away! Go have a shower and clean your teeth. Now!"

He hung his head and turned away to the bedroom.

I went to the kitchen sink and spat in the basin. It wasn't saliva I was getting rid of, but the question that had been lingering in my mind through Anthony's explanation. Why hadn't he deleted the photos? I was too afraid to even ask the question. It wasn't that he had them in the first place, so much as why he hadn't deleted them. I ran the water in the sink to wash the words away, and heard a yell from Anthony as the shower went cold.

He emerged from the bedroom in only his boxers. I sent him back to get dressed properly. He had become as needy as a baby. I said to his back, "Anthony, have we – can we have – a future together?"

As he pulled the t-shirt on, he said, "Please, if you'll have me."

I led him to the couch where we could sit quietly. I took the home phone off the hook and placed it gently on the table. The mobile was not even switched on. This was going to be a difficult conversation.

Chapter 12

Pouring wine, I began. "Tell me whatever you can, Nee." (One of my pet names for him was Nee, as in Antho-nee). "I've had a lot of time to think this week – but all I have are questions, no answers. Please give me the answers. Start anywhere – start with the photos."

He hesitated. I watched him bite his bottom lip. "Hon, I'll try. You want to know why I got the photos and why I didn't throw them out. I'm not sure I have the answer, but I think it lies in my past somewhere. I don't know where to start, so it will probably be in the middle. There's lots of stuff about my family that I never told you. You know my mum – surely you can see there's something odd."

I rolled my eyes. "Yes, there is something about her. But whatever it is, you should have told me."

He nodded. "I should have. I'm sorry. But it's not my mum that's the real problem."

We were sitting close together on the couch, and I linked my arm in his. "Go on then. Out with it. I have to know."

He sighed, then took a deep breath. "Well, my dad left when I was about four or five. Mum got a new boyfriend almost at once, and he sort of moved in. I was about seven when Mum got pregnant. As soon as she told him about the baby, he just left. It devastated Mum. She turned to me like I was the man of the family. I did all the things a father should have done. I looked after her."

He leaned forward and picked up the glass from the table, gulping the wine thirstily.

"Sometimes she asked me to sleep in her bed, and I woke up to hear her crying."

"Did she ever… touch you? Or do anything?" As a child, he must have felt powerless against Leila, who could be quite dominating and scary. If I felt that about her, what must it have been like for a kid?

"God no!" Anthony seemed mildly amused by the thought. "She was quite scared at night without someone there. We just lay on the bed and she held my hand, and we drew imaginary pictures on the ceiling from the water stains that were left after the roof leaked one winter. She said it was a comfort to have me there. And then Jarrod was born."

"That was a problem?" I knew his brother. He was a slow learner with ADHD. He had left school early and been unemployed on and off most of his life. There had been problems with the police; I thought it was drugs and theft, but no-one had ever told me. Jarrod wasn't living at home; we never saw him.

"Not exactly a problem, but Mum stopped thinking about me. All of a sudden I was a nuisance, and she only cared about the baby. Even when she asked me into her bed, the baby had to come as well. Then she yelled at me in case I rolled on it and squashed it. I didn't understand why she had changed."

"You shouldn't call the baby 'it'! He's your brother!"

"Well, from the time he was born, he was just a total nuisance. Things were bearable till he came along."

I joined him in sipping, then refilling the glasses. So far, nothing he had said came anywhere near an explanation that satisfied me. I encouraged him with a nod to continue.

"Jarrod was about two years old when my dad reappeared on the scene. He just turned up one day and demanded to see me. I didn't even remember him, I didn't know who he was and why Mum insisted I speak to him. She had another boyfriend by then, so she sent me over there to stay with Dad whenever she wanted privacy."

"I've never met your dad. He didn't come to the wedding. I didn't even know you had contact with him."

"I don't, and I don't want you to either. Please just listen. I was about nine then, and I remember going to Dad's house in Brunswick. It was a rundown weatherboard council house, and it stank. God, I remember that smell! Must, urine, dust, rats scuttling around. But it was all he could get. I suppose no-one else wanted it." He shuddered. "It was revolting. In summer, we spent a lot of time outside. Then another bloke joined us. Dad said it was his brother – my Uncle Sam."

I raised my eyebrows at the addition of yet another family member previously unknown to me.

"He was no relative. I found out later that he was Dad's partner and that the reason he had left mum was that he was gay."

My face must have shown how incredulous I was, because he went on.

"Yes, I know. It's hard to believe, but it happened. I hated Sam. He used to talk about 'us three boys' – me, him and Dad – as though we were kids. And he said it was too hot inside the house, and we should camp outside. It would be fun. He got this tent and put it up in the backyard and we all slept there on the weekends when I was there.

"At first, I was really excited. What kid doesn't enjoy camping? But after the first time, it got a bit creepy. Dad and Sam slept naked, dropping their clothes in the house and stalking around the backyard making an exhibition of themselves and laughing. I hated it, but I couldn't say anything to Dad – he wouldn't have listened. He would have just made fun of me." He stopped.

I prodded him gently. "Go on."

He stood up suddenly and walked to the back door and looked out at the garden. He turned his head towards me. "This is too hard. Can we just leave it for a bit?"

I frowned at him. So far, his story was not much different to thousands of other children whose parents had separated. Having a gay father was perhaps unusual, but in this day and age it was perfectly acceptable. I wondered why parents couldn't be honest with their kids. Didn't they realise how much damage they could do? But I had to try to understand. Otherwise, there could be no forgiveness, no support. He had to explain.

"No, Anthony, you can't stop there. I have to know where I stand, have to start working things out in my head."

He nodded a little sadly and bit his lips together. Sitting back on the couch, he took a deep breath and went on. "I don't know how many times we slept in the tent, but one night, Sam... touched me." He stopped.

"Touched you? What do you mean, touched you?" I thought I knew, but I didn't want to jump to conclusions.

"I mean, he interfered with me. He was sleeping next to me, and I woke up when he fingered me through my boxers. I think I screamed and Dad sat up and asked what happened. Sam gave me this filthy look, so I said it was a nightmare."

Anthony stopped, and I took his hand. He had his little finger in his mouth and was tearing at the skin by the nail. I thought he was going to cry.

"More wine?" We had nearly finished the bottle by now.

He shook his head. "I want to tell you this bit, now that I've started." I nodded.

"Anyway, after that it got worse. Every night we slept in the tent, I felt his hand working down my chest and feeling me through the boxer shorts. One night, he slid a finger under the elastic and then put his entire hand down there. I just lay still and prayed for it to stop. I thought God must have been punishing me for not going to church. I shut my eyes tightly and waited. It seemed like forever."

He turned his head away. Neither of us spoke for a few moments. I tried to imagine what it was like, tried to put myself in his place and get the sense of fear and revulsion, but I couldn't. It was so foreign to me.

"Go on." I didn't want to hear, but I needed to know.

He shut his eyes tightly. A tear squeezed out and dropped onto his shirt. "I can't. I can't say it. Sorry."

We clung together, his head buried in my chest as I patted him on the back. I had to put my feelings aside while he got this out. Then I needed to think about it.

There was a pause. "In the morning, he'd give me money – not much, just fifty cents – and say it was for lollies. I said nothing to anyone. Mum asked where I got the money and I told her Dad had given it to me. She didn't believe it. 'Hmph!' she said. 'He never gives me anything for child support!' But she didn't know about Sam."

He sighed, and so did I. I felt sick at the thought of what had happened to him. My parents protected me from anything bad. They never allowed anyone to hurt me. I had never known anyone before with a story like this, and I was confused about how I felt. But maybe it explained some of his actions – if he had an early experience of sexual assault, and homosexual assault at that. I looked at him, patting him on the back like I was bringing up a baby's wind, and gave him an understanding smile.

"Thank you for telling me. I am glad you trust me. It can't have been easy. But this is just the start. I have to understand everything that happened in order to feel I can support you."

He nodded. "There's more, but... maybe later."

I stood up. It seemed the right time to change the dark, sombre mood.

"We have a lot to do anyway, Nee – or rather, I do. You'll have to stay home while I get the internet cut off and do other stuff. Shall we have something to eat and then I'll run some errands? We can talk again later."

"Sure, hon. I'm actually feeling pretty exhausted by all this. I haven't talked about it before and it's bringing back some pretty horrible stuff. What do I do this afternoon, then? Can I come with you?"

I looked at him in disbelief. "Didn't you see the photo in the paper this morning? You're not leaving the house, that's for sure. You can read a book or weed the backyard or cook dinner."

He looked at me with wide, pleading eyes, which I ignored.

"And how about you get a salad ready for lunch while I change?"

I was tired. It's amazing how quickly the body adapts to change. Last week I had become accustomed to being on my own, doing many strange new things. And now things should have been just like they used to be, but the foundation underpinning our lives had collapsed, taking us with it. Now Anthony was home – for however long – and I had to adapt again, this time to babysitting.

It seemed he had the stuffing knocked out of him and was looking to me to make the decisions, waiting for me to tell him what to do – not a role I was used to. In our relationship, I realised it was him who had usually taken the lead; he worked out where we ate and who we invited over, and what we should plant in the garden. He told me which of my friends he liked. The change in roles scared me.

The cupboards were looking a bit empty, and I wanted to stock up on things. As I was backing the car out, I looked in the rear vision mirror and got a fright at my appearance. I looked much older than I had a month ago.

The shopping centre was crowded, and I thought people might recognise me. My photo had never appeared in the paper, but nevertheless, I was worried.

The supermarket seemed busier than usual. I took a trolley, loading it with cans and long life provisions. Aisles were jammed as people stopped to chat in inconvenient locations, causing others to reach across them to select cartons of eggs or containers of yoghurt. Oblivious, they talked on, occasionally throwing annoyed glances at people who stepped in front of them as they conversed.

Hesitating in front of the milk cabinet, I saw a father and three boys; I assumed they were his sons. There was an argument raging about the size of the chocolate milk carton – Dad was in favour of small, the boys were arguing for giant. I smiled inadvertently and wondered where Mum was. Then a cold chill ran through me. The boys were aged about nine to fourteen, the age range that Anthony had photographed. These boys, bickering amiably about flavoured milk, could have been some of the very children who had been involved. I would never know.

The smile evaporated from my face and was replaced with a tear. I put my head down and hurried down the frozen food aisle, where I picked up a small packet of frozen peas and cooled my cheeks with it, then felt compelled to put it in my trolley.

Now everywhere I looked, there were happy families shopping. Mothers with children, young people hand in hand, an elderly person on a motorised scooter. All of them might have been Anthony's victims, or their relatives or friends. I hurried through my tasks so I could get safely home. I bought enough to withstand a siege, paying for it on credit we didn't have.

Once back in the car, I realised how ridiculous I was being. It wasn't me who had done anything wrong. Why should I feel so guilty? But if I was identified, the media might follow me. So far, we had not seen any sign of them, but that was before the photo was published. If they found out where we lived, I was sure they would stalk us. My mind raced ahead to television crews interviewing the neighbours, graffiti on the fence, broken windows, being forced to move house because of chanting crowds holding signs saying 'Child Molester'.

I don't remember the drive home. I gathered the grocery bags from the car and put them on the verandah while I wrestled with the front door. There was no sign of Anthony at first, then I saw him sitting outside, looking at the back fence. Dumping the bags on the kitchen floor, I put my head out the back door.

"Watching the ivy grow?" He turned his head quickly, startled, as though he hadn't heard me come in. I couldn't help but go to him. "What is it? You look terrified."

He clung to me. "I was daydreaming that I was back in prison. I was alone, and no-one came near me. It was god-awful lonely."

"Was it really bad in there?" He nodded and said nothing for a few seconds. "Tell me," I prompted him.

"I was terrified the whole I time. I was by myself mostly, but I was always afraid that someone would come in and share my cell. The noises, the strangeness, the smell – and the guards – it was awful. I know the officers were just doing their job, but it was 'them or us'. The cell was so tiny, and I was locked up for so many long hours a day. It's all stuck in my head and the thoughts go round and round."

"Maybe you should speak to someone about it?"

He just shook his head. "Only to you. I don't want to see a shrink."

Hearing about prison brought things too close. I turned on my mobile. It made comforting noises as it went through its rigmarole and alerted me to new messages. There were lots. Most I ignored – I only looked at Nellie's.

"RU OK? Call me!"

"Oy! Put yr phone on!"

"Where RU? If u don't answer im comin ova."

And finally, *"Im at our usual café. Not going till you join me"*

The last was sent less than half an hour ago, and I immediately texted back *"wait im comin"*

Anthony hadn't moved. I put my hands on his shoulders.

"I'm going for coffee with Nellie. Be back later."

He looked up quickly. "Can I come? I'm sick of being home alone. I need some company. Please?"

"I can't take you, Anthony. I want to see Nellie. You have to get used to being home by yourself. You can bring the shopping in. It's on the verandah."

"But I could wait for you in the car or something."

"No, you can't! Give me a break. Bail! You have to be in my sight when you are out of the house. I've spent the last week running around trying to get this mess straightened out."

He looked downcast, putting on an expression he knew I had trouble resisting. But that was a week ago. Now I was stronger.

I kissed him on his bristly cheek. "Bye."

Chapter 13

Nellie was sitting by the window. The café had some comfortable couches and we always grabbed these when we could. Nellie wore one of her own homemade creations, a striking vision in black and white with a red bandana. I loved her zaniness – she was creative, often outrageous, and she generally didn't care what people thought of her. I admired that.

She had ordered me a large latte, which was waiting on the table. I sank into the couch and smiled at her. "Thank you! I haven't had my mobile on. Sorry!"

"You're forgiven. Can you catch me up? And how are you?"

"So much has happened, and yet in a way it's nothing compared to this past week. It's all a blur. I can't even remember what I told you last!"

I sipped the hot coffee while I thought. Nellie just looked at me and gave me space. I had learnt in the last few days how valuable it was to be able to stay silent, and how difficult. Finally, I was ready.

"OK. He's out on bail at the moment." My voice must have been louder than I meant, because some ladies at the nearest table stopped talking and looked at me. I lowered my voice. "Did you see it in the paper?"

She nodded. "It was an awful photo. Not like Anthony at all."

"I didn't read the story, but I saw the photo. The Prosecution didn't want him to be let out, but the Magistrate said he could, as long as he kept to some strict conditions. He isn't allowed out of the house unless his mother or I are with him. That's going to be really hard. And he has to sign in at the police station every single day. And no internet in the house. Such a nuisance! Oh well. I was spending far too much time on the computer, anyway."

Nellie sipped and sighed. "Yeah, but it's a bit of a drastic way to cut back!"

I had to broach the subject eventually. "Nellie, I need to ask you something." I felt weird, gathering my courage to ask my best friend something that last week would have been so easy.

"Fire away." She smiled at me.

"Anthony wanted to come with me today, but I said no. I have to ask you whether you mind. He said he wants things to be like they were."

I had hoped Nellie would just automatically tell me not to be ridiculous, that of course she still loved him and me just as much as ever. I could almost hear the words, and I willed her to say them. They didn't come. Instead, there was silence. I didn't know whether to look at her, say something, or just wait. I waited. I drank coffee. I dabbed my eyes, which had unaccountably sprung tears. The longer the silence, the more I worried.

"Bugger," she said. "I don't know quite what to say."

Silence again. I didn't want to make it easy for her to say no. Anthony wasn't the only one who wanted things to be like they were before. That included us having fun times together, the three of us.

She took a deep breath. "Look, it's really hard. I would love to just say yes, everything will be fine, and to promise to act like it is.

But I'm not sure if I can. I don't know how I feel. I don't want to hurt you, but I am not sure that I know Anthony anymore. I thought I did, but I didn't see this coming."

"And you think I did?" I was suddenly angry with her. "You think I asked for this and I am helping him out because – well, why exactly?" I wanted to hurt Nellie, I wanted her to strike back at me, almost something physical, so that I could see cuts and bruises. You get sympathy for a broken arm, but none for a broken heart. "This mess was not of my making, but I'm the one stuck in the middle. And my friends need to support me, and to do that they have to support Anthony! And if they don't, then I don't want them as friends!"

Nellie went white, and I knew I had hurt her, but I was glad. Someone else needed to feel my pain, to be a part of what I had been coping with. Nellie was the only person I could trust. There are not many people you can hurt and know it will still be OK.

"Is it a case of 'Love me, love my husband', regardless of what he has done?"

"It is! Like it or not, I am his wife. I married him for better or worse, and you don't get much worse than this. But he needs me. He needs treatment. So I will help him through this. I will make sure he gets to a doctor who can fix him. I will make him better."

She looked into my eyes and saw what I was trying to hide. It was as though, in that instant, she had reached behind my façade and found how deep the wound was. The anger suddenly left me.

"Oh Nellie, I'm sorry. I'm so sorry I hurt you. I was just striking back at anything I could. I'm so mixed up."

"I know. It's OK Erica, I'll be your emotional punching bag!"

That started the waterworks. Luckily, the two ladies at the next table had left before they were treated to a real scene. I became hysterical. Waiters brought me clouds of napkins to mop up the floods. Nellie waved them away.

"There, there, you silly sausage. I can't even begin to comprehend what it must be like for you. But you asked me a question. Do you want to hear the answer?"

Dry-eyed now, I bit my lip and nodded.

"OK. I am prepared to meet with you and Anthony. I need to discuss what happened with him. And I want to support you, now and in the future, if you let me. But there are issues of trust that he has torn down, not only with me, but with his friends and family. And I need to see if he can repair those, so it's not a decision I can make straight away."

"I shouldn't have asked you today. It's too soon. If you can forgive me for the hurtful things I said, then let's just put this in the 'too hard' basket for the time being, OK?" I put out my hand and we shook.

She kept hold of my hand and covered it with hers. "We forget this part of the conversation. Agreed?" I nodded.

There was a moment's silence, then Nellie continued with casual chit-chat. "What else happened apart from the bail thing?"

"Anthony told me some stuff about abuse in his childhood. It explains a bit."

"He needs to do some explaining to more than just you. Is he seeing a psychiatrist?"

"Mr Szili is making appointments for us with… I think it's called a forensic psychologist. I don't quite know what they will do. And we are seeing the priest."

"Father Nick?" I nodded.

"Sounds like you're pretty organised at the moment?"

"Well, in terms of getting things underway, yes. But not in terms of answers. Look Nell, I'd better go. Anthony was pretty upset about being left at home, and I feel a bit guilty when he's been locked up for a week."

"You go do what you have to. I'll be there for you, short meeting or long. And you know you are welcome to stay at my place if you need." We shared a long hug.

Before I went home, I called in to see my parents. I needed to be loved and cosseted. Mum hugged me and put the inevitable kettle on. Dad was out in the vegetable garden, and Mum sent me out to join him. "I'll bring the tea out in a little while."

Dad was digging away at his patch with a three-pronged hoe which he'd had for years. The handle was all worn and had splinters sticking out, but he swore it was the best one he'd ever had. Personally, I thought a hoe was a hoe.

He was running a bit behind with the crop because the corn and tomatoes had just kept on flowering and fruiting, and he hadn't wanted to pull them out. But now they were gone, and he was adding potting mix and fertiliser to the soil, ready for the next crop to be planted.

"*Lánya gyermek.*" He greeted me with a kiss on both cheeks. My parents had never made me learn Hungarian, though I knew a few words. *Lánya gyermek* meant daughter, and it was Dad's pet name for me. Sometimes he called me *"cica"* or kitten. "Come and sit with me."

He leaned the hoe against the garden shed and led the way to a rustic bench. He had made it years ago so that he could sit and watch for cabbage moths, scare the starlings away from pulling up the seedlings, or do a snail patrol by torchlight. He kept a close eye on pests, and his vegetables were always insect-free.

"Now, *cica*, I want you to listen to me and not interrupt. Remember, your dad only has your best interests at heart and he loves you so much."

"I know, Poppy. And I know you are always right – at least in your opinion!"

He smiled at me. "Your mother and I have talked this over for hours. And I know you will have been thinking about it non-stop. There's no easy way out of the situation. But I can't forgive Anthony for doing this to you." He held up his hand as I went to interrupt. "Let me finish first. Just listen to me, *cica*." I tucked my hand in his arm, and rested my head on his shoulder, partly so I didn't have to look at him.

"Your mother and I think Anthony should give up this bail idea. It's too hard on you. You won't have your own life as long as you have to be his babysitter. If he went back into jail, you could come and live at home with us, and rent out your house. We thought that money for the mortgage is going to be tight without you both working, so the rent would be a help. And what wasn't covered by the rent, your mum and I could top up with our savings."

I had almost stopped listening when Dad had suggested Anthony going back to jail. But this last sentence caught my attention. I knew they didn't have much money, but their savings were for a trip back to Hungary to visit relatives. Dad hadn't been back since he came to Australia thirty years ago. He had escaped from Hungary rather than be called up for national service, and it was only recently that he had a letter from the Hungarian Embassy in Canberra stating that he would not be prosecuted if he went back. It was the reason he had not gone home sooner, even though he was an 'old' man and they would never make him join the army now.

They were saving hard to make it a trip that could last about three months. They had never visited the graves of their parents, and there were cousins, aunts and uncles spread around the country, most of whom I had never met, though they often asked us to come and visit as a family. I couldn't take that money from them. I said as much.

Mum arrived with tea and biscuits and joined in the discussion, handing Dad a mug. "But darling, we don't plan to go to Hungary while all this is happening, anyway. And you could pay us back when things got sorted out."

"We've had a talk." Dad dunked a biscuit, and Mum looked at me enquiringly.

I shook my head. "It's really kind of you, and I do appreciate it. But I can't. Anthony needs to be free so that we can work out what's going to happen. And he has to go to appointments and things."

Mum chimed in, making it clear that she didn't wholly support the scheme. "This plan of your Dad's, it doesn't have to be tomorrow.

It could be in a month, or two months, whenever. I'm sure Anthony only needs to go to the police and hand himself in. It's going to be really hard on you to be his keeper. It wasn't fair of the court to make that condition."

"I agreed to it, Mum. I got up on the witness stand and told the Magistrate I would do it. I have to stick to my word."

My parents looked at each other and sighed. "Told you, didn't I?" Dad hissed at Mum. "Stubborn, just like her mother." He turned to me. "Just think about it, that's all we ask. We'd be happy to have you home so we could look after you."

Just for a moment, I was tempted. Then I remembered Anthony's face as I left. I shook my head. "Thank you, dear, kind parents. But no, certainly not at the moment. Now I have to get on. I need to go home."

They glanced at each other, then stood up and walked me to the car. I was hugged and kissed and reassured. Dad put his head in the car window. "Come round any time. But please don't bring Anthony. I don't want him here."

The statement punctured the warmth that I was feeling. I didn't say anything – just drove off, but my angst was back and raging. I put the statement aside to examine later.

Chapter 14

When I arrived home, Anthony was flicking idly through the daytime TV shows. His face was already bristly, his jeans and t-shirt stained and crumpled. "Nothing but crap," he muttered. "I thought you'd never come. Where have you been?"

He sounded churlish, but I ignored it. The shopping bags were still on the floor in the kitchen, and I asked him to put things away while I changed. He did it, but with a roll of the eyes.

"What's up with you?" I sighed. I didn't have the energy to cope with a sulky husband behaving like a child. Thoughts kept jumping into my mind – *'If it hadn't been for you, our life would be still going along as normal. So like it or lump it!'* – but I knew that was no help, and I tried to cultivate patience. It was hard.

Anthony kicked a cupboard door shut with his foot. "What's up with me? What the hell do you think is up with me? The police raid the house and arrest me, I've been locked up for a week without a clue what's going on, I finally get home and you disappear for hours on end, chattering with your friends, and leave me here alone! Then I tell you about the biggest trauma of my life and you just up and leave! How do you bloody think I'm feeling?"

He stood with a shopping bag in each hand, and I could see the muscles in his arms bulging. A tic twitched in his face. I meant to keep my temper, I really did. I had every intention of being calm and collected and showing him understanding and care. But when he acted like the wounded warrior, it was too much.

"Well, I'm sorry for not being considerate enough! I'm sorry for not appreciating having my life ruined by you. I'm sorry for using all my holidays in order to fix up your bail and be your babysitter. I'm sorry for wanting some part of my life to be a bit like it was before the police came looking for you and your bloody photos. Obviously, I am an unreasonable human being who doesn't deserve to have you in my life. Obviously it's time I left!"

I couldn't make a dramatic exit because he was standing in front of the door, so I turned towards the back door. Out of the corner of my eye, I saw him faint and slide to the floor. There was a crash as the remaining shopping bags dropped to the floor, and bright red pasta sauce flooded onto the tiles, mingling into his black hair like blood. My anger was banished by guilt and fear. I ran to help him.

He hadn't lost consciousness, but he was groggy. I tried to think of what little first aid I had learnt as he stirred and tried to sit up. I helped him to the couch, and sat on the arm of the chair next to him, smoothing his hair with one hand and patting his arm with the other. He opened his eyes, and they took a second to focus on me.

"Are you OK?" I asked, wondering if he had really hurt himself. He nodded, but didn't look certain − his eyes were bleary and unfocussed. As I looked at him, I couldn't help but laugh. "You look so delightful with pasta sauce in your hair! But really, are you alright? Should we go to the doctor?"

He gave a wan smile. "I'm fine. It takes more than a mere fall to knock me out. I'm sorry. I think I'm a bit overwrought. I felt faint, and next thing I was down. I'm really sorry. I was selfish."

"I'm sorry, too. It's been a long few days. We must try to be patient with each other. Are you sure you don't need an ambulance?"

He gave a minimal shake of his head. "Give me a few moments, I'll be right. Maybe a cup of tea?"

I got up. "Just lie there and I'll be back." I spread a towel to prevent a stain on the sofa, and thought how considerate I was.

Our tempers seem to have been knocked out by the fainting episode. We drank tea, and he had an aspirin. Then he watched me finish unpacking the groceries in silence, pushing the remaining items into any spare space I could find. So much for my tidy cupboards.

When that was done, I sat back in the comfy chair. "Is it OK to talk?" I asked him. It didn't matter which of us said it – we were both thinking it. We sat in silence for a while, neither of us wanting to start.

Finally, Anthony began. "Did you really mean what you said about leaving?"

I thought for a moment. "Nee, sometimes I get so angry with you I can't bear it. I can't help but think that it's your actions, not mine, which have brought us to this. At times like these, yes, I do want to leave – but I agreed to see this out, and I will. But you must allow me free rein to do what I want, when I want. You're the one on bail. You have to cop the staying home. If that doesn't work, then maybe we can talk to Mr Szili."

He fixed his gaze on my face, shoulders slumping. "What about? There is only one option: I go back to prison. Don't think I don't realise that! It's never far from my mind." He ran his hand through his hair, then wiped off some pasta sauce on the towel. "I don't think I could stand it." He bowed his head as though in prayer.

There was no choice about prison, if that's what the judge decided – but it wasn't helpful to say it. I took his hand. "Mr Szili might have other ideas. Maybe we could apply for a change in the bail conditions, ask for more freedom so you could go places by yourself. Or maybe other people could supervise you. They might let you get some work. Mr Szili said to wait a bit, and if you did everything right and proved you're trustworthy, they might consider changes to the conditions."

He brightened. "Did he say that? Really?" A smile spread across his face. "After two days of house arrest, that sounds like heaven to me. You know, sometimes I wake up in the night and it's like this is a dream, that all this never happened. And I'm so happy, and then it comes back in a rush, and it's worse than ever." He blinked rapidly.

I squeezed his hand, and he leaned over and rested his nose on my arm.

"Yes, well, you're not alone in that. Maybe we are sharing a nightmare."

My shirt muffled his voice. "I can't believe that I'm not even allowed out of the house! It seems so stupid, when a week ago I was going to work, going out, doing anything I wanted and no-one had a problem with it. Now, suddenly, I'm like a leper." He looked up at me.

I puzzled about that, too. You read about 'innocent until proven guilty' and all that, but when it comes down to what actually happens, the police and the courts have the power to do anything to you.

I sat up. "Look, Nee, I need to understand what happened. These things they have charged you with, they're horrible. I don't even want to think about them. Why didn't you tell me? That stuff about being scared of losing me – didn't it ever strike you that you were more likely to ruin our relationship by keeping secrets? Trust is a pretty big part of a relationship. Didn't you ever think that these were wrong things to do? Going on the net to find a child porn ring?"

He just stared straight ahead, biting his lip. I waited as patiently as I could for a response. None were forthcoming.

"Anthony, I need an answer. I need to understand. Healing our relationship depends on us being able to trust each other – and I haven't done anything to abuse our trust. You have. You need to do the work." I stood up and roamed around the lounge, plumping up cushions, straightening rugs, running a finger along the shelf to check for dust. Anything to reduce the tension.

He started biting his nails. They were already gnawed right down. He didn't look at me. "Hon, if I could explain it, I would. The police said I was sick, sick in the head. Maybe I am. Had you noticed?"

"You kept it well hidden, if you are. To me, that means you're not." I thought to myself if he wasn't sick, then he must be just bad, and I couldn't stand that. But I didn't say it. "We go to this expert Mr Szili is arranging and hopefully he can help you." I sat on the couch opposite him.

"What expert? A shrink? I don't want to go to a shrink!" He started to panic and become agitated. He flushed, then abandoned biting for pulling his hair.

I pulled a cushion from behind me and hugged it on my knee. It was soft and somehow comforting. "Hey, you!" I kept my tone neutral. "Take some deep breaths. It will help." As we breathed together, I felt more settled, and he lost the red blotches on his face. "You have to go to a doctor. Mr Szili said the court will require a psychiatric report. He has given me the name of the top doctor in this field. It's expensive but there's no choice."

Anthony looked up, brow furrowed. "Will you come with me?"

"If I'm allowed. I don't think they'll let me into the appointment, though. But I have to come with you anyway, because of the bail."

His face fell. "I keep forgetting. But, hon, do you think I am sick?"

I didn't want to answer this. Somewhere in the back of my mind, I had divided the offences he had been charged with into two categories. I was only dealing with the first. I could only just manage to think of Anthony getting porn images of children from the internet. I knew there were people who did that. I could even manage to think of him looking at them, though I didn't want to go into what he was thinking when the images were on the screen.

But actually having children there, in front of him and having sexual fantasies about them – that I could not bring myself to deal with. I only knew a few snippets the police had told me, but the words 'bondage' and 'nudity' stuck in my mind. What did it mean for me, for us, if these things were in his mind? How could we ever have a normal relationship? And how would I know if he was still thinking like this? I had some cousins in primary school, delightful boys – what if they had to deal with the actions of a man like Anthony? It hurt me too much to think about it, and I pushed the revulsion away. I couldn't tell him what I was thinking, not yet. Everything was so raw. If I talked about it, I would have to deal with it. I was determined that it was going to stay boxed up in my mind for as long as possible. I opted out of a brutally honest answer.

"Honey? You haven't answered my question. Do you think I am sick?"

Swallowing hard, I chose my words carefully. "I have personally never had any desire to look at the sort of images the police tell me you had on the computer. The police showed me some of them. It would horrify me if anyone offered them to me. I can't understand what you found so attractive about them. So yes, that makes me think you have an illness, a twist in your brain. Maybe it was caused by what you went through with Sam, I don't know. I'm no expert. I'm hoping the doctor can explain it."

He was silent. Then he stood up and walked to the window overlooking the backyard. "I haven't told you everything yet."

My heart sank. "Oh. Do you want to? Now?"

"No, not really… but …"

I almost screamed at the prospect of hearing more, but it was important to contain my feelings so I could understand. I nodded and sat down. "Go on."

He stayed looking out of the window and I couldn't see his face. He took a deep breath. "I'll just give you the bare outline, then. My mother and stepfathers were abusive to me, physically and verbally, right throughout my childhood. My father often beat my mother before he finally left. I hid in my room, pretending I couldn't hear, in case he came in. But I could hear her screaming at him to stop." He recited the facts as though he had learnt them off by heart. "Maybe this gave me some warped and twisted idea of sex."

I'd had enough. I stood up to bring this to a conclusion. The right thing would be to go over and hug him, but I couldn't. "That's enough for today. Let's open a bottle of wine and drink it all!"

I picked up the remote and clicked it at the TV. There was a cricket match on, which was brainless enough for anyone. I was ready to leave the topic. But it was a bit too abrupt for him, and he turned to look at me, biting his lip. I left him to watch the match in silence.

Chapter 15

The next few days formed their own sombre pattern. I slept in the spare room, taking a pill each night. Anthony slept in our room. When we woke up, we got our own breakfast, then walked to the police station for Anthony to sign in. There had been no more publicity, so I felt safe enough to walk instead of drive. Conversation between us was sparse and confined to facts. "Is there more milk?" "What would you like for dinner?" – that sort of thing. I missed our relaxed relationship, but had no idea if or when it would return. After the sign in, I went to Mum's to check emails, then went shopping and had coffee with Nellie.

Sometimes we had an appointment with Mr Szili, and other times I took Anthony to see the priest. Father Nick had agreed to meet him twice a week. At first he thought he couldn't help him, but I pointed out that, at the very least, Anthony needed reconciliation and prayer, and Nick was the one who should provide it. I didn't care whether Nick consulted the bishop or whoever his supervisor was to get permission – so long as, at the end of the process, Nick stood up in court to say that Anthony had been a regular penitent.

All this I negotiated without Anthony being involved. However, when I told him, he wasn't quite as compliant as I had anticipated. "Why in hell did you do that?"

I stared at him. "Don't you understand the situation you are in? Don't you realise that in court you are going to need every positive statement that you can get, and that priests are generally highly regarded? In any case, you have nothing else much to occupy your time with, so you may as well pray!" I couldn't understand why I he was so reluctant to get help.

He wasn't impressed. "Priests are usually the ones who get the publicity for their own child abuse! What makes you think they will be highly regarded in court?"

I couldn't believe it and found my anger rising quickly. "How dare you make any implication like that about Nick? Just because you're a fool doesn't mean you can go around bad-mouthing other people! You wouldn't dare say that in front of Nick, so what makes you think I'll tolerate it?"

"I didn't mean it that way. You know I didn't. It's just that I don't want to be forced to spend hours a week talking to a priest, for God's sake. Surely you understand that?"

I didn't care what he said. "Either you see Father Nick twice a week or you don't go out at all." I put my shaking hands in my pockets to hide them.

He reluctantly agreed. I figured I was safe enough leaving him with Nick, and in any case I was not allowed in to the sessions, so I had some private time, which helped restore my equilibrium.

On the first visit to the forensic psychiatrist, Anthony had to complete a long questionnaire (a diagnostic tool, I think it was called) and didn't really speak to the doctor at all. No lying on couches and being psycho-analysed. I think that's what we both expected. I was disappointed and eager to get things underway. Anthony wasn't so keen, and I had to keep reminding him of the court orders. We made appointments for future sessions, but not until the doctor had assessed the answers to the questionnaire. I don't know how a questionnaire can tell you more about the person than they can tell you themselves. What's stopping people from lying on the questions, anyway? Surely it's better to talk to the person and observe them? But hey, what did I know?

Anthony had resigned from his job. He didn't have much choice, really – it was that or be sacked. It was understandable. The Recreation Centre had copped some adverse publicity, and the local papers raised questions like *"How safe are your kids?"*, *"Is there a shark at your child's pool?"* and *"What's happening when you're not around?"* It was pathetic. I hadn't read the articles myself, but Nell told me about them. If I saw a local paper in the letter box, it went straight to the recycle bin.

A couple of weeks into the new regime, I started looking in the employment section of the paper. We could both consider different jobs. There were several for telemarketers and also a few for salespeople. I didn't say anything to Anthony, but I thought long and hard about the chances of him being able to work. I decided to get him organised first, then look for something for me. It was another indication of how our marriage had changed, that I was the one doing the planning for everything. It was less of a partnership and more of a hierarchy.

One day when he was signing in at the police station, Sergeant Price came in and greeted me with a wave. I should have been suspicious, I suppose, but I trusted him. Anyway, we had nothing to lose.

I asked him straight out. "If Anthony could get a job in something that didn't have children anywhere near, would you be prepared to vary the bail conditions?"

Anthony wasn't listening. He was at the other end of the counter waiting for the bail sign-in book.

Sergeant Price paused for a moment. "What did you have in mind?"

"Like sales, or phone marketing?"

"Let me think about it. I'll let you know. In the meantime, we've finished with some of your gear. You'll need to sign for it before you take it home."

I was encouraged. At least Sergeant Price would consider the job idea, I was sure of that. We collected the digital photo frame, the albums, my laptop, and a few other bits and pieces. I made Anthony carry most of them while I took my computer. Sergeant Price had said I could keep the internet on it, provided it was never in the house. He said I could keep the computer in my car, but it was preferable for it to be somewhere else. I decided to take it to Mum's. Anthony wanted it at home to play games on, and suggested we took access to the net off, but I had used it for work and I didn't want to lose any documents. I thought it best not to stuff around with the hard drive or I might never get things back the way they were. Anthony knew about these things, but I didn't want him to touch it. I thought maybe the police might fingerprint it one day to see if he had used it – that's how neurotic I was getting.

A few days later, Sergeant Price called. He said Ms Obermeyer had agreed to the change in bail conditions to allow Anthony to work, provided we gave them the contact details of the employer and the times that Anthony was working (assuming he got a job, of course). When we had these, Sergeant Price agreed to apply to the court for the change.

I felt as though an enormous burden had been lifted. No longer would Anthony have to mooch about the house. If he could pick up a job in a call centre or a plant nursery or a big store or somewhere, then he could earn some money. God knew we needed every cent, and it would help to keep him busy. I was grateful to Sergeant Price, who could have just ignored my request.

We searched the papers for suitable jobs, me with more enthusiasm than Anthony. He reluctantly went to a couple of interviews, though he was overqualified for them. When he started talking about waiting to see if anything better came along, I got really angry. I noticed how short-tempered I was getting.

"You'll take the first place that offers you a job, Anthony. I don't care if you love it or hate it." I knew it wasn't fair, but it was getting too much for me.

"But they all pay much less than I was getting, and they'll be boring!" he complained.

"Don't care. You're doing it."

As it happened, he was offered two jobs on the same day, and once he had decided which one to take, we approached the police. The Magistrate altered the bail conditions after making sure the police agreed. We didn't even go to the court.

Chapter 16

Within a week, I was seeing Anthony off on the train to the city, and I was free. The loss of his independence had hit us both hard. I was not at work, and he was. I could have some head space to myself. Sometimes he came home complaining, but I refused to listen.

The casual sales job was good because it meant Anthony could take time off to go to the psychologist or the priest. I had to take him to those places because the bail variations only covered work, but I could cope with that.

In the time created by not having to supervise Anthony, I slowly began my own healing. There wasn't much I could do about my dad's attitude, not at the moment – he was adamant that he never wanted to see Anthony again, and he didn't even want to talk things over with me.

I started seeing the psychologist from work. She was helpful, and when I ran out of free sessions, she kept seeing me as a private client.

While some people say counselling is useless, let me tell you that the right person at the right time can work miracles. I don't know how I would have coped if I hadn't had her as a sounding board. I talked to her about the feelings of panic and loss of control that I felt, and described a couple of incidents where I thought I was losing my mind. She reassured me that I was processing the trauma and told me to keep breathing deeply when those events happened.

I told her about Anthony's experience of sexual assault, and she helped me reminisce about my own experiences. By comparison, nothing bad had ever happened to me. I told her how out of control I felt. I couldn't see how I could simplify my life, how I could restructure it, except by eliminating Anthony, and that wasn't an option. He needed me and I had to be there. How often had I sat through that message in church? But she challenged me on it.

"You say you can't 'eliminate' Anthony. That sounds very final and dramatic. What do you mean?"

At first an answer didn't come easily. "I love Anthony. He's a kind, good man. Our marriage has been happy. It's given me independence and my own life. I've never felt any doubt about our relationship. And in our religion, you marry your husband for life. I knew that. Since this happened, of course I have tried to think about what life would be like without him, but I'm so used to having him around."

"You say you love him. Can you describe what that means? You mention it in relation to independence. Do you see a connection between marriage and independence?"

I found myself breathing heavily and sighing. Was I really in love with the idea of marriage, rather than with the person I had married? Surely not. It had felt 'right' from the time we met. My parents had taught me this love thing was about caring more about the other person than about yourself. And I cared about Anthony. I thought he cared about me. He had to stay.

I told her I needed to strip away unnecessary things, that tidying up and throwing things out made me feel better. She said that was only a superficial solution and didn't change things, but I disagreed. In a fit of activity one day I had cleaned out the garage and taken a load of stuff to the tip. I felt much calmer afterwards. I was sure that reducing everything to essentials would help. Despite the counsellor's advice, I made a list of things I could downsize. I started by cleansing my acquaintances. I had already taken us off Facebook and Twitter, and anything else I could find that shared us with the world. I removed phone numbers from my mobile, and then went to my email. I sent a message to everyone in my address book:

"Hi. You will no doubt have heard about our personal crisis. I am going to be a hermit for as long as it takes. Feel free to contact me but don't expect a reply."

I expected people to email back with sympathy and consideration. I thought my friends would stand by me. In fact, pretty much nothing happened – it was as though I had not emailed at all. A week later, I just deleted everyone who had not replied. I figured they had made the decision that we were not worthy to be called friends, and I should unburden myself of them. Later I discovered that there were many reasons people didn't reply. Some had changed their email addresses, their computer had been 'down', they were out of the country, or a number of other legitimate reasons. But most importantly, some people took me at my word and left me alone. They were being considerate in their own way and giving me the space that I had more or less demanded. However, at the time, I decided to shed them, so they were deleted. It hurt, but it also felt good.

It was like cutting myself, a habit which I'd had as a teenager and to which I had returned during this time. I didn't tell anyone that I had started cutting again. I knew it would devastate Mum. She had been so worried when I was at school, in case cutting turned into suicide attempts. But I didn't do it for that reason: I wasn't trying to kill myself – I was trying to see if I could still feel, and that the feeling was pain. And if I felt physical pain, I could cope with the mental pain. It sounds stupid, I know, but that was my thinking. Cutting was always in the back of my mind. I still have tiny white scars on my thighs and stomach. The blade was my constant companion.

Sometimes just looking at the scars brought back the pain and then I put the blade away. But sometimes nothing could stop me. I had to cut. I had to. I didn't do my arms, usually only the top of my thighs, where no-one saw it. Usually it was about six or seven little cuts in a row, and then I laid a tissue over them, and looked at the pattern of blood. The cuts were neat and orderly, all the same length. Afterwards, I felt like shit. But at the time, it seemed like the only thing that worked.

However, shedding people certainly made my life simpler. Generally, I was in contact only with my family, Anthony's mother, and Nellie. It was a small circle, but the energy required to speak with other people was too much. Facing them was too difficult. After all, what was there to say?

I couldn't believe that it had only been about eight weeks since the raid when I actually settled into an alternative routine. How adaptable we are as humans. My relationship with Anthony had reached a sort of stasis, where we had tacitly agreed not to talk about the case, at least not for the moment. He was learning his new job and came home tired and often grumpy. We knew we couldn't avoid the topic forever, but neither of us wanted to upset what had become the new status quo. I tried not to resent him for the situation we were in.

I recognised our relationship had moved from one of equality to one where I was looking after him. I felt it evolving, and it wasn't pleasant. I wanted to love him as desperately as I used to, but shut off any thoughts of being intimate. I slept in the spare room, got up and had breakfast, also making it for Anthony if he had an early shift, then went to see my parents. A bit of shopping, house cleaning, lunch, and then 'me' time, which I constantly needed. Sometimes it was a long, lingering coffee in a discreet shop near my parents, sometimes it was a visit to Nellie, or a massage. Some days there was an appointment with the psychologist, the lawyer, the priest, the bank, or whoever else had a slice of my pie.

On one of my free days, I decided to make a start on regaining some fitness. Since the raid, after an initial week of eating barely anything, my appetite returned double or even triple – but not for anything remotely nutritious. I tried, oh I tried, but looking at broccoli and carrots, zucchini and beans just turned me off. Instead, I sought out pasta and spaghetti, fried rice and sweet, tangy noodles. I followed these with cold Coke or lemonade, a hot jam donut or cream cake. In between came chocolate, chips, maybe a hamburger. I calculated that the emotional energy I used more than compensated.

You might refer to it as comfort eating, but there was nothing comfortable about it. It led to a rapidly expanding figure, which was never sylph-like to begin with. I didn't care. Life was shit, and the hand it had dealt me sucked. What did it matter how big I was? It was more important that I enjoyed my food and got some pleasure from it.

To help dissipate the disapproving looks from my dad, I went to the gym. Anthony and I had, at one stage, joined a health club. We paid an exorbitant amount of money, got a personal trainer and a list of scary sounding classes such as Pilates, Strength Training, and 'Love Your Body'. But, as with about 99% of other new joiners, we only went once or twice. Our personal trainer had given us a strict program to follow. We'd written it down carefully and stuck it on the fridge, then promptly ignored it. I had gone to the gym once, Anthony had pulled some weights, and we went to a water aerobics class, but that was it.

I decided to have a swim at the local pool, where I thought I could both exercise and relax. I felt very self-conscious in among the beautiful people. Although it was enjoyable, afterwards I realised I was ravenous. I hot footed it to Mum's, where I downed a large plate of her homemade ravioli, topped with heaps of grated cheese. It was exactly the garlicky, tomatoey, cheesy dish that I was crying out for. I felt almost content as I drove away. I felt almost as though I had got on top of things.

Almost.

But the pain struck without warning and sent me spinning away, out of control. There was no cause, no incident that warned me to be careful and alert. It just hit.

I remember being on my way to Mum's. The traffic lights turned red at a big intersection, with three lanes in each direction. I was jammed in. On the passenger side was the curb; to my right was a petrol tanker; behind me, a large truck. Ahead was a workman's ute, with some planks secured and hanging over the edge, and a dog tied by a leash to the framework. It was a kelpie, or heeler, and it stood firm on all four paws, eyes fixed on me.

I sat patiently at the lights, willing them to change. My eyes were drawn to a movement from the dog as it strained on the leash. It started to bark at me, and I was afraid. I locked the car doors, breathing quickly and starting to feel panic set in. The dog frothed from its mouth, tiny white bubbles. With each breath it inflated in size, snapping its jaws and snarling at me. I watched in horror as it doubled in size, skin tight, looking ready to burst.

A blast of horns from behind me brought me suddenly back to reality. There was no dog. The ute had pulled ahead as the light turned green, and I found I was holding up traffic. Shaken, I made a sudden left turn and pulled over. Breathing heavily I wondered what had actually happened, and rang Mum, asking her to come and get me. I realised I had experienced a panic attack – something I had heard of, but didn't expect to have myself.

It was an enormous relief to see the familiar figures of my parents running towards the car. Mum came over and helped me out. "Come on, love, we're going to take you to the doctor. Your dad will take the car, so don't worry about anything. OK?"

The outcome of my visit to the doctor was some tranquilisers and a referral to a psychiatrist. I filled the prescription, but the bottle sat unopened on the bench and I didn't make an appointment with the psychiatrist. I preferred to rely on my counsellor, who had been such a rock over the past weeks. I made an appointment with her for the next day and talked at length about the horror, the fear, and how irrational I felt after it was all over. She was calm and sensible and helped me think more clearly.

I was alarmed that she thought the attacks might happen again, but at least I was prepared for them this time. She explained the physical symptoms and how the mind can just race into overdrive. It all made sense. After that, I tucked the tranquilisers into my bag, and decided to take them if I needed to. I didn't want to have that experience again.

I didn't tell Anthony about the panic attack. I didn't think he would understand.

Chapter 17

One night over dinner, we looked at each other and knew it was time to continue The Talk. It was strange how we were so attuned to each other in that way, but so far apart in the secret life he had been leading. He opened up the discussion when we had poured a glass of Baileys each and sat in the comfy lounge chairs.

"Hon, I feel like you are punishing me, sleeping in the spare room. I miss you lying next to me. You know I might be… away… for a while. I'm lonely. Would you consider coming back?"

He took me by surprise. I was thinking we would talk about court and tactics, and that he would tell me what the psychologist and priest had said. I had asked him a few times, but he managed to avoid answering in detail. He just said, "They talk about stuff with me," and "Father Nick does a lot of praying."

I had not really considered the issue of sleeping together again. It just seemed natural to have some distance while we got to know each other again, even though it was lonely in the spare room. I had quickly got used to sharing the bed once we were married.

I said as much to him. "I understand what you are saying, but I'm not sure that I know you anymore. And I don't generally sleep with people I don't know." I thought it was a pretty logical answer, but he had a comeback.

"But hon, it *is* me. I haven't actually changed. You have seen a part of me I kept hidden from everyone. I was protecting myself. But now I can't do that. And I need support and I need to feel loved. We had… *have* love, you and me. You know that, I know that."

Another Baileys went the way of the first. Can you get drunk on two glasses of Baileys?

I paused. "I thought we had love. I believed we did. But where does trust come in, if our relationship was built on less than complete honesty?"

He stopped nibbling cheese for a moment while he considered that. "Does it make sense for me to say that I never deceived you intentionally? That what we had, the love we had, was between the person I was then and the person you are now, and that hasn't changed?"

Something about his logic was twisted, but it made sense to me at the time. I took a moment to breathe by getting up and clearing away the plates. "Are you suggesting we could just go back to square one?" I asked. "I don't think I can. When you think you know the totality of a person and you find that 25% is not even showing, it shakes your confidence a bit."

He put his arm around my shoulders and pulled me towards him. He often used to do this. The familiarity of it was bittersweet. I didn't move away. "Could you try?" he asked. "I can't change what has gone before. I can only try to retrieve what we had and rebuild it. Aren't there things you have kept from me? I think everyone has secrets. Anyway, there, I have asked you. The decision is yours. I'll go to bed now and give you some space." He dropped a kiss on my head and departed.

I took the glasses over to the sink and slowly rinsed them before opening the dishwasher drawer and cramming them in. I pressed the start button and stood listening to the whoosh of the dishwasher. The sounds of the machine mingled with those of Anthony cleaning his teeth, flushing the toilet, opening and closing the wardrobe – such familiar sounds, yet in such an odd situation. He was right. There were things I had kept from him, small things, but nothing that compared with this.

In the spare room, I undressed slowly. It seemed like giving in to just crawl back into bed with him, yet his arguments were logical. I could understand – to a degree – that he thought he had shown me the whole, and that if I had truly been in love with whom I thought was Anthony, then it made sense that I should still love that person. Nothing had changed – he had been like this before we were married, I just hadn't known. I had loved the façade he had shown. But when I remembered the raid and the police interview, and the revelations that had come out, then it didn't seem logical at all. But Father Nick said God loved us all, warts and all. Who was I to judge?

In the morning he went to work, and I went to see Nellie. I wanted to talk over what had happened. As usual, she was eminently sensible.

"Time, my dear. Give yourself time! Remember he has lived for years with his secret, but you haven't. He knew about it, so it wasn't a surprise to him!" Nellie didn't judge, condemn, disapprove – or if she did, she didn't make it known.

And because of that, because it was my decision, I felt the next night that I could return to our bed. I crept in after Anthony was asleep, turning back the covers on my side before he went into his old habit of lying sideways across the entire bed. In the morning, we awoke at the same time, and I found my hand was holding his. "Thank you," he whispered.

We resumed a sort of normality. There was always some tension and a sense of unfinished business in our lives, but we managed to erect a façade that served in a makeshift fashion until we were ready for the next step.

I didn't suffer any more episodes as severe as the one in the car. There was a horrible one at the supermarket, when I was about to wheel the trolley across the road. Suddenly it felt like I was pushed from behind, and the trolley headed out by itself into the road and was hit by a car. The groceries went flying in the air, including a dozen eggs. The cardboard container sprang open and eggs became airborne. I dived into the road, trying to pick them up. There was a voice by my elbow.

"Are you alright, dear?" A middle-aged lady had stooped to where I had crumpled on the pavement. There was no trolley in the road, no eggs. It seemed I had just fainted, and the woman had grabbed my trolley to prevent the very accident I had envisaged. I stood up shakily.

"Sure. I mean, thank you. I just felt faint for a minute."

"Come and sit on the bench. Shall I call someone?"

"No! I mean no, thank you." I allowed her to lead me to the bus stop just behind us, and gratefully sat for a moment.

"Are you sure?"

I nodded. "Thank you so much. I'm fine now. I didn't have breakfast, I felt sick, and I think I might be…" I don't know where I got the inspiration, but she got the hint.

"Oh, how lovely! Well, you take good care of yourself and the little one! Make sure you have a checkup. Maybe you have low blood pressure. That sometimes happens with pregnancy!" She hurried off, waving at me from across the road as she clicked her car door open. A few people had gathered during the incident, but now a bus pulled up and they all piled on, since there was nothing more to see.

I continued to feel uncomfortable in busy places like shopping centres, and I avoided anywhere it might be difficult to leave. Mum was worried, but I reassured her I would just pop a pill if I felt myself going nuts. I had been really scared by that episode. It showed me how vulnerable I was, and I determined not to allow myself to freak out.

Sleeping in the marital bed made our relationship feel nearly normal again. Not that it was – if I was lying in bed, I had only to think of the smell in the police interview room, or the taste of the sweet coffee, or the photo in the paper, and I was back in the horror of the raid and the court again. It was a relationship hanging together by a single thread. Some days when I started to feel we were a normal couple, I had only to look at the list of bail conditions hanging on the fridge and I was instantly transported to the morning they carted him out in handcuffs.

But, to be totally selfish, the really good thing about sleeping in the same bed again was that Anthony rubbed my feet. We climbed into bed and I stuck my feet in Anthony's face. He obediently started massaging them. He always worked hard on the little knobby bit on the right foot, which was quite painful sometimes when I walked.

One night when he was working away at my toes, I felt confident enough to bring up the troublesome topic. "Nee?" I was tentative in my approach, since most of our arguments had been over this subject. "Do you have any idea how we are going to pay for the lawyer? I mean, your new job barely brings in enough for the train fares and lunch, and I'll run out of paid leave soon. And I don't think I could face going back to work – not at my old place, anyway."

He stopped rubbing, and I wriggled my toes to remind him of his duty. "I have asked my mum," he said slowly, "and though it's hard for her, she's prepared to pay for everything upfront, but we have to pay her back." This was extraordinarily generous of Leila, since she was usually pretty tight with her money, but it didn't actually address the question.

"Yes, but how are we going to pay for it eventually? Especially if…" I didn't know how to get the words out. "If you can't earn an income for a while."

He stopped rubbing again. "You mean if I am in prison." He said it as a statement, not a question.

I leant up on my elbow and nodded. "We haven't talked much about it. But it is a possibility, isn't it? The police said they expected a jail sentence. But Mr Szili said he thought it might not be."

"I'm trying not to think about it," Anthony said, then squeezed my foot. "If I don't think about it, then I won't get too upset. I will when it's closer. A week locked up waiting for bail was enough for me."

I didn't pursue that, but returned to the issue of money. "When does Leila expect the money back?"

Anthony didn't reply for a while. "I don't know. I'll talk to her again. We've paid Mr Szili up to date so far, but there's the psychologist still to go, and I think if he gives evidence in court he'll charge a few thousand."

"What do you think the total cost will be?" I didn't want to know the answer, really, but I had to at some stage.

"I think about $30,000," he said in an even tone. "Maybe a bit more." The amount echoed around the bedroom.

"$30,000?" I was unprepared for this. I sat up, almost kicking him in the face as I pulled my legs away. "I was thinking about half that amount. Where are we going to get that to pay your mother back?"

"It could be closer to $40,000. Mr Szili didn't know. It depends on a few things." I couldn't believe how casual he was about it.

"Like what? What does it depend on?" I couldn't keep the cynicism out of my voice, though I was surprised – I didn't think I had anything left in me to be emotional about.

"Well…" he hesitated, but caught me glaring at him. "The cost of the lawyers for a trial is high. The case could go for a couple of weeks, he thought. But he said that if I plead guilty, the chance of a jail sentence is higher than if I get acquitted."

"Obviously!" I made my tone bitingly sarcastic. "If you get acquitted, there won't be a sentence of any sort!" I felt like screaming with the stupidity of it all.

"I do understand that, hon." He was being patient with me, and pulled my feet back towards him. "But Mr Szili suggested I might plead guilty to some charges and not guilty to others. Then we need a barrister in court, as well as Mr Szili. But he said that in the interview I gave a lot of admissions and that it would be a bit awkward to plead not guilty, given what I said on the tape."

I gave this some thought. "What happens if we plead not guilty?" Now I was the one sounding stupid. "I mean, then they need witnesses and things, don't they? Who would be witnesses?"

Anthony sat up in bed, pulling the doona over his legs. "That's the problem, hon. If I plead not guilty, they might dig up anyone who didn't like me and wanted to take me down. And they could say whatever they liked and people might believe them because they wouldn't like me. I mean, because of the photos and things, they think I'm a pervert."

I was still processing the rest of the implications. "If you plead guilty to everything, you are likely to go to jail – but the cost is less. And if you plead not guilty, and they believe the witnesses, you could go to jail for longer?" I wasn't sure what it meant if the jury believed the witnesses.

"Mr Szili said that if I plead not guilty, then get convicted, the judge might give me a longer sentence."

"But that's not fair! You're entitled to plead not guilty if you want to! It's up to the police to prove things, isn't it?" Thank goodness I had watched *Law and Order*.

"But if I plead guilty to some of the charges I might get locked up anyway. I think I should just plead guilty to everything and get it all over at once. It's much cheaper that way. Mr Szili said the cost might double if you go to a full trial, because we have to get a barrister as well as the solicitor, and that could be thousands of dollars each day."

I didn't think that money should be the issue when our future and his freedom were at stake, but I did see the point he was making, since his mother was stumping up with the funds. I didn't want him to go to jail, but he was talking as though it was inevitable. I reversed my position and plumped up the pillow, ready to try and sleep, though I knew my head would be whirling for hours.

"It's complicated. When do we have to decide?"

He pulled me closer to him and nestled my head into his chest. "You don't know how good it is to hear you say 'we', hon. I dreaded that you might abandon me."

I wish it had been that easy. This was the man I had given my life and love to. Now I had to decide whether he had shown me the real person, the real damaged person that he was. Or was there more? And could I fix the damage by staying?

"I think we should see Mr Szili together and talk this out. Is that OK? I know you normally see him alone, but can I come?"

It was agreed.

That night we slept in each other's arms, like we had when we were first married. It felt good.

Chapter 18

Mum had been visiting Father Nick regularly. She kept trying to get me to go by myself, and eventually I agreed to see him – not that I had anything against the priest, but I worried about what he might say.

Father Nick normally met his parishioners in a room off the vestry, but for my mother, the meetings were at his house – a small cottage really – attached to the church by a covered walkway. I drove while Mum chattered away next to me.

"What do you expect me to get out of this, Mum?" I was still trying to wriggle out of the appointment.

"Darling, Father Nick knows things. He understands. He is a really good listener. You'll feel better for seeing him. It isn't confession!"

"I have no objection to confession. I haven't been for a few months, but I still believe in it and the church. I guess it's just that this whole thing has put my view of God at risk. I suppose I could talk to

Father Nick about that!" It horrified Mum that I might criticise the church in the presence of a priest, so I had to reassure her I still had a modicum of tact.

The outside light was on, and Nick opened the door with a smile. I called him Nick, Mum called him Father. Nick and I had an agreement about this that we'd made when I was a teenager at youth group, much to Mum's disapproval. I had hesitated over the formal title, and he said simply, "Just call me Nick." And from that time on I had, but Mum thought it was disrespectful.

He ushered us in to his kitchen, where he had a table set with a cloth and some mugs. The kettle was just switching itself off as we entered. "Coffee for you both?" He knew how we liked it. I watched and listened to my mother, and I finally saw why she thought Father Nick was such an earthly saint. He listened carefully to everything Mum said and agreed with her, or at least didn't dispute anything.

"Father, thank you for seeing us. You know how I value your opinion and your wise advice. My little baby here, she needs to talk to you and listen to what you have to say. And maybe she will come to confession as well."

"You know I welcome all members of your family, my dear, especially at this time. And I am happy to listen, to advise and to support in any way I can. I hope that at some stage Anthony will join us."

I nodded, as Anthony and I had discussed this and he certainly saw the usefulness of having the Father as a character witness. He was seeing him individually, but if Nick could see how the three of us interacted, it might help heal the rift that was sitting there between Anthony and my family. I hadn't mentioned any of this to Mum.

"I will certainly see if Anthony will come," I said to them both. "I am sure he'll consider it. He needs all the help he can get, and he realises that."

Mum basked in the priest's earnest gaze. "Now, Father Nick, I'm worried about my girl. I don't think she is looking after herself. She is stressed and anxious. Her father and I have suggested to her she come and stay with us, but she is so stubborn! She insists on staying with Anthony, and her father won't allow him to visit our house, so it gets quite awkward. What should we do?"

Nick cast a long look at me, raising his eyebrows in question. I half smiled and shrugged. He turned to Mum.

"I can see you are trying to be everything a mother should be – caring, considerate, and prepared to put yourself out to help your daughter." I watched Mum smirk and preen a little. "But she is only doing what you have taught her to do – to be a good citizen, to respect her marriage vows, and to take her own course in life. This is something that a mother both worries over and is proud of. Her dad is acting according to his own principles, which is really what your daughter is doing as well. You see how well you have brought her up to be an independent thinker!"

He was good, by God, he was good. He hadn't actually expressed his own opinion at all! I watched as the ANZAC biscuit my mother had dunked in her coffee started to wilt and fall over. When she noticed it, she crammed it into her mouth all at once. When she had swallowed with a gulp, she gushed at Nick.

"You understand so well, Father Nick! That's exactly how things are! And you can see how difficult it makes it. We were such a loving and united family."

"We still are, Mum!" I piped up. "I love you and Dad, and you love me. And there's nothing that will change that. But Nick is right. You have to let me decide. At the moment – I am not saying forever, but at the moment, I am 100% supporting Anthony, and that's how it's going to be. I understand why Dad won't let him visit, but I can come over to you and Dad never makes me feel unwelcome. So, as far as I am concerned, we don't need to make Nick spend hours fixing our problems! But..." I turned to Nick, "I think I will come and see you, if that's OK."

He beamed at me, and I felt warm and comforted. "Of course. Any time."

We chatted on for a while and then stood to leave. While Mum was in the bathroom, Nick asked me quietly, "Come over without your Mum some time? I got the feeling there were things you want to say?" I nodded. "Tomorrow, or any Wednesday," he said. "Any time."

Mum reappeared, so we stopped our cryptic conversation. It wasn't that I objected to Mum knowing, but she would be curious about all that was said and what the outcome was. At the moment, it was between Nick and me.

Chapter 19

The amount of money the whole court thing was going to cost weighed on my mind. It didn't seem to worry Anthony. For him, the fact that his mum was paying seemed to be the answer, and the problem of repayments was easy to ignore. Maybe he thought it wouldn't be his problem if he was locked up. But for me, the mortgage and the car repayments were the first things to cover, and then the other bills. When both of us were earning reasonable salaries we didn't have a problem, and, like other young people, we spent little time considering the future. We just paid our bills and spent the rest. Our funds had been eaten up by Mr Szili on the first day. I was still being paid from my job with my leave entitlements, but Anthony was on a small wage with very little commission. A few more mortgage payments and my funds would run out. I was worried.

"We need to talk money, Nee!" We were stacking the dishwasher after dinner one night. I scraped the plates. He put the dishes in.

Somehow he always managed to cram in more than me, and there were never any smears or baked on bits when he did the stacking.

"Uh-huh." The response was automatic. Sometimes I thought he didn't even hear what I said.

"I think I should go back to work." That got his attention. He stood up, dish in hand.

"No way, darling! Look at you, you little stressball! This is the first time you haven't actually had to be at work, and you are running around trying to help me. You can't fit work in! Anyway, I thought you didn't want to go back to that bitchy office?"

"I don't. I'm thinking of looking for a new admin job. I can get extra money for a bit – we need it all. I could temp for a while. Then I can leave days free for coming to appointments with you. And temping pays quite well."

He undid my apron strings and lifted the blue-striped fabric over my head. Folding it, he led me to the couch, patting the seat next to him.

"I think you need to take some time off. I really do. Starting a new job is hard – I'm even finding it hard, and this is an easy job. You'd be working in different offices every day or week, and having to speak to lots of people and be nice to them. It will be a real strain. I'm worried about you!" He was really considerate, most of the time.

"But I am worried about the money," I said. "If I was working, there would be less time for worry, and I'd bring in something useful as well." I didn't add what was really on my mind – that if he went away… no, say it… if he went to prison, then his meagre income would stop and we certainly couldn't afford the mortgage.

"Well, whatever you think, hon. But let's just give it a few days, OK?"

We left the subject at that, but I brought it up with Nellie later when we met at the café.

"How are things, my sweet?" She had ordered the coffees, and we were sitting outside in the glass-covered area to reduce the biting chill of the wind.

"Pretty much as you'd expect, I suppose. But there was something I wanted your advice on."

Nellie put on her serious face, which made me laugh. I told her how Anthony thought I wasn't ready for work. "I'm worried whether we might have to sell the house and rent somewhere. We can't manage the repayments once my income stops. Anthony doesn't seem to understand that. Maybe he thinks my parents could help. His mother is paying our legal costs, as a loan."

"And would your parents help?" She knew them well.

I had asked Mum the same question, and she had, in turn, asked Dad. "They have different views. If we changed the house into my name only, Mum will help. Dad is really set against helping Anthony at all."

Nellie's expression softened, but she held my gaze firmly. "I don't think your dad wants to be seen to be supporting Anthony. But that means he can't support you either."

"He said to just leave, just walk out. But I can't!"

I wanted her to make me feel better, but she was just making me question things I didn't want to face. Why couldn't she understand I wanted her to say I was doing the right thing? What was so hard about that?

Nellie sat back. "You talked about going back to work? What was the end result?"

I sipped and sighed. "I haven't done anything about it. I've put it on hold, for a while."

"You don't sound happy about it."

"I am tired. I want some time off. But I am desperately worried about the money, and the amount we will end up owing his mother after it's all over. He might go to prison, and how could he get a job afterwards with a criminal record of that sort?"

Nellie signaled to a hovering waiter for more coffee. I decided on a chocolate milkshake instead. Nellie tapped on the table with her spoon to get my attention. "Listen, pet, I want to say something. I want you to listen and not say anything straight away. Promise?"

I was suspicious. "Okay."

"I've been thinking. I was wondering how you would feel about taking a bit of a holiday with me? We could just go away to Queensland or somewhere for a week or so. There are some great bargains at the moment. But…" she glared at me, "I will pay for you." She saw me open my mouth and put her hand up to stop me speaking. "You agreed to listen! I can get a great deal for a resort, on one of the islands. I have heaps of savings and I don't need it all. What do you say?"

What could I say? I was overcome by her kindness. I felt the tears start, and with Nellie it was OK, so I cried. She just handed me serviettes as I needed them and waited for the torrent to stop.

"I take it that's a yes?" I nodded, though my smile was watery. "Are there any dates I should avoid? Have you appointments already scheduled that I should know about?" I shook my head. Momentarily I thought about my duties as bail wardress. Anthony would have to live with his mother for the week. She'd love to have him.

"Then consider it done!" Nellie smiled at me. "I know you are worried about Anthony. You don't need to be. He's a grown man who can look after himself."

I slurped loudly on the dregs of the milkshake and for once didn't care who turned their head and looked at me.

On the way home, excitement hit me. I could hardly wait to pull into the driveway. Throwing open the door, I took a running jump at Anthony where he sat on the couch, knocking the wind out of him.

"Guess what! Nellie and I are going to Queensland for a week! She's paying for everything, just to give me a break! Isn't she wonderful?" I kissed him noisily on the cheek. He was silent and unsmiling. I pulled back and looked at him. 'What's up? Aren't you pleased for me?"

He produced a half smile. "Of course, darling. That's great! I'm very happy. When are you going?" But I could tell it was false.

"What's the matter, Nee? Come on, out with it!"

He pushed my legs down off his lap and cast his eyes at the floor. "It's nothing, babe. I guess I'll have to stay with Mum, that's all. I had just got used to us having our marriage bed back together. Don't worry, pet, you go and enjoy yourself. I'll be fine."

I was contrite. "I'm sorry, but I really need a break. I'll stay home though, if you want me to." I tried not to feel disappointed – life was difficult for us both at the moment.

He smoothed an imaginary wrinkle in my blouse. "No, no, sweetheart, no way. You are going on this trip and you're going to love every minute of it. Now I come to think about it, I can sign in at the cop shop on the way to work during the week, and on the weekend I can stay with Mum. No problems. In fact, I might enjoy it!" He looked a little mischievous, but I suspected he was acting to cover up his hurt.

"Really, though, Nee, now I come to think of it, I should wait till after... after the case is over. There might be things to arrange, things to see to. You know how these sorts of problems come up just when you don't expect them. I'll tell Nellie in the morning that we should wait a bit. OK?"

He looked down at the floor again, then just glanced at me for a brief moment. "Thanks, hon." His voice was quiet and subdued. "I just want to spend every moment with you until the government sends me away on an all-expenses paid holiday. Just like your trip really!" He sparked up at his attempt at humour, but it made me cry. We ended up in each other's arms on the bed, just trying to make the most of each moment we had together. In that moment, I felt we could make it.

I sent a text to Nellie in the morning, telling her I couldn't come, but she replied she had already booked the holiday. *All done, leave in ten days. Start packing.* I had to tell Nee.

He nodded. "Of course I understand. She's paying all the expenses. You can't let her down. I'll be fine, really. Don't worry!"

But I did worry, of course, but there was nothing I could do about it. Deep down, I knew it was important that I had some time out. I booked a time with Mr Szili for when I returned, and set off unannounced to see Nick for a chat. But he wasn't available. There had been a death in the parish, and he was out on compassionate visits. He left a note of apology. I didn't get to see him till after the holiday with Nellie.

Chapter 20

I tried to think of ways to make it easier for Anthony while I was away, to smooth away some of the guilt I felt at leaving him. First, I thought I would write him a letter or card for each day. Then I remembered the advent calendars I loved as a child – the ones where you open a little window each day leading up to Christmas – and wondered if I could make one for him, maybe showing photos of us when you opened the little doors. It might cheer him up.

I checked the publishing programs on the computer, and found something that I thought might work, though it took a lot of fiddling around. But eventually I printed it onto cardboard, cut out the doors, put the photos behind them and secured each little window with a tiny piece of tape. I was really impressed with how it looked, and it did me the world of good just to have a craft project that was so personal.

The days leading up to the trip passed quickly and almost routinely. Anthony and I didn't really discuss the holiday again before I left for the airport, though there were veiled references to 'being away' and 'having a great time'. I gave him the calendar the night before we left. It was after dinner, and I was in the bedroom checking my case was packed, though I knew it was – I had packed and repacked many times in my excitement. I could smell him before he spoke – the heavy scent of the sweat from under his arms told me he was stressed about me going. He was leaning on the doorframe, watching me.

"I think I'm all packed."

"There's nothing left in the wardrobe, so I think you must be!"

We were both fake. I moved to him, and he put his arms around me. "Have a great time, sweetheart. I'll be thinking of you, but I want you to be relaxed and happy, OK?"

I unwrapped his arms and held his hands instead. "I made something for you, to keep you company while I am away. Wait a moment!" The card was quite large, so I had hidden it behind the chest of drawers, and now I presented it with a flourish.

"Here you are! Now, you are only allowed to open one little door each day, no more! I have put the date on each one, so no cheating. And you can't start till tomorrow!"

We sat on the bed together, and his eyes filled with tears as he looked at the card. He blinked rapidly, then pulled me towards me and kissed me gently on the cheek.

"You are the sweetest thing. Thank you, pet. Promise I won't cheat. You made this yourself?" He sounded impressed. I nodded. "You're clever. I couldn't do any crafty things like that. I will hang it in the hall and look at it every day."

I tossed and turned all night while Anthony snored a regular, rhythmic bass. Usually it was enough to hypnotise me back to sleep, but not that night.

Nellie and I had to take the airport bus from the city. Although Anthony could have driven us out to the airport, he could not have gone home by himself. We discussed it, but the risk was too great.

If the cops stopped him – and they regularly patrolled the freeway – he would be sent to jail for breaking his bail conditions. We kissed goodbye at the front door. "I'll be fine, darling," he assured me. I chose to believe it.

The airport bus picked us up in the main street, and I gazed out the window as though seeing Melbourne for the first time. I was so excited I practically danced down to the departure gate, first in the queue. I was determined to enjoy every minute of the escape.

We arrived at the island in time for a late lunch. Tall, bronzed islanders dressed in shorts and t-shirts brought the bags to our cabin, one of a row of grass huts facing the beach. We unpacked and bounced up and down on the two queen-sized beds. When the excitement of this had worn off, we boiled the kettle and made tea, sipping it in the chairs outside the cabin, facing the gentle waves of the beach. I chose lemon tea, and Nellie had blackcurrant.

I smiled at my friend. "Thank you, Nellie. I feel much more relaxed already, and we've only just arrived."

"I'm glad you are grateful, because it puts you in my debt! You will have to accede to my next requests!"

"Oh dear. What have I let myself in for now?"

Nellie put her cup down and turned to face me. "I have seen how dragged down you have been over this whole business. I thought that for this week, you should give me your mobile phone, and allow me to take any calls or texts. And if there is anything urgent, I promise to tell you." I thought for a minute and it seemed reasonable. I nodded.

But then she went on. "And one more thing. Internet access is quite expensive. If you like, I could check your emails, and I promise not to open anything that doesn't look urgent. You just need to give me your password. That way you can be truly out of contact with the world."

Again, I didn't see any harm in this. I had severely reduced my contacts that few people emailed me, and Anthony didn't have internet access, so he wouldn't be writing to me.

"One more thing."

I rolled my eyes. "Now what? Haven't I agreed to enough?"

She smiled. "You'll like this one. We are both scheduled for an hour's massage at four o'clock today!"

For that, I had to get up and hug her. "You are the best friend, Nellie! Thank you! Let's walk along the beach and then head to the massage place."

That was the plan we followed. The beach was just like I'd imagined – crunchy sand, waves, pretty shells and palm trees. People were out sailing and snorkeling, and swimmers were dotted around the ocean and the resort pools. I thought a week might not be long enough for me. Already the cares of the last few months seemed less important. The memories of police and courts seemed to be in a past life. I could almost forget the coming trial.

The massage cabin was a grass hut just like ours, but with two tables and some screens. Annie was my masseur, while Nellie had Paul. They looked vaguely Polynesian, and Annie had a pink hibiscus tucked behind her ear. She started working on my shoulders and back, using a fragrant oil, and I realised just how tight I was. The magic of her fingers working up and down my spine and sweeping across my ribs left me feeling floppy and light-headed. The only sound in the cabin was an occasional sigh from Nellie or me, or the gentle padding of feet as the masseurs worked their way around the table.

The hour passed in a flash, and Annie said at the end of it, "I think we had better get you back tomorrow. There's a lot of work for me to do on the knots." I booked an hour every day there and then.

By this time it was past five, and we were getting hungry. We wandered back to the hut, changed, and went for the smorgasbord dinner. I piled my plate high with seafood, then went for the mud cake, fruit salad and pavlova. Food had never tasted so delicious! But I found myself yawning, despite the lively ukulele band and the dancing girls. Nellie wanted to wait for a bit and see the rest of the dance numbers. I excused myself and went back to our hut.

In the bar fridge was a collection of bottles, and a handwritten note on resort paper. *"Help yourself. It's free, but once it has gone, we won't restock it."* I chose a peach Vodka Cruiser and took it outside to sit on the comfy chairs and watch the ocean. It was very soporific – the waves, the balmy air, the sound of the birds nesting for the evening, and I found myself dozing off.

I was rudely woken by the bottle slipping out of my hand and falling on my foot. Startled, I looked straight out at the beach. Joggers panted past, and an assortment of couples strolled by. I felt nostalgia for our honeymoon, but before I had time to indulge myself, my attention was caught by a young man and woman walking hand in hand along the beach. She was looking up at him, and they were talking earnestly. I couldn't hear what they said. Just as they were in front of me, the girl turned, slapped the guy on the face and marched off.

He stood there for a moment, feeling his cheek, then noticed me staring. He smiled ruefully, then came up to the path and called out to me. "Do you have any advice to give on women?"

I smiled back, and he came closer, leaning on the railing which was in front of our hut, commonly used for drying towels. I noticed how attractive he was – tall, lean, lightly tanned.

"What seems to be the problem? I couldn't hear what you were saying, but I noticed the whack on the cheek!"

"I guess it was my fault." He rubbed his hand across his face. "This is our first time away together. We've been going out for nearly six months. She was really happy to come away, and I thought… well I thought that when we got here, we would… well, you know!"

"Make love?" It wasn't hard to guess.

He nodded. "But when we got here, she kept wanting to do stuff, you know, recreation stuff, so I had been swimming and playing tennis, and I thought we were never going to… do it. I suggested the walk, and then I produced a packet of condoms and said 'Boy scout! I'm prepared!' That was when she slapped me. The rest you saw. Should I go after her?"

For some reason, this struck me as hilarious. From just smiling, I giggled then laughed, and I couldn't stop. I think I became a bit hysterical. Finally, I wound down to a chortle, then stopped. The guy looked on a bit bemused. "I'm sorry," I choked out at him. "Just the way you told it, I could imagine it so clearly! Yes, go after her! See if there is a peace offering at the shop – chocolates, or flowers or something! And don't ask her for sex until at least tomorrow!"

He nodded at me and smiled. The island was like that – everybody was a friend. As he moved away, I started to laugh again when Nellie appeared, throwing herself into the seat next to me.

"I'm glad to see you're so cheerful! What's up?" Like so many things that are amusing, the telling of the story was very flat, and Nellie barely raised a smirk.

That night I slept like a baby. Actually, that wasn't really right, because babies often wake in the night and cry. I just slept – deeply and, as far as I could tell, dreamlessly.

I woke next morning to the sun streaming in through the door, where Nellie had left it open. She came in, hair dripping from an early morning swim.

"Come on, sleepyhead, it's gorgeous in the water!" Laughing, she dragged me out of bed and threw my bathers at me. "See you at the beach!"

I pulled on the costume, threw a towel over my shoulder and went to join her. The water was warm and caressing, and easy to swim in. I wallowed in the shallows, and did some lazy breaststroke out to an artificial reef and back again. I felt good.

There was plenty to do at the resort, even if it was plenty of nothing. Our days alternated between swimming, lying on the beach, eating, reading, massage, sailing, snorkeling, and going to some classes – crafts, yoga, art… there were heaps to choose from. I didn't see the guy from the first night again, though I wondered whether he had managed to make up with his girlfriend. I wouldn't have minded meeting him again, even though I'd never steal someone else's man. It was pleasing just to know that I could still attract men.

Each morning I asked Nellie about texts or emails, and she always assured me that there was nothing to be concerned about. I trusted her. I didn't want to hear any bad news, anyway.

Chapter 21

By the end of the week I was brown, and I was sure I had lost a couple of kilos. There was a spark back in my step. Nellie noticed it, and I was glad for her sake that the money she had spent on me had been worth it. I was sad to leave the resort and couldn't thank Nellie enough, but she just brushed off my gratitude.

The island had been a haven for me, a place of healing and a chance for a time away from the strain I had been under. It reminded me of a different life, one I'd once had, and I wondered if there could ever be a life like this for me in the future. The thought of returning home was not all that enticing.

I had a slight panic attack on the plane. The flight was quite turbulent, and even though the pilot told us over the microphone that it was going to be a bumpy ride, I found it a bit nauseating and held the sick bag at the ready. Then I got the shakes and felt hot and cold. Nellie noticed what was happening and spoke to me calmly.

"It's OK. Just breathe slowly. Ground yourself. Look at the back of the chair. Notice the texture of the fabric. See the clip of the tray on the back of the seat. Think about how many meals and cups of coffee have been served on that tray. It has survived many bumpy rides. Good girl. Nice slow breathing. Keep it up." The attack gradually passed, as did the sick feeling. I gave Nellie a weak smile as we landed. She winked.

I realised as we taxied in to the parking bay that I had not actually missed Anthony as much as I expected. But when he met us at the airport – driven by his mother – I flew into his arms. There was something in his expression which told me he needed reassurance – maybe the way his eyebrows tweaked, or the hooded lids of his eyes. As we kissed, I noticed Leila watching us, nodding and smiling.

We dropped Nellie off, then Leila took us to our house. She expected to be asked in for lunch, but I turned to her at the front door and said, "Thank you Leila. I really appreciate you coming with Anthony to pick us up." I shook her hand and she had really no choice but to say goodbye and leave. It was a minor triumph, but it gave me confidence.

The calendar was hanging in the hall, just as he had promised it would, with all the doors open.

"I didn't cheat! It was lovely to have a new photo every day, and I took to heart some of the things you wrote." He hugged me. I looked at the calendar and thought maybe I had gone a bit overboard – *"Love puts obstacles in its way"* and *"Love will keep us together"*.

Anthony showed little interest in the holiday. I guess he was jealous. I asked him how work had been and he said it was fine, but that he had got lonely.

"I thought it was mean of Nellie not to let you talk to me," he commented as he was chopping vegetables for dinner. I was lying on the couch.

"Did you call? Nellie was minding my phone. She wanted me to be really relaxed. I feel much better now, and ready to tackle the hard stuff."

He raised an eyebrow at me. "What do you mean, hard stuff?"

"Well, we have the appointment with Mr Szili, and your psych person, and I want to start looking for some work, and we haven't even finished talking about the things that have happened in your life. That's the most important thing for me to understand."

He kissed me on the cheek. "First things first. It's Mr Szili on Tuesday. I'm at work every other day this week." The subject change was obvious and clumsy, but I let it go.

On Monday, I went to see my parents, showed them the holiday photos and told them everything we had done. They commented on how much better I looked.

I was pleased. "I feel good. Better than since this whole thing began."

Dad smiled at me. "Have you given any thought to the offer your mum and I made, *cica*?"

My smile faded. "I haven't had time, Dad. But I am staying with Anthony – that's for certain. When the case is over, then I might think about it – when I know what's happening. That's what gives me the biggest headache – not knowing."

"I thought the biggest headache was getting to know the rest of your husband." That was Dad being really sarcastic – unusual. It told me how deeply upset he was for me.

I took a deep breath. "Dad, is there any chance of you being reconciled with Anthony at all? Ever? I don't mean now. I know, I've lived for the last few months with what it means to have a partner who has a mental illness – that's what it is – but can you see that sometime down the track we might be part of the larger family again?"

He paused. "Sweetie, you will always be my little girl. I will always love you dearly and deeply. But I have to tell you the truth. No matter what punishment the courts give Anthony, no matter what treatment he has, I will never forgive him for what he has done – not only to you, but to those children, to your friends, to our families. There is no longer trust. I could try to be polite to him for your sake," he said, looking at me and holding my hand, "but I could never be sure that he was not thinking that way again."

It was a long speech for my father, who preferred to communicate through a hug or get my mother to say things. I felt my lip tremble and the joy of the holiday evaporate. I had hoped so much that things might be repaired. Now it seemed that was not going to be possible. Mum put her head through the door, saw the intensity between us, and disappeared.

"I understand, Dad. I know you will always love me, and I thank you for that."

We sat on the couch, his arm around my shoulders. I saw his eyes were full of tears, and I cried for all that I had lost.

Chapter 22

The name of the firm – Szili, Szili and Kiss – was the funniest thing about the place. It was a normal office – not ostentatious, just functional. I thought about that first phone call I had made to them from the police station, and how glad I was now that I had chosen this firm. Mr Szili had organised everything for us. Maybe any solicitor would have done the same.

A middle-aged receptionist gave us coffee while we waited. I accepted, even though I was nervous and the coffee would go straight through me. Anthony was quite calm. Mr Szili was a busy, bustling man, wearing a vividly striped shirt and clashing spotted tie. I didn't care about his dress sense as long as he did the right things for us. He courteously ushered us in and pulled up a second chair for Anthony. There were things I needed to know, but didn't want to ask. I hoped his intuition and experience would speak for me.

"Mr Grey, Mrs Grey. We need to talk about a few things today. The police have advised me they are changing some of the charges and adding a couple more. I haven't actually seen what they have done, but from what the informant said, they are adding 'procuring' to the list of charges. From our point of view, that is not ideal, but the outcome might well depend on how you decide to plead, Mr Grey."

"Hang on a minute, please." My brain was having trouble coping with all the information that he flung at us. It was like listening through a fog. "Could you explain that again? Who's the informant?"

He took his glasses off, rested his elbows on the table and laid the tips of his fingers together, tapping them lightly. He spoke slowly and clearly. "The informant is the police officer, Sergeant Price. He called me yesterday and said the wording of the original charges had been adjusted. You don't need to worry about this. It just takes account of the number of images they found, and the sources. But they are adding charges of 'procuring children for the purpose of pornography.' This is concerning, because they are more serious."

My stomach fell through the floor. Just when I thought I knew what was happening and was starting to prepare for the trial ahead, and now this. I looked at Anthony. "Did you know this was likely?" My voice was shaky. He shook his head. Mr Szili looked at him for a long moment, then went on.

"I will talk over the consequences of the new charges with Mr Grey. You are aware that the first process is through the hand-up brief. That is, we will be sent all the witness statements and no witnesses will be called at that time. This hearing is coming up in two or three weeks. What I need to talk about today, Mr Grey, is your plea. There are several things to consider before deciding."

Anthony's eyes were now roaming up and down the bookcase filled with bound legal tomes, not fixed on the solicitor. "What sort of things?" he mumbled. I could see it was going to have to be me who talked about the issues. Anthony was zoned out in some other land. Lucky him.

Mr Szili continued. "If we work backwards, we should first consider the possible sentence in the event of a guilty verdict. The court generally takes an early guilty plea into account."

I interrupted. "Early?"

"Early means now, before the time of the hand-up brief," Mr Szili explained. "It saves the police and the court a lot of time. It allows other cases to be booked in. It also saves emotional distress for the people – in this case mostly children – giving evidence. As far as you are concerned, it also saves money – the cost of barristers – and it means a shorter trial." Mr Szili paused. "You should also be aware of the publicity that can result from a case that lasts several days. The media often sit in. Pleading guilty means there is no jury – and frankly, it will be difficult for us to get a sympathetic jury in this sort of case."

I preferred him not to be so frank. I was well aware of the sort of case this was. I hit Anthony on the thigh to get his attention. He rubbed his hand over his face as though he had just woken up.

"What else do we need to consider?" I was scribbling notes on a scrap of paper so I could remember things later.

He turned to Anthony. "Mr Grey, if you decide to plead not guilty to some charges, you will go to trial on those, and there is the chance you might be acquitted. Clearly, then, you won't be sentenced on those charges. If you are thinking of pleading 'not guilty' to any charges, you could consider pleading 'not guilty' to all of them, despite the admissions you made in the interview, and despite the evidence the police hold."

Mr Szili waited for Anthony to speak, but he just looked at me. It was indicative of the helplessness he had developed. I had to ask the question. "And do you advise that course of action?"

"To be frank, no, I do not – though it is your decision. The admissions, combined with the actual images, are sufficient to convince a jury despite any explanation we could present. That is, I don't believe we have a defence to offer, but if Mr Grey has any other explanation, we should explore that now. We can offer some mitigating circumstances, but that only affects the sentence, not the verdict."

Anthony now had his gaze fixed on his wedding ring, but he dragged his attention back to the solicitor after another nudge from me. When he spoke, there was a tremor in his voice. "When you ask for one image, you often get heaps more. I never stopped to count them, and it was like junk mail – they just kept arriving. But the police said it was the fact that they were there at all that made it an offence."

"That is correct. The offence is possession of the images, not how they arrived. The police found many files with different download dates, so they don't believe they all arrived there by accident. In addition, they were saved in hard-to-find places on the desktop. That shows deliberate intent to hide them. But please, if you have an explanation that we could offer to the court, then let me hear it! I can't advise you properly if there are things you have not disclosed."

Anthony was silent, and so was I. My stomach was feeling distinctly queasy. My head was spinning. In his visits to Mr Szili, Anthony must have heard all this before, but he had never discussed it with me. It sounded much worse than I had thought. Up until now, I had thought it was just a few nasty pictures, but the way the solicitor was talking, there was a lot more to it. Anthony hadn't explained to me how the images had got there, and I couldn't believe he did it himself.

"Then where do we stand?" I wanted to finish the conversation and get out of there.

"It is something you and Mr Grey need to discuss, but at the moment, you should give some thought to pleading guilty to everything. In that case, there will inevitably be a conviction, but the advantage is that the judge will take the plea into consideration when sentencing. We have discussed the likelihood of a prison sentence." He paused. "I think there is little doubt about that." I had to swallow hastily as a mouthful of saliva welled inside my mouth. Images flashed in front of me – Anthony in handcuffs, prison walls with barbed wire, speaking to him through a phone. I blinked to try and get rid of the pictures, as Mr Szili was going on.

"It might be of consideration to you that the children in the pictures will not have to be involved, nor will a jury. And of course, the cost is a factor. A trial will cost thousands of dollars more." He sat back in his chair and looked at us.

There was too much to think about. I wondered if it would make any difference if the judge knew about what had happened in Anthony's past. I didn't know whether to tell Mr Szili about it, and had no idea what difference it might make to the case. I cast a meaningful glance at Anthony, but he raised his eyebrows at me.

I decided I should at least ask. "Mr Szili, Anthony has told me about some stuff that happened in his past. Should we tell you? Will it be useful?"

Anthony put his hand on my arm and shook his head. "I don't want to say anything about that, hon."

Mr Szili looked at first me, then Anthony. "If it might be useful to the defence, you should disclose to me anything that might be relevant. As a communication between solicitor and client, it could remain confidential, unless we use it in the mitigation."

I made Anthony look at me. "It's up to you darling, but Mr Szili knows best, don't you think?"

He opened his eyes wide and glared at me. "I don't want to."

"Well, it's up to you. Talk it over and let me know." Mr Szili sounded a little annoyed.

I paused. "One other question, just quickly. What are the other sentence possibilities?" I didn't want to know, but I had to.

"As I said, I think it almost inevitable there will be a prison sentence."

My heart felt like lead. I was sure Mr Szili knew what he was talking about. It was time to stop pretending that this all might go away, and that we could pick up life how it used to be. It wasn't going to happen.

I pulled my attention back to the solicitor as he continued. "Since Mr Grey has no prior convictions, the court could possibly consider an intensive corrections order, community service, a fine or probation… but the prosecution will certainly ask for a reasonable amount of time to be served. The maximum for these offences is ten years. Chances are, with a guilty plea, it won't be much more than five. But the prosecution will want a jail term. Society demands it."

Five years. Five whole years. That would make Anthony approaching forty, and me… well, not far behind. I wanted to have children. And what would happen in five years? How would he change in jail? And how would I change? How would we cope?

I looked at Anthony, then back at Mr Szili. "Do we have to decide now?"

"Not at all. You don't have to decide until we get the hand-up brief, and you can always change your mind, anyway. Bear in mind that if you decide to plead guilty, the earlier the better. If you intend to plead 'not guilty', then we should approach a barrister. The man I want is quite busy and the case will have to be deferred for some time until he is free. I'll be briefing him anyway for the hearing, but if it is a two or three-week trial I need to book him as soon as possible. Your bail should be continued, but the charges will not be resolved."

I stood up. "We'll talk it over and let you know. Is that OK, Anthony? Or do you want to decide now?" He shook his head. I turned back to the lawyer, who was on his feet.

"Thank you, Mr Szili. Anthony will ring you as soon as we have discussed it." I had to get out of there before I fainted or threw up. I didn't know which was worse.

Anthony wanted to have lunch in Melbourne, but I needed to get away from the city where I felt stifled. We ended up driving down to St Kilda Beach and walking the beachside path, despite the cyclists weaving in and out of their marked lane.

"What do you want to do?" I felt I was pestering him, but it was a decision which had to be made sooner or later, and peace might be easier to come by if it was done.

"What do you think, honey? What should I do? You seem to have a clearer head than me."

"I can't make the decision. You have to. I gather Mr Szili thinks you should plead guilty. I don't know much about the legal system, but it seems to me that if you plead guilty to some charges and not to others, then the jury might be more likely to think you did everything. And then you might get more than the five years. But it means a definite prison sentence." I held tightly on to his hand.

He stopped and put his arms around me, ignoring the danger of being run over by lycra-wearing, bell-ringing cyclists. "Darling, if you and Mr Szili have the same opinion, then I'll go along with it. I'll plead guilty and get it over with. The sooner the better. God knows I don't want to go to jail, but it sounds as though there's no choice."

I expected to feel better when the plea decision had been made, but I felt worse. I tried to accept that prison was definite, but at the back of my mind there hovered just a wisp of hope that the judge might take into account the good things about Anthony. I started to cry softly. The tears gathered and fell without any decision on my part.

"Let's go." Anthony took my arm, and we walked towards the car. I think we were both aware that this could be one of the last few times when we could go home together.

Chapter 23

The trip to the solicitor unsettled me. I developed an anxiety, a depression, and even an anger that I couldn't shift. Mundane household tasks which used to give me satisfaction did nothing to lift my spirits. The thoughts kept coming back. I had nothing to do but brood.

I couldn't get the image out of my mind of the happy couples in Queensland, ambling along the beach under a full moon, just like Anthony and I had on our honeymoon at Sorrento. I couldn't help but think back to that magical time, and how different things had been then. We had hired a basic old beach house for our honeymoon, with a view of the gentle waves of the front beach. After the reception, Anthony had driven us there, meandering along the Rosebud foreshore road as we reflected on the wedding. I remember that it felt strange to just be alone, without at least one of our family chaperoning us.

It had been winter, and we'd snuggled up before an open fire – at least one of Anthony's boy scout activities had come in handy! The second night, a violent storm had blown in from nowhere. We'd climbed into the huge queen sized bed, fluffed up the pillows and pulled the doonas tightly around us. Rain beat on the roof and we could see lightning flashes, even through the thick curtains. Lying in bed, we curled up together in the newness of our physical proximity, legalised by the Church and the law. The wind rattled the windows, pleading to be let in. We cuddled closer, not making love, just staring at each other and touching.

The next morning, it had been a whole new landscape. Trees had fallen across roads and paths, and the beach was littered with seaweed that had been violently uprooted and tossed about in the waves. The sand was full of jellyfish, torn to pieces, segments of their bodies sparkling in the weak sun. The waves were still unsettled, crashing onto the surf beach as though trying to get away from an angry mother sea. Some piggybacked on others in unseemly haste to reach the shore.

We'd walked from one end of the surf beach to the other, surrounded by a symphony of crashing waves. Then I'd sat up on a rock while Anthony wrote "I love you" in the sand with a stick.

While he was writing, I'd looked out over the sea and wondered where the waves had been. Did they just get recycled in this area? Or had these very droplets been evaporated and dropped back into Antarctica as snow, or in the Pacific, or as rain in the forests of South America? How could hydrogen and oxygen combine to make this ocean? This was where I found my certainty in God. The orchestration of nature had to come from a plan. I was part of the plan, and in time I, too, would be recycled.

On one of Anthony's days at work, I decided to make a return visit to Sorrento to try and recapture some of the spirit of our honeymoon. Of course, being alone, and with Anthony's charges hanging over our heads, it would not be remotely like that happy week, but I had felt at home there and I hoped I might again feel that serenity.

I didn't tell anyone where I was going. This was to be my escape. As soon as Anthony left, I set off in the car – no lunch, just bathers, towel, and a drink bottle. I took $50 in a little purse. The day was sunny and warm, even though it was late winter, and the hour or so drive was pleasant and quiet.

The nice thing about the Mornington Peninsula is the choice of beaches. I parked in Rye to buy a cheese roll and a bottle of Coke, then walked along the sand, munching and listening to the seagulls. It was mostly deserted during the week, though the occasional dog walking couple or jogger passed me. The sea was everything that it should have been – sparkling blue and gentle. I meandered along the water's edge and enjoyed the feel of the thousands of tiny crushed shells under my feet. A little pain never hurt.

Then I drove on to the Sorrento front beach. I bought a bucket of chips from the café, and walked to the end of the short pier. The Queenscliff Ferry was approaching, and I watched while it manoeuvred its fat backside into the ship parking bay. There was a whining sound as the tailgate was lowered, then cars and a few delivery trucks started emerging from its belly. I watched until the ship tooted mournfully and pulled out, motoring its way back to Queenscliff. I mused for a while about the courage of the early explorers who sailed to what they thought was the end of the world. How brave they must have been.

I sat on the steps leading to the boat ramp. Little boats were dotted through the shallow water. It was easy to retrieve your boat – you just walked out. The waves at the front beach only got to waist deep after about 200 metres. On our honeymoon, we'd sat at this very spot and watched a tribe of pelicans sitting on one of the boats, their droopy bills nestling on each other affectionately. Later, someone told me pelicans were bad luck. I didn't believe them – not then, anyway.

Next, it was time for a vanilla slice and coffee at the famous bakery in the main strip. Expensive, but worth it. I sat alone at an outside table and spooned up every last crumb of the creamy cake. When no-one was looking, I wiped my finger across the plate to collect the final dregs of custard. My mother would not have approved.

My last stop was at the Sorrento Surf Beach. I drove down the hill into the National Park, as always admiring the view of the strip of sand, the rocky outcrops at each end, and the giant rock that stood about 300 metres offshore. It was just after noon, and the beach was uninhabited. Gulls swooped hopefully around me as I parked the car next to the ramp down to the beach. I walked down to the sand, spreading the towel and sitting, hugging my knees. Suddenly I started crying. It was right here that Anthony had written in the sand, and I had thought how lucky I was.

A little further over, waves were almost at surf height and I saw a couple of surfers at the far end of the beach, paddling out near the rocks. I assumed they could steer away from them if they caught a wave in. The slight breeze dried my cheeks.

I walked to the end of the rocky beach, away from the surfers. It was nicer to be alone. Mine were the only footsteps I could hear. There was a crusty top on the sand, which was pleasantly warm on top but cool underneath. I could see the waves far out to sea in a smooth line. At some point, part of the wave broke and started to turn, and the rest of the water followed it obediently. Then it gathered strength again to come crashing down on the shore. As it finally reached the beach, the incoming waves argued violently with the ebbing flow, as if fighting to keep the water from reaching the shore.

Shedding my shorts and shirt, I walked down the sandy slope in my bathers to the water. The waves hit my knees violently and I had to brace myself so as not to be knocked over. It was exhilarating. I walked in further, despite the chill as the water got deeper.

Turning back to face the beach, I was almost knocked over by the waves coming in behind me. I jumped up so they could go under me, and turned again to face the vast ocean. A huge wave headed towards me and I dived under it, almost laughing. Playing with the waves was liberating. They had so much power, and I had so little.

They could toy with me, throw me in the air, do what they wanted. I floated on my back and let my body rise and fall with the motion. The clouds above me were swirls of white cotton wool, which expanded and swelled as though they were taking a deep breath. The waves were noisy, drowning out my thoughts. The harsh cry of the seagulls was jarring against the sound of nature's ocean.

I relaxed with the water. A shadow fell across me; it was the huge rock. Looking up at it, I could imagine having a house right on its flat top. How perfect it would be! Just be enough room for a helicopter to land with supplies, and I could be totally alone. Just me. Only invited guests could visit, no-one unwelcome. Truly, I could be the master of my own home.

Moving was effortless. Now the water felt almost warm and caressing. I kicked hard. Droplets heavily laced with salt flew up and landed on my face. I felt as though my skin was getting burned. Lazily I turned onto my stomach, dipped my face in the water, and then my head.

I felt the pull drawing me down. I lifted my head and took a big breath, then dived under the waves, deeper and deeper, holding the last morsel of oxygen until it wasn't possible to hold it any longer. I opened my mouth and let the water rush in. I resisted at first, spluttering for air and swallowing salty water. But the current was mild and supportive, carrying me further from the beach, almost gently now. The waves developed a mind of their own, calling me deeper. I felt pain in my chest and a banging in my head, but it didn't matter. It was beautiful here. Up above, the sun sparkled on the surface of the water, but further down at my depth it was an incredible deep blue, tinged with aqua, but unlike any colours I had seen before.

I felt pain everywhere, incredible pain, but I knew it was what I deserved. In its own way, the ocean was showing me I was loved, accepted, welcomed. I didn't fight it. We understood each other, the sea and I. It was giving me what I really wanted. *Peace.* Time had no meaning.

Below me I could see some colourful fish. I dived a little lower to see if I could catch them, but they darted away. I was sad. I didn't need to breathe anymore. Maybe I was turning into a fish, breathing through my gills. I laughed at the thought, and again the water rushed into my mouth. It didn't matter. Nothing mattered. The ocean had claimed me as its own. We were as one. It was a feeling too beautiful to describe.

Suddenly, my arm was firmly pulled by an unseen hand. Hauled to the surface, I hit out at my captor, my mouth full of water.

"No," I tried to cry out. "Leave me! It's peaceful here!" But I couldn't speak. Above me loomed a rubber dinghy. I was pushed towards the boat and more hands hauled me up and over the edge. I didn't help them. I tried to tell them I was happy in the water. One turned me on my side, while the other started up a putt-putt motor and the boat started moving. Salty liquid ran out of my mouth, and I vomited sea water. The boat beached on the sand, and more hands lifted me out and laid me down.

Incredible sadness, then anger forced the peaceful feeling away. I panicked and struggled as they lifted me onto a stretcher and into the back of an ambulance. A man and woman in uniform attached things to my body.

"I'm Anna," the woman said as she attached a pressure cuff around my arm and held my wrist. "This is Brendan." The man stuck a plastic tube near my nose and told me it was oxygen, then spread a crinkly space blanket over me. I was shivering. Then they pestered me with questions. I refused to answer, sulking.

They moved away towards the back of the cabin and murmured, but I could hear them.

"What do you think, Anna?" Brendan's voice was deep and pleasant.

"Not sure. She had nothing except a towel and the car keys. Looks like it was deliberate."

"Has she asked to call anyone?"

"No. I offered, but she refused. Something's not right."

I kept my eyes closed to hide the fact that I was listening.

"Did you call the police?"

Anna sounded unsure as she answered. "No, not yet. I don't think there's enough to go on. She's denying intent, but she's calm now."

"Let's give it a few more minutes and see what happens."

I had to convince Anna. Thank goodness I'd overheard the conversation.

Brendan bent over me. "We're going to attach a heart monitor to check things are OK."

"Don't bother," I said. "It's broken." He looked puzzled, then smiled uncertainly.

I turned my face away, and he took it for consent.

Anna sat by my side. After a while, I turned to face her. The anger had gone. Her face was kind and her eyes gentle.

"You had a tough time out there in the water." It was a statement of fact, not an accusation.

"It was fine. I was peaceful. I was enjoying myself." I somehow knew it was a lie, but a convenient one. I had probably been drowning, and I hadn't cared whether I lived or died.

"You got caught in a bad rip. The surfers saw you go under and called the lifeguard. Luckily, they were doing some maintenance in the clubhouse, and they came right out to get you."

"It didn't feel bad. It felt good. I was free. I was OK."

She smiled and shook her head. "That peaceful feeling, it's often reported by people who have been rescued from drowning. It's like the brain decides there's nothing more that can be done."

I tried to sit up. She saw me move, and propped another pillow under my head.

"Was I nearly drowning?" I asked innocently. "I thought you would fight all the way if you were drowning? That's why I wasn't worried. I was enjoying it." The memory of the pain was fading, and I was conscious only of convincing Anna that I had not intended suicide, or she might call the police.

Anna chatted on for a while, just trivia about the weather, nothing personal. I guess she was checking on my mental state. "We'd like to take you to Rosebud Hospital and just run a few tests. If everything checks out, we won't keep you in."

I shook my head. "No. I'm fine. I tell you, it was nothing. I was just exploring the sea."

"You came quite close to drowning, and if the lifeguards had not got to you when they did, you might not be here. It's really important that we confirm things are fine. We can only do so much here in the back of the ambulance."

"No! I'm not going to hospital. You can't make me." A sudden doubt came over me. "Can you?"

She shook her head. "No, we can't make you, but we can strongly advise you this is the best thing."

Images flashed across my head – Anthony and my parents getting a phone call, them racing down to the hospital, Dad meeting Anthony by my bedside, a huge argument and punch up in the ward, Mum crying, nurses separating them… no, it wasn't worth it.

"Can you take these things off now, please? I'm feeling good and I want to leave. Thank you for your help, I really appreciate it."

She tried again to persuade me, but finally gave up. A few moments later, I was upright and walking around at the back of the ambulance, which was in the car park at the beach. A couple of surfers were watching, staring. I glared at them and they turned away. I wondered if they were the ones who had called the lifeguards.

While the man was packing things away, Anna said, "Please see your doctor and get checked out. Will you do that?" I smiled at her and promised. I wouldn't, of course.

I sat in my car and watched the ambulance pull away. I reversed out of the parking place and followed the ambulance to the roundabout, where it suddenly put its lights on and accelerated away. It felt like desertion. They should have stayed, should have made sure I was alright. Couldn't they see I needed them more than whoever just called them?

On the drive home I got the shakes and stopped at Rosebud for coffee. Suddenly hungry, I ate a large bun, then a pie. I gobbled them quickly and felt bloated.

I didn't tell anyone what had happened. In a way, I was ashamed. It was embarrassing to be rescued and treated by paramedics. But what concerned me more was the acceptance I was prepared to give to death. I didn't think I was suicidal, but what else could it mean when you don't care whether you live or die? There must be more to life than this, or I would take that route to peace.

Damn it, there *is* more to life than this, and I am going to find it. Damn the police! Damn Anthony! Damn the courts! I'm going to get through this and move on with my life. The experience strengthened my resolve to see this through.

Chapter 24

The money situation constantly nagged at me. I forced away the anger I felt towards Anthony at the thought of my suffering financially and emotionally while he was safely tucked up in prison. I told myself that it would be horrible for him, but I still kept thinking that I'd be faced daily with the stress of just coping. I anticipated his mother constantly nagging me about the money she was lending us, just because Anthony wasn't there. He wasn't keen on me getting a new job, but for my own sake I had to try. Before I got any applications in, though, Anthony came home beaming all over his face.

"Guess what!" His animation was pleasant compared to the usual expression on his face when he returned home, after a day of trying to sell the unsellable.

"Tell me!" It was obvious he was going to anyway.

"My boss said I was wasted just on the floor, and he wants me to do some admin work for him. He'll give me a try this week. I come in an hour earlier and stay later a couple of times. If I go OK, he might give me a morning each week to do some of his work!"

I was as pleased for him as he was for himself. "How exciting! But he knows you are on bail, doesn't he?"

"Yes, I told him, and he isn't worried as long as it doesn't affect my work. He could see I was far more capable than the normal people they get working there."

"Do you get any extra money?"

"Honey!" he protested. "Why is money all you ever think about? I've been bored stiff, and I was sure you would be pleased that I was getting something better."

My temper flared unexpectedly. "Bored? Well, what about me? Last time I checked it wasn't *me* that was arrested and bailed, but I've given up my job and I'm sitting around all day waiting for you to swan home!" I knew it was unfair of me even as I said it, but sometimes the thoughts you have been suppressing just bubble up without warning.

His smile faded, and he went quiet. "Of course. It's not that I don't appreciate all you are doing. But I thought you didn't like your job anyway and wanted to resign?"

"To leave on my own terms, yes. Not use all my leave with no actual pleasure out of it. All my sick leave, long service leave, gone! We were saving that for when we had a family."

"I thought it was good for you to have a rest. I was worried about you long before all this came up. You haven't seemed to be happy at work for ages. If I had known how you felt…"

"Which you might have, if you'd cared to ask!" I was still angry. He took my hand.

"I'm sorry. That's all I can say. I'm truly sorry." And with that he left and went to the bedroom. I felt a real heel because I had taken all the pleasure out of his little announcement. Somehow, he could always make me feel guilty. I followed him and we lay together on the bed, holding hands. That night, we made love.

Anthony started his admin training the next day, and pretty soon he was coming home a good two hours later than he had been. This gave me more freedom and also more time to think about searching for my job. I updated my resume and had trouble with changing fonts. I was really annoyed and made a mental note to take the laptop to a computer person. I knew it should have been easy to fix myself, but I didn't have the energy. It went on the 'to do' list.

First, I looked online for temp jobs. I had temped when I first started work, so I knew about the pitfalls – don't take a one-day job, don't take a maternity leave job. Take a job where there is an unknown outcome, for example the worker is ill. Then, if they don't get better and you like the position, the business has a ready-made replacement. I went to a few interviews with agencies and waited for the results.

Meanwhile, there were other issues to deal with. After the episode at the beach, I took care not to be alone in case I made another impulsive decision. I spent hours with Nellie, either at a café or at her place, and also at Mum's. Dad seemed to avoid me – Mum said it was because he didn't want to be obvious about not asking about Anthony. He spent more time at his club. Sometimes when I let myself into the house, I heard Mum and Dad fighting. Usually my name was mentioned. I was sad, but I didn't want to let them know I had heard, so I just quietly closed the door and left. Most times, it was just Mum at home. We made pasta in the machine, watched TV and just chatted about anything that wasn't to do with the case.

One evening, Anthony and I went out for pizza. In the old days, we had gone out to dinner about once a week, and Anthony had been complaining about being stuck at home.

Once the pizza had arrived and I was busy trying to bite off a long string of melted cheese, Anthony asked me about Nellie. "We used to do so many things together. It'd be nice if we could all go out together again, just the three of us. I know she didn't want to earlier, but maybe now?"

"She's never mentioned it again. I can't answer for her, but I'll ask."

It was something I didn't want to do face to face. Nellie wasn't totally understanding of my decision to stay with Anthony.

I chickened out of speaking to her and emailed instead. My computer had been sitting in its case in the wardrobe for several days. When Anthony was at work I used the internet at home, despite the bail conditions meaning I shouldn't. I thought I had been punished enough for something I didn't do. I rarely used it anyway, except for the spreadsheet I used for the bills. Today, for once, I thought I'd use the computer while Anthony was there.

Since I had chopped most of my contacts, there was hardly any email. I started the computer and went to log in. My password had gone out of my head for some reason – maybe having to keep changing all those PIN numbers had confused my poor brain.

"Anthony! What's my password for the email?" He always knew these things.

"Saltandpepper hon, unless you changed it." He was watching some reality dancing thing on the TV, which I couldn't stand. It reminded me of how uncoordinated I was.

"Thanks." I tapped in the password and then realised that normally my password was already there, in little asterisks, and I just had to press the Enter button. Oh well, the mysteries of the internet. At least now I could remember my password. I opened up the mailbox and thought for several moments before I started a message:

Hi Nell, how are you?

I just have a question. Actually, it is a request from Anthony. He said he misses the times we had together and wondered if we could go out like we used to? You were a bit iffy last time we asked, but I'd love it if we could. I am sort of shuffled between seeing people and seeing Anthony. No-one wants to see me and him together.

There was no reply for a day, which was unusual. When I opened the email, I noticed fourteen messages in Spam – they were always about enlargements, vitamin tablets or fake Rollex watches. You'd have to wonder how many people actually bought stuff that way.

Anyway, the next day, Nellie replied. The heading in the title was "Um". Not a good start.

"*Dearest,*" the email read, "*I knew you would ask this some time or other. I really prefer to talk it over face to face. Any chance?*"

I emailed back immediately. "*I feel really awkward about it*"

We swapped a few more emails, which hedged around the subject. It was like two boxers sparring before the first punch was thrown. And when it came, it threw me:

"Look, I don't want to hurt you. You are one of my oldest friends. Please read what I have to say carefully and don't react to it defensively.

I have thought long and hard about this. I guess I can't reconcile my conscience with being friends with Anthony, as though this never happened. I thought I knew him, but then I found out that I didn't. That makes me not trust my own judgement about people.

At the moment, I don't want to see Anthony. But I do understand why you are doing what you are doing. You feel you have to be there for him. And I want to be there for you in exactly the same way. Because no matter what happens, you may need support.

Does that make sense? Can I be your friend but not his? I know he doesn't have many friends left, but that is inevitable. I know that affects you, but it can't be helped.

Please let me know your thoughts. Your eternal friend, Nell."

As I read the email, I started to cry. It raised issues that I had put aside as being too hard. I didn't reply to her for several days. I needed to think.

While I was thinking, I sampled a few of the bottles we had in the cupboards, mostly gifts for our wedding. Whatever was there, I mixed and swallowed. It helped at the time, but the next day I had to cope with the hangover. And every morning, after I calmed the thumping in my head, my first thought was that Anthony never had any friends of his own. All our friends had been mutual acquaintances, or my friends, who had become our friends. So why didn't he have any friends? I'd never noticed that before.

Nellie emailed and sent text messages, but I ignored them. It hurt, but it was easier not to have this discussion with her.

Instead, I took myself into the city, intending to visit my old work, and say hello to the colleagues who used to be my friends. I was pretending I was normal. It was a grey day, and I loitered outside the building, trying to get the courage to go in. It wasn't cold, but I shivered just the same. Then the swinging door opened, and I thought I saw my old boss, Kerry, coming out. I panicked and ran downhill, very inelegantly. Whoever was in my way stepped aside. As I ran, I felt the taste of vomit in my mouth and wondered if I would have to stop and be sick. But I swallowed hard, and the feeling passed.

I sought shelter from my emotions in a bookshop. I caught my breath, hanging on to the display stand near the door. Heading to the self-help section, I scanned the titles. What I wanted was a book titled *Is Your Husband a Pedophile?*, but instead I picked up three books whose titles promised help. *Fix It in Five*, *Managing Problems for Dummies* and *If You Are in a Life Crisis You'll Be Very Angry If This Is Not The First Book You Read*. I paid for them with my credit card, oblivious of the cost. At those prices, the authors were indeed helping themselves to happiness – if money could buy happiness.

When I got home, I crawled into bed, exhausted. Anthony found me there when he got home, turned out the light and quietly shut the door. He knew better than to talk to me in this mood.

I emerged about seven o'clock that night. Anthony had cooked pasta for dinner and kept some for me. I zapped it in the microwave and shovelled it down while he watched on.

"Bad day, hon?" He was sometimes good at stating the obvious. "What happened?" Before giving me a chance to reply, he went on. "I had a great day! The boss was really pleased with the work I have been doing, and he has given me a company mobile phone to use for work! I was so missing my phone!"

I slammed down my fork. "He GAVE you a mobile? Please don't tell me it's got the internet. Please don't say that."

He frowned slightly. "Why not, hon? It does, as a matter of fact. It's brand new, and he said I can use it as long as I work there! And he said he'll pay the bill, before you ask!"

"He does know you are on bail, doesn't he?" I knew he did, but wanted Anthony to wake up to the problem. "Is this man an idiot? Even if you didn't tell him what you've been charged with, surely you must have known not to take it."

"Of course he knows about the bail. He didn't ask why and I didn't tell him, but he knows."

"Then why, you stupid, bloody idiot of a man, did you accept the phone? What the hell did you think you were doing? Don't you remember the battle over the bail conditions? And the one that says no access to the internet? Just being in possession of the bloody thing breaches your bail! If they find out, you go straight to jail for goodness knows how long!"

He slumped in the chair. "I didn't think of that. I only thought that now we could call each other without any hassles, and I could send you texts and smiley faces. But it doesn't matter!" He cheered up. "It's in the company's name, so the cops won't know, anyway!"

I groaned. Could he really be this stupid? Or was it naivety? "Has it never struck you that the police can easily check on the messages that I receive? And that they can trace them back to a phone and then to the owner of the phone? Your boss has only to say 'Yep, I gave it to Anthony.' For crying out loud, get rid of the damn thing! Like now would be a good idea!"

His shoulders drooped. "Shit." He sighed. "Of course. I'll give it back to him straight away. I've just felt really out of touch. Sorry. Wasn't thinking."

"Yeah that was obvious!"

"Please don't be nasty. I didn't mean anything. I've been enjoying work – it's such a pleasant change after spending days on end playing Freecell on your computer, and now I have a job, and getting a phone back, it made me feel normal for the first time in months. I'm sorry. What else can I say?"

I sighed and stomped back to bed. Honestly! Sometimes I wondered how intelligent he was. But without realising it, he had answered an unspoken question – now I knew how my Freecell percentage kept going down!

The next day, I flipped through my new purchases, but they turned out to be a load of crap. If I was writing a self-help book, I wouldn't be so damned self-indulgent. I tried drinking myself into a stupor to work up the nerve to call Nellie, but that didn't work either, so her last message stayed in my inbox, unanswered.

After we had the internet cut off, I bought a thumb drive with internet access. It constantly amazed me how technology people thought of everything. This tiny device connected me with the world. In the early days after Anthony's arrest, I used to leave the computer in the car, but now it just stayed in the house. Having the thumb drive saved me going to Mum's every time I wanted to get on the net.

There was one message in my inbox – from the travel centre we had used ages ago. I deleted it and tried to write to Nellie again. Every time I wrote a reply, the words didn't come out right, and I deleted them. I made one last attempt, but it sounded a combination of sanctimonious and snobby, so it went the way of the others. Instead, I just sent her a brief message saying that Anthony had been given a mobile phone with internet access and I was furious!

I started to close the computer, then thought I would try to locate the problem with the fonts. I started off in C Drive, and worked my way through all the files. I was sure the fonts were there somewhere. A whole lot of mysterious files with numbers instead of names came up, but nothing I recognised. I was just about to give up when I came to the final folder, Windows. I opened it, and there it was! Fonts! I felt very proud of myself. Now I knew where to look for my missing letter style.

C Drive was not on the internet, so I didn't need to stay in the car to try and fix the problem. I closed the laptop and popped the thumb drive into my pocket. I had to remember to drop it in my handbag when I got inside. Even when Anthony wasn't home, I tried not to use the drive inside. I really worried that the police were monitoring us somehow.

Inside, I settled down with a coffee and the computer. Anthony was at work and I had the house to myself. When he was home, it made a big difference to the feel of the house. The thought of actually being alone there – after the trial – was intimidating. A house feels far more occupied when more than one person lives in it, even if you are the only one at home.

Logically, the missing font should have been there, and somehow it had been deleted. I went into the Fonts file and scanned down the list. I found a folder called Fonterama. When I tried to open it, there was a message that required a password. I thought it must have been something the Windows people put there, but I idly typed in our standard 'saltandpepper' password. Rejected. Our other main ones were cinnamonbuns and yummymeatballs. All food, you might have noticed! However, it was a surprise when yummymeatballs opened the folder.

I knew in an instant that there was a problem. The folder was full of photos. I knew the icons. But equally I knew they should not be there, and not in a password-protected file, buried within a rarely used folder which was supposed to be devoted to fonts. I shivered, not with cold, but with dread. I looked around, afraid that Anthony might walk in on me, though I was doing nothing wrong, and I knew he was at work. Now that I had come this far, I had to know what was in the photos. I shut my eyes and double clicked an image at random.

The picture filled my screen, and I shut my eyes and looked away. It was a photo like the ones I had seen in the police station. Same style, same sickness. I shut the photo and clicked another at random. Same type of thing. Shit. I closed the files, logged off, and shut the computer. What on earth should I do? My head started pounding, and I could almost hear the thud of my heart. Where had these images come from? Why were they hidden?

Many questions came to my mind, but before anything else, I needed to speak to Nellie. I sent her a text asking if we could meet. Her reply message was brief. *"I'll wait for your call. Any time. Nell xx"*

I rang her mobile immediately. I could hear the delight in her voice. Ten minutes later, I was in the car, and twenty saw me in the café. Nellie was wearing her 'fortune teller's outfit' – a kaftan-like creation in orange, with a matching headscarf with the tails dripping on each shoulder. We hugged, and the embrace went on for ages. It felt good.

"Before we talk about the Other Thing," I said as I waved at the waiter. "I have another problem to ask you about." She nodded. I stirred sugar into my coffee absentmindedly. I had got quite used to sugar at my police station café.

"You know how Anthony had lots of images on his computer?" She nodded. Suddenly I didn't know how to go on, and tears welled up in my eyes.

"What's happened?" Nellie leaned forward, concern in her eyes.

"I don't know. That's the trouble. I was just looking in some folders on my computer, and I came across..." I stopped, and remembered I had brought my laptop. "Look, I'll show you."

It didn't take long for the computer to wake up, and then I showed Nellie how I had come across the file. "And the thing is, Nell, it's password protected, and it's OUR password. And that frightens me, it terrifies me. I can't see any way that these photos got there unless Anthony put them there himself." And that was as far as I could get before I found myself sobbing into a hanky.

Nellie pulled the computer towards her, and I guess she opened some of the photos. I heard her sigh heavily and I snuck a glance at her face. She was biting her lip and scratching her head as though in puzzlement.

"What should I do? Just delete them? Or should I talk about it with Anthony? Maybe they got there by mistake. You know how computers sometimes go haywire? Maybe they came unsolicited, and he didn't know what to do with them? And they might have been there for years, you know, because Anthony often used my computer, and I don't know..." I tailed off because Nellie was shaking her head at me.

"Drink your coffee." We didn't talk while we emptied the cups for the first time and ordered a second.

"What am I going to do, Nell? I can't talk to Anthony. I can't face his response. I can't go to the police. But I can't ignore it either. I know you hate Anthony, but he would never, ever do that to me. Not again! He promised, and anyway he didn't have... he didn't ..."

"Are you going to say he didn't have internet access?" I nodded, tears filling my eyes. "But he did?"

"Only since yesterday, I think. Work lent him a mobile. I made him give it back. He's taking it to the boss tomorrow. Tell me what to do! Please!"

"Would you like me to look at the dates on these photos? Then you would know if they were there before all this started."

I thought about it. The risk was that if Anthony had acquired them in the last day or so, then my question of support for him became a whole lot harder. In any case, I had questions about how they had got onto my laptop. But maybe he didn't put them there. Maybe someone else had, and he didn't even know about it. Passwords were not all that secure after all. Anyone could have hacked in. This seemed quite a likely scenario, because Anthony knew exactly what was at stake. Feeling reassured by my own argument, I looked at Nell.

"Someone might have hacked in and put them there. Probably the police would be happy to know about it, so they could find the sender and maybe stop them."

"The police could likely trace the source. How would that help you?"

"Well, they might be able to catch the guys. Then some children might be helped, and might save people from being in Anthony's position."

Nellie wrinkled her brow. "How do you figure that?"

I opened a stick of sugar and poured it on the table, drawing things in sugar with my finger. "If they track the source, like they did for the ones on Anthony's computer. It might take them a while, but in the end…" Without her speaking, I saw in her face the fears I had pushed away. "The source… you aren't thinking… NO, Nell! That's not fair! I know if they are Anthony's that they are old photos."

"And if they aren't?" She didn't say it in an accusing way, just as though she was curious. I felt like a butterfly pinned to a board and couldn't meet her eyes.

"But if I reported it to the police – and it was Anthony – that's the end of everything. He would lose bail, be locked up, and face other charges. Shit, shit, shit! But it isn't him. He could never do such a thing!"

"Listen, pet, I'm not going to make any suggestions. You have to decide for yourself, or ask Anthony. And by the way, I don't hate him. I just think he has an illness. But we need to get this thing sorted out first. Then we can talk more."

We parted with another hug, and I felt our relationship had been saved. I was relieved.

I couldn't face talking to Anthony when I got home. I snuck into bed and lay still. Anthony was snoring steadily. Thoughts kept whirling round my head. Doubts and fears were ousted by indignation that I could even think such a thing, but they crept back nevertheless.

At about two in the morning, I allowed myself to think about the possibility that Anthony had indeed used my computer to download the photos. Now I thought about it, there was no earthly reason why he couldn't have bought a thumb drive for the internet just like mine. Maybe he planned to get the things onto a disc before I saw them. I gave up trying to sleep. Sliding out of bed, I went to the lounge where I sat in the comfy chair and covered my legs with a rug.

What were my options? Ask him or not ask him. If I asked him and he denied it, could I believe him? Up until today, I had always thought I could. He had explained to me how the photos were on his computer, and it was a reasonable explanation. I was still confident that at court this would be accepted. In all other aspects of our life, he had been upfront and truthful. He had never cheated on me or flirted with other women. Logic demanded that I believe him.

But whether or not she meant to, Nellie had planted a seed of doubt in my mind. Why would he do such a thing? Surely he knew it was a risk that I would find them. How could he get access to them, anyway? I left my computer in the house, confident that there was no internet access. He'd even asked me to leave it sometimes. I'd always thought of him as an intelligent man – but then he had accepted the mobile from the firm without considering the bail conditions. That wasn't smart.

What if I asked him and he admitted it? Then I had a real problem. I wasn't sure whether knowingly allowing him to break his bail conditions was an offence on my part. I should find out. What if the police were monitoring my mobile? I firmly banished the panic that was developing in the pit of my stomach.

In the end, I decided to wait and see if more photos appeared in the folder. If they did, I would ask Anthony, and when he answered, then I could decide what to do. It was a wimpish decision, but at three in the morning it was the only one I could make.

I must have drifted off to sleep in the chair, because Anthony woke me at six as he was getting his own breakfast before heading off to sign in at the police station and continue on to work.

"Couldn't you sleep, darling?" He was attentive and gentle and brought me a cup of tea. He was in a white shirt and blue trousers, which looked a bit tight on him. I wondered if he had put on weight.

"No. Woke up and wandered the house for an hour or two. I can nap today."

He kissed me goodbye and, as I watched him leave, I wondered.

Chapter 25

There wasn't much temp work around, and I waited impatiently for calls. I hoped for something long term, maybe four or five weeks, but eventually I was offered a three-day gig at an insurance company in the city. Anything was better than nothing, so I accepted with alacrity. I was familiar with this type of work, and I hoped I could cope with the pressure after weeks away from a daily routine.

The thought of going to work was terrifying, even though I had almost a decade of experience. I'd lost all confidence over the last few months. The alarm went off at seven, but I was up and dressed in my work clothes long before that. I felt sick with anxiety. The entire way into town by train, I felt queasy. At Flinders St Station I felt my way off the train, eyes closed, and leaned my forehead against the cool of the ramp walls. Behind me, I felt the impatient rush of people hurrying. If they were that late for work, why hadn't they caught an earlier train?

I opened my eyes once the crowd had dispersed. I trudged up the ramp, but sped up as I remembered the coffee stop in the station vestibule had great lattes. I joined the queue, then tackled a large coffee and felt better.

I hoped to remember everything that I needed to know about Accounts Receivable. Surely it wouldn't have all been knocked out of my head! What if I had a panic attack like the last one I had in the city? I couldn't talk to anyone about Anthony. No-one could possibly understand, and I didn't want anyone to know.

As I approached the building towards the Spencer Street end of Collins, I felt my muscles tightening and realised my hands were shaking. I shut my eyes for a moment but felt dizzy, so I opened them. It was only half-past eight, so there was plenty of time. I didn't start work till 9 and there was no sense in arriving too early. Another latte and muffin at a nearby cafe seemed to settle the feelings. Then I marched inside and took the lift to the tenth floor without giving myself any more time to think. I reclaimed my stomach after the express ride in the lift. Turning left, I found the reception desk.

"Good morning, can I help you?" The young woman behind the desk wore a lanyard with the company logo and "Naomi" in readable-sized letters.

"I'm the temp," I explained.

"Thank goodness! We're in such a mess! Come through and meet Mandy."

She led me through to the offices behind her desk and introduced me to Suzie and Jackie, the team she had allocated me to for the next three days. They sat me down and explained the program they used. I was familiar with it, and gradually my heart slowed and my shoulders relaxed.

Suzie gave me a pile of papers to process – it seemed the person whose place I was taking had not been doing their job very well. It was peaceful and monotonous work, and I loved it. It took the edge off having to think. They asked me to join them for lunch in the staff canteen.

"Thanks! When I left home, I hadn't thought about lunch. Is there a canteen here?"

Jackie nodded. "The staff café is great – prices are cheap and the food's good."

I had a salad and a huge slab of chocolate cake. My eating habits had been shot to pieces anyway, so I justified the cake by having the salad. We chatted easily over lunch, and the hour fled. I felt as though I had known them for ages. They wanted to know about me, but I deflected the conversation back to them. It was a situation I needed to face in the future, but not yet.

Mandy came to my desk about four o'clock. I looked up, having not realised how quickly the time was going. "Slow down or all the work will be done before your three days are up!"

I smiled. "I'm sure there is lots of work for me to do."

Mandy was about to move away, but at that, she stopped for a moment. "You know, you're probably right! We'll have to see."

It was a great feeling. I was wanted! I was achieving! I realised how lonely I had been. I had never linked my self-esteem to my work, but when everything else in your life is in ruins, work can be a safe, predictable refuge. It had been a good decision to accept the assignment.

On the train home, people kept smiling at me. I looked carefully at my clothes – nothing wrong there. No buttons undone, no odd shoes. Then, as the train went under a tunnel, I saw my reflection in the window, and realised that I had been grinning. My mouth felt strange and tight. Probably because no smile had crossed my face for weeks.

Anthony asked about my day at work, but not in a way that showed he actually wanted to know.

The next day I felt much more confident and almost enjoyed the slow and claustrophobic train trip. It was interesting to look around the carriage and see how people passed the time – headphones, newspapers, Kindles, laptops, reading, staring and sleeping. I was willing to bet that no-one else was in my position, though.

At work I finished the pile of accounts, and they put me on the reception desk over lunch, so I couldn't sit with my friends from the previous day. That was OK, though, because reception was busy and I had to locate people, give directions and answer phones. The hour fled by. After lunch, it was back to Accounts again.

Mandy came over at five, just as I was packing up. "You've finished what we had lined up for the temp," she said with eyebrows raised. "We don't really need you tomorrow. But the boss said that you had done such a great job that you should come in anyway and we will find you something, since you were promised three days."

I was elated. This was fantastic! My old work had never appreciated me like that.

On the third day they put me in Policy and Assessment, and taught me about the procedure for issuing policies. It was interesting work and the time flew. I joined my new friends Jackie, Suzie and Josephine for lunch, and at the end of the day I was sad to say goodbye. Mandy promised to ask for me at the agency if they had another temp position.

Anthony was pleased that I had gone well, but also happy I was finished. He leaned on the bench as I finished clearing up the dishes. "You looked very tired yesterday, and today as well. At least you can rest tomorrow."

I glimpsed myself in the mirror in the family room, and saw no signs of tiredness. In fact, I felt more energised than I had for months, even before this all happened.

"Do you think so? I'm feeling great!" As if to emphasise my statement, I did a little jig with the tea towel, which was still in my hand.

Anthony smiled, but frowned at the same time. "Well, I'm keeping a close eye on you. And I know you have been sick with anxiety. I don't want you to wear yourself down. I've seen how you droop after dinner and fall asleep in front of the TV."

"If there was something more interesting on TV than another cooking program, another so-called reality program or a crappy soap opera, I could stay awake!"

"Look, hon, you're running yourself ragged over me. I appreciate it, but I don't want you having a nervous breakdown either."

I gave the kitchen bench a final swipe with the cloth. "Nee, I haven't been at work for weeks. It's always tiring after holidays, too – just getting back in the swing of things. And I brought home some money!"

He led me to the couch. "Money isn't everything."

I looked at him. "Yes, it *is*."

He put his arm around me. "When I think of all you are doing, and then trying to work on top of it, I get really upset. I wish you'd take a break."

"This placement is finished anyway and there aren't any more offers in the pipeline, so relax, OK!"

He smiled at me with the melting little-boy smile I loved. His eyes softened. "OK."

I snuggled up to him on the couch. He put his arm around my shoulders and rested his chin on my head.

Chapter 26

During the days at work, my laptop had stayed in the house. The decision to check the Fonts folder again could not be put off forever.

I rang Nellie and asked if I could call in and see her. I planned to ask her to check the folder. I walked up her drive, clutching my laptop. I hadn't told Anthony where I was going. I didn't care at that point.

She welcomed me in and we sat at the kitchen table. I avoided her gaze. The laptop sat in the middle of the table.

"What am I going to do?" My voice wavered. 'Can you look at the folder? Should I talk to Anthony?"

"Erica, listen to me." Nellie's voice was firm but kind. "Let me look at the folder. I'll check the dates on the photos. If they are after Anthony was bailed, then you have a decision to make."

"What decision? What should I do?"

"Let's look first."

I opened the laptop and swung it round to her. I heard the little clicks and whirring sounds as it followed the commands. I shut my eyes and waited.

"Erica. I've looked at the photos. There are many that are dated in the last week."

The statement fell into the room and sat there. The consequences of reporting to the cops started to filter through my head. If they could trace them to Anthony, then he would be in much more trouble. It meant a longer jail sentence. I couldn't pretend that things could ever be normal between us again. I would not be able to pretend that *he* was normal. I said as much, and after a moment of silence, Nellie nodded.

"If Anthony obtained the photos," she said, "then he has continued to betray you in the worst possible way. If that is the case, he has taken the help you have given him, all the support, the love, the kindness, and thrown it in your face. It still doesn't mean he is bad, but it does mean he is very ill."

I closed the laptop and sat back. I felt more in control and calmer than I had earlier. At least now it was confirmed. The only way they could have got there was from Anthony. I turned to look at Nellie. "What should I do?"

She wasn't giving me orders. "What do you want me to say? You have to live with the decision, despite what I think."

"Are you going to tell me what you think?"

She shook her head. "It's not my business. As I have said before, I am here for you. Whatever your decision is, I support you with the consequences by being there for you – if you allow me. If you choose not to go to the police, you will have to decide how you approach Anthony. If you do go, you know what might happen. Do you feel he needs a chance to explain? Or deny it?"

I sat up straight and took a deep breath. "I am going to confront Anthony before I talk to the police. He might have an explanation. I want to give him that chance. I still don't believe he did this."

"And then? What will you do then?"

"One step at a time. I'll tell you what I think will happen. Anthony will deny knowledge of it. I won't tell him I am going to the police. I'll see Sergeant Price. He will investigate it, I'm sure. Then I will wait calmly for something to happen. Then it is out of my hands. It isn't as if I am betraying him. Does that make sense? I was hoping and praying and half believing that it was all a mistake. Now I know it probably wasn't. And if it did come from him, and he couldn't stay away from temptation even while he was on bail, and he was seeing the priest and the psychologist, then I can't help him anymore."

"You will leave him?" Nellie asked the question, but didn't really expect me to say yes.

"Haven't decided yet. Thank you Nells. Now I need to go home."

Chapter 27

I pushed open the front door. The house was quiet, but I knew he was there – well, he had to be, unless he was out with his mother. I walked past the lounge and into the family room. It didn't take more than a glance to see how upset Anthony was. He sat on the edge of the chair, head in his hands, and looked up as I said his name. His eyes were red and swollen.

"What's the matter?" I dropped my bag and ran over to him. "What's up?" The last hour was forgotten. He didn't speak, but gestured behind him to a pile of papers on the table. I picked up the top one. Mr Szili had written with the details of the court proceedings.

"What am I going to do? God help me, what am I going to do?" Anthony groaned and buried his head in his hands again. His voice trembled. "I hoped it had gone away. I tried to forget it. Things were sort of just getting back to normal, and I could almost pretend…"

I patted him on the back, making a hollow thumping sound. "We knew this was coming, Anthony. In a way, it's a relief. It will be over, and we will know where we stand."

"You mean I'll be locked up and you'll be free? There's no relief about that."

"Well, yes, I guess that's the case." I tried to sound lighthearted but my palms were sweaty and my heart was pounding. "But let me read the letter, see what he says." I reached for it, but he stopped me.

"Before you do that, could I have a hug?"

He stood up and we embraced, slowly rocking around like waltzing bears at the circus so that eventually we were facing the opposite direction. Just having his arms tightly around me was amazingly comforting; I hoped it was the same for him.

The issue of the photos was pushed to the back of my mind. When I saw him like this, any doubts I had faded – this was the man I trusted and loved. He needed looking after. In the company of cynics like my parents, I naturally tended to think the worst. They say that no-one knows what goes on inside a marriage except the two people in it. That's true. My parents didn't know the real Anthony, not like I knew him.

I lifted my face, and he kissed me lightly on the lips, then more passionately. Eventually, I untangled myself and pushed him away. "Please show me the letter." His arms fell from me, and I left him standing in the middle of the lounge. "Could you make a cup of tea?" I asked him. He paused for a moment, then started towards the kitchen.

The letter was short and formal.

Dear Mr Grey, I have been informed that the committal date will be 1st September in the County Court. When we last spoke, you indicated you intended to plead guilty to all charges. If you want to change this position, please contact my office immediately."

There were a few more administrative details about what to bring and what time to be there, but it was the date that stood out – the day our lives were to be changed forever.

"Are you going to see Mr Szili? Can I come?" I wanted to be there for one last briefing. "Is it OK for both of us to see him?"

Anthony nodded and poured the boiling water into the pot. I liked my tea fresh and hot. Any idea of talking about the emails had flown out of my head for the moment. The court date took priority.

Mr Szili could see us next afternoon. I met Anthony in town after spending the morning in bed, feeling off-colour. Sleep had been hard to come by, and when it did, bad dreams accompanied it.

"Mr Grey, Mrs Grey." We were ushered into the comfortable leather chairs in front of his desk. "Mr Grey, I want to remind you that what we say here is confidential, and to make sure you are happy for Mrs Grey to be here?"

Anthony gripped my hand and nodded.

"Very well then. I want you to sign off on the pleas, just for my records. Of course it does not bind you, but if you decide at a later date to change your plea, I may not be able to represent you. I have cleared the proposed dates, but I have several large cases coming up which will not give me much flexibility. If this should occur, someone from our firm will represent you." He beamed around at us as if we should be pleased.

"Now for convenience, I have divided the photos, which are the source of the charges, into various sections. The photos from the computer, via the internet, are grouped in year order. If you could just sign next to each year, that will be satisfactory." Anthony signed on each dotted line.

Mr Szili removed those pages and gave him a new page. "Now for the other photos, the ones which were not sourced from the internet." He looked at me from under bushy eyebrows. "Those are also in yearly totals. Again, please sign next to each." Anthony cupped his hand around the page and it was harder for me to see the paper. Anthony signed and returned the page.

"Thank you, Mr Grey. Now, on the 1st of September, you will need to be at the County Court by 8 am, preferably a little earlier, to surrender to your bail. Mrs Grey, there is no need to come. Mr Grey will be taken into custody from the time he signs in, and you won't see him until he appears in court. Do you understand that?"

I nodded.

Chills went up and down my spine. What had seemed to be a future event was suddenly right before our eyes. Images flashed through my mind – Anthony at the court, a backward glance at me as he went through a door accompanied by the police. I shivered, and Anthony put his arm around me.

Mr Szili cleared his throat. "The court hearing will be brief. There may be media waiting and there is no back door to the County Court. If ongoing bail is granted, you will have to come out the front door. If they want to photograph you, they will wait as long as it takes."

"How do they know the date?" I asked. How innocent I was!

"The Court website. And they most likely have contacts in the police. Mr Gurney is the barrister I have briefed on your behalf – Mr Grey has met with him several times. He has all the information he needs. You should be aware, however, that with a guilty plea, the judge may remand you straight into custody, Mr Grey."

We moved instinctively closer together, as though the prison authorities were already trying to prise us apart. "Why? Doesn't that come later?" I pleaded with Mr Szili, though it was out of his hands.

"Just be prepared – in case." He stood up, as if to indicate the interview was over. Time is money, I suppose – our money.

"Thank you so much. Um… Mr Szili?" I hesitated about saying anything, but Anthony had already gone to the door, so I took the chance. "Could I have a private word with you?"

Anthony turned and looked at me. "What about, hon? What's up?" He came back. "Anything I should know about?" I shook my head, but felt my cheeks flush. He just shrugged his shoulders at me and went out. Mr Szili stood, not making me feel at all welcome.

"Mrs Grey, I should remind you I am not bound to keep anything you say confidential. You are not my client – your husband is. If this has anything to do with his case, you should seek independent legal advice from another firm."

I hesitated. Perhaps I shouldn't say anything. "Can you recommend someone?" I asked.

He shook his head. "It's best that you go through the phone book or the Law Institute." I didn't move. "I think that is the correct course of action, Mrs Grey." His tone was grave, but kind. I wondered if he suspected – no, how could he? I was getting neurotic. He opened the door for me, and I joined Anthony by the lifts.

Once on the street, Anthony turned to me. "What's going on? Why did you want to see him alone? You asked him about divorce, didn't you? You're going to leave me!" He was going red in the face, and his voice was getting loud.

"Shhhh," I said. "Keep your voice down!"

"Why? Why should it be a secret that the moment I get stuck away for God knows how many years you walk out and leave? Typical!" he fumed. "Just when I thought we were OK. When you accepted me for what I am. Thanks a lot."

He stalked ahead, leaving me stunned. I didn't know how to react. Laugh? It was an ironic misconception. Ignore it? Run after him pleading? We had come in on the train. There was no opportunity to carry on the discussion until we reached our station. He remained silent the whole train trip like a sulky kid, and strode down the platform ahead of me. He was sitting in the driver's seat by the time I got to the car.

I climbed in. "Have you quite finished?" He started the ignition and shot away between the rows of cars. "Anthony! Don't be so childish!" He ignored me. "If you drive stupidly, I'll get out at the next set of lights. Slow down! We can't afford an accident right now." I could walk home from here – the house was only about two kilometres away. He slowed down, though he said nothing.

When we got home, he put the car away while I went in and sat at the table, ready for a discussion. I folded my hands in front of me, and I suspect I looked very stern.

He threw the car keys on the bench, looking a little sheepish. "Sorry," he muttered.

"I should think so. Talk about jumping to conclusions!" I felt righteously indignant, even though the real topic I had wanted to raise was worse than divorce.

"Well, if it wasn't divorce, what was it? We don't have any secrets. Tell me what you wanted to talk to him about."

Maybe it was my guilty conscience that got the better of me, I don't know, but I felt a sudden rush of blood to the head and yelled at him.

"We don't have secrets? We don't have secrets? No, we don't! *You* do, though. It's OK for you to hide this… this… illness from me for the whole time we have known each other. It's OK for you to expect me to support you through this police business… it's OK for me to have to cope with the financial burden, the shame, the loss of trust? All that is OK, because you have to go to jail to pay for it all. So I should only feel sorry for you? Oh, please!"

I really didn't mean to explode like that. Immediately after I finished I felt horrible. He just looked at me and dropped his eyes. When he went all defenceless on me, I always gave in. Sometimes I think he played on it a bit.

I reached across the table. "Sorry. I think we are both a bit uptight. The court and all that. I'm sorry, love, really. It will be horrible for you in prison. I'll manage OK out here. Can we just forget it and go to bed?"

He was silent for a moment, then looked up. "You won't tell me?"

"It was nothing. Just an idea I had. It isn't important." I thought he was going to pursue it and I frantically tried to think of a reason I might have wanted a private conversation with Mr Szili, but nothing came to mind. He looked and me steadily, and I held his gaze.

Eventually, he shrugged and stood up. "If you won't tell me, you won't tell me. I'm not in a position to argue. Bed?"

He went off to work as usual the next day, and I made some phone calls to solicitors. I chose one about three suburbs away and got an appointment later that week. Mum had rung, so had Nellie, and I had to tell them I had not carried out my plan. I know they were disappointed.

Just after Anthony left for work the next day, the agency rang, offering me three weeks' work, starting just before the committal hearing. It was with the insurance company where I had done the last temp position. I was pleased to accept the job, but asked the agency to tell them I was waiting on confirmation of a medical appointment and might have to have a day off. I couldn't tell them the real reason.

The following Wednesday, I set off for the solicitor's appointment, but all the way I was arguing with myself over whether to go or not. In the end, I chickened out. What was the point? After all, if it was Anthony's doing, then it didn't really matter because it looked like he was going to be jailed anyway – and if it wasn't, then what a horrible accusation for me to make. He couldn't trust me anymore. Anyway, if I was honest with myself, I didn't want to have an answer to my question. I could always make another appointment. The computer sat accusingly on the passenger seat. I tried not to see the disappointed faces of my parents in my mind.

The days rolled along with almost a monotonous regularity. I had become so used to the highs and lows after the initial raid that to have nothing happening was almost boring. It was a real trap. I sometimes nearly forgot that I had a husband who was accused of child sex offences. I sometimes nearly forgot that he would most likely be in jail before the year was out. I sometimes nearly forgot that my life would be changed forever, even once his prison sentence was over. However, most days I felt a deep sense of foreboding, a hot flush that spread through my body as though I was heading for an early menopause. I was hypervigilant, always on the alert for something to go wrong. And of course, it did.

A week later, a primary school cleaner was arrested for placing cameras in the girls' toilets and recording the children. Big headlines, editorials, letters to the editor, calls for capital punishment for child sex offences. The media was on the warpath – and in the mix, they republished the horrible photo of Anthony and called for severe penalties for people convicted of these types of offences. I was terrified. With Anthony's name back in the media, people might try to find out where we lived, follow Anthony, start a campaign. He might end up with a bigger sentence because of the publicity.

I stayed in the house for days on end. I didn't dare go out in case someone recognised me. Meanwhile, Anthony just went off to work as though nothing had happened. Every time I went out, though, first I opened the door, peered out, made sure there was no-one there, then hurried to the car. I became anxious that I wouldn't be able to go into the city to get to the job, so I set some goals, gradually making myself do tasks outside, and eventually got myself on a train without flinching.

I went back to the insurance company in the last week of August. I was welcomed just as I had been before, and this time they gave me far more responsible tasks to do. I was as happy there as I had been in any job.

The first week flew by, and I explained to my boss that I had a medical appointment and could not come in on 1st September, but I would either make up the time or take it without pay. She insisted on paying me, and said that I worked so quickly I was efficient enough to catch up the day missed. I felt slightly guilty that I was deceiving her about where I was going. I said I would come in for the first hour and leave at 9.30 am. She was impressed by my dedication.

Anthony wasn't really keen for me to do this, but as I pointed out to him, we would go to court together at 7 am, and once he went to book in, there was nothing else for me to do until court started. I might as well work.

Chapter 28

I dressed carefully for the court appearance, though there was no real need. My work clothes were usually a skirt and jacket, and for today I added a silk scarf and slightly higher heeled shoes. Leila was making her own way in. It was 'just the committal' according to Mr Szili, and not really necessary that either Leila or I be there, but we had been to every legal proceeding and it didn't seem right not to go to this one.

Anthony and I caught the 6.30 am train together, and were a bit confused when the court building wasn't open, but Sergeant Price appeared from somewhere. I kissed Anthony and watched him go through the police entrance, then hurried down to the office, biting my lip to stop myself from crying. It was a relief to have work to take my mind off things.

At 9.30, I put my head in to Mandy's office and told her I was leaving, then walked up the street to the County Court. It was a foreboding building – modern, with lots of glass.

I kept an eye open for people I might know, or the press. There was a group of people just outside the door, mostly dressed in jeans and t-shirts, smoking. Lawyers in flapping black robes strode into the building, followed by a retinue of assistants with wheeled trolleys or suitcases, presumably filled with court papers.

I put my bag on the screening belt and walked through the security doorway without incident. Straight ahead of me was the display board with the court allocations on it. I already knew Anthony was in Court 7 on the fifth floor. The building was buzzing with people. The robed barristers also had to go through security, but they didn't have to open the suitcases. They all looked hard-faced, as though years of court appearances had made them cynical.

There was a choice of escalators or lifts. I wanted to stay anonymous so I chose the lift. As the doors slid open, I saw a group of people in the carpeted corridor gathered near Court 7, and heard the animated voice of a woman. A green-coated official was barring her way into court. Behind her stood a group of about six or seven solemn adolescent boys.

The woman was right in front of the court entrance. Rather than draw attention to myself, I wandered away from the court and found a hard wooden bench. I could still hear the woman.

"Listen, the courts are open to the public. I checked. You can't keep us out! I looked on the internet and I rang the court. So don't try!"

"Ma'am, normally the courts are open, but this is a case involving sensitive issues and the children will not be admitted. You may come in, but not them. I'm sorry."

"You should be sorry. I know damn well what sort of case this is. Why do you think I brought the boys in? They are the victims. I promised them they could see that the police took this seriously. Now, if you're going to try to keep us out, you ask the judge. See what he says. Please!"

I froze. I wanted to run away, but I was fixed to the seat. The green-coated man disappeared into the court, and the woman got the boys to sit on the seats next to mine. She came and sat down next to me.

"Are you here for the Grey case as well?" she asked as she settled herself beside me. I couldn't escape, and was terrified of being recognised. I frantically tried to recall if my photo had been published anywhere. I was sure it hadn't. She couldn't know me, surely. I had to think quickly.

"No, I'm waiting for a friend." I zipped up my handbag and went to get up, but she kept talking.

"I brought the boys in to see what happened in that case. That bastard, that Grey, he's ruined the lives of these boys. Do you know what he did?"

I couldn't move now, even if I wanted to. I needed to know what she claimed he had done. I shook my head.

She opened her bag and pulled out an envelope, battered from having been handled many times. As she spoke, she took a sheet of paper from it. "This man, he's been charged with a whole lot of offences against children. Some of them were boys from my swimming group. This man told them he was an agent for a big movie producer in Hollywood. He told them he was the casting agent for a new film of *Lord of the Flies*. It was to be set in Australia in modern times, and he needed to film the boys in various poses and positions, mostly in their underwear or swim suits. He said that was so the American casting people could look at them and choose the right ones to play the parts." She stopped to dab her eyes with a hanky she took from her pocket.

"This is the letter he sent to the parents. I let my boys go and be filmed. I just… let them go. I told their parents about it, and I gave permission for them to be exposed to this… monster. And of course, there was nothing. No film. No fame. He only did it so he could see the boys' bodies. He deceived them. He cheated them of their innocence. He got their hopes up that they could be film stars and earn lots of money and be famous. Here, read the letter." She thrust the letter into my shaking hands.

Lies suddenly came easily from me, with no thought. "The friend I am waiting for, she is actually a journalist. Do you mind if I go and show her this so she can scan it? Maybe she can get some publicity?"

The woman smiled at me. I felt sick. "Really? Do you think this could be in the papers? It might help the boys get over things, just to see their story so that other kids might think twice. They feel so betrayed and angry. They don't know who to trust any more. Neither do I."

"I'll be back." I almost tore the letter from her and ran down the hallway. The lift doors were just closing and I forced them open. The lift was empty. I pressed the button for the next level down. I had to vomit. I had brought a muesli bar in a plastic bag to eat during the day. I was able to get the muesli bar out and open the bag in time to catch the stream of thin, hot liquid.

There was a toilet just opposite the lift, and I ran for it. No-one was in there, and I vomited into the toilet and flushed it away, leaving only the lingering odour. I wiped off a speck that had landed on the letter, and hoped the woman wouldn't notice. Then the thought struck me that I needn't return the letter – that I had evidence in my hand that perhaps the police might want. I could dispose of it and they would never even see it. The idea took hold in my mind.

But the memory of the quiet group of boys and the woman with tears in her eyes stopped me. I asked at the office whether I could photocopy one page, and was pointed to a machine. I refolded the letter and sat on a bench, thinking about what to do. If I went upstairs again, I would have to return the letter. If I just kept walking, no-one would be any the wiser – except me. And I wasn't to know whether she had other copies of the letter anyway.

I stopped thinking, and automatically headed upstairs. I trembled and felt cold and clammy, but by the time I stepped out of the lift, I had regained a certain measure of control.

There was no sign of the woman, but the boys were sitting in silence on the benches opposite the courtroom. I was worried now about the time because I couldn't go into the court in case Anthony showed that he knew me. Then the woman would know I was involved with the case. Damn! I paused, thinking what to do, and the boy sitting nearest got up and came over.

"You're the lady with the journalist friend." He made this a statement, and I couldn't refute it. I just smiled. "Mrs Shearer was allowed into the court, but we weren't. She said to wait outside and she'll tell us what happens. I think it's shit that we aren't allowed in."

I gave another small smile, which he must have taken as encouragement. God knew I didn't want to hear any more, but he walked down to the next bench and I found myself sort of shepherded along. We sat together.

"Can I tell you what happened? And you can tell your journalist friend?" He looked up at me with so much eagerness in his eyes that I couldn't tell him that I didn't want to hear his story. I nodded again.

"No-one really wants to know. They just tell us to forget it. But it's hard. We were just finishing our swimming lesson one morning when Mr Grey came along. We knew he was the pool manager, 'cos he had to organise replacement lessons and stuff if we missed them. He called us over, that was the five boys in the junior squad. He said that he had an important letter for our parents and it wasn't about swimming, but about being in the movies. The way he said it, like, it was so real! He said that he was this agent guy for some Hollywood crowd, and he'd sent them videos and stuff and they had often picked kids out for movies from him, so they trusted him. He said some of the Harry Potter extras were boys he'd found."

This was something Anthony had never mentioned to me. The other boy came up. My informant waved him away.

"Anyway, our parents signed this consent form. They were pretty excited for us. Mr Grey got us to meet in the Rec Room at the pool. It was sort of off to the side and down the corridor, so it was quite private. He said it needed to be quiet so he could take good video." He paused, and I hoped he had finished. I watched his face as he bit his lip and blinked rapidly. Then, looking up at me, he went on. "Then he got us… to take our clothes off, down to our jocks, and dance around, 'cos he said that was what's in the book, *Lord of the Flies.*"

I murmured something, nothing, I don't know what. I was mesmerised now, and couldn't move. It was as though I was reading a murder mystery and was about to find out who the murderer was. And, like a work of fiction, reality was suspended.

"Then he picked one of the kids, the biggest one, Darren, and said we had to tie him up, like they did to someone in the book, I think it was 'Piggy'. We got this rope he had and tied the kid up, and he hated it and kept wriggling. Mr Grey told him to be still, 'cos the part of Piggy was really important and he wanted him to get it." The boy's eyes filled with tears, and I blinked away some of my own.

"And he made us do this dance around Darren and do war cries, and then… we had to… take off our undies. It was really embarrassing. At first no-one wanted to do it, but Mr Grey said we had to show our bums, that's what they wanted in America. After we did it, Mr Grey said it was great footage and he promised to give us a DVD when he had edited it. But he never did. When we asked, he said he had sent it to Hollywood and now it was their copyright or something, and we couldn't have it." He looked up at me as though I could help him. I wished I could tell him that it was really me that needed the help. "Then he told us to go, but Darren had to stay. Darren hasn't ever said what happened."

I tried to imagine Anthony doing these things, and I just couldn't. Or maybe I didn't want to.

"I liked Mr Grey. He was always nice to us. But after that I never felt comfortable. It was, like, the way he looked at us."

What could I say to that? "Maybe Darren needs to speak to someone." I was thinking of how my counsellor had helped, but I didn't have time to go on, which was just as well, since it might have given me away.

The door to the court opened and I saw people starting to come out. I had to get away in case Leila and Anthony came out. I didn't want them to see me. They would want to know why I wasn't in court. The boy looked up eagerly, searching for Mrs Shearer.

I took the opportunity to slip into the small interview room and shut the door. There was no lock on it, but I pressed myself into the corner, hoping I was not visible from the glass panel in the door.

I couldn't take in everything the kid had told me. I heard Leila's voice, muffled by the door, and I hoped she was leaving with Anthony. I hadn't promised to come to court; I said it depended on my work situation. I expected them to leave as soon as they could. I peered out of the corner of the window. As far as I could see, the hallway seemed clear. I opened the door and stepped out cautiously. The boys were heading towards another courtroom, led by the green-coated official. Mrs Shearer was at the back of the group, and she looked around and saw me.

Smiling, she turned and came quickly towards me. Taking my hand, and pressing it with both of hers, she bit her lip. "Thank you for talking to my boy. I noticed the difference in him straight away. He looks like a great burden has been lifted off his shoulders. He hasn't talked about it, you know. We've been offered counselling, but he just refused to speak. But for some reason, he trusted you. Are you a counsellor? Could he see you again?"

The irony of it didn't really strike me at the time. I was trying not to show my amazement. "I'm sorry, I'm just a normal person. But I am glad he is happier."

"Thank you so much." She pressed my hand again, then turned to see where the boys were. "The man is showing them another court, an empty one, and explaining what went on. I must go and join them. Thank you again!" She smiled at me and I managed to grimace back at her. I went back to my little room and sat on the floor. This time the tears flowed.

The door opened and Sergeant Price put his head in. He saw me and spurted out "Oh, sorry," before he recognised me. He came in and squatted next to me. "Mrs Grey, are you OK? I didn't see you in court?" I shook my head, but couldn't speak. "Have you got anyone with you?"

I shook my head and croaked. "I'm OK, thanks."

He didn't look convinced but spoke quietly. "Just call me if there's anything I can do. I mean that." I nodded, but didn't look at him. I thought about showing him the photos, but as soon as the thought came into my mind, I banished it.

I suddenly felt as though I had to get out of there before I died. Brushing past him, I ran without stopping until I reached the train station.

Chapter 29

On the way home, I rang Father Nick and asked him if I could come straight away. Dear man, he said, "Of course, and the kettle will be boiling."

When I arrived, he asked me whether it was confession or a talk that I wanted. My mind was in such confusion I couldn't even answer that question. Nick just led me inside. "We'll start here then, and go to the church if we need to. Shall we start with a prayer?"

I nodded, but have no recollection of what he said.

Over a cup of tea at his familiar wooden kitchen table, I tried to tell Nick all that had happened. He had been called away that first appointment we had made and somehow I had never got around to making another. I had been to church, of course, but not regularly. I started talking, but he gently patted my hand. "I see your mother often, so I know what's happening. If it's any help, you can just tell me the latest."

The tears were dry on my cheeks. There was no feeling left in me. I could tell Nick calmly about the episode at court. He listened intently, elbows on the table and chin in his hands.

"Up until now I had been able to distance myself, to pretend that it was all really OK, and that this had been a big overreaction by the police to something that was not so important or dreadful. And I know I had ignored the charges about photos that were not from the net; I just pretended to myself that all of them were from the net.

"Then suddenly I was talking to a kid, a boy who was suffering because of what Anthony had done. And the suffering was deep, and he was ashamed. The *boy* was ashamed, Nick, not Anthony. Anthony has never said he was ashamed. The only thing he said was that he didn't mean it.

"And Anthony never said anything to me about this thing at the pool. Never! This kid, he felt let down and deceived. I'd never considered that before. He was a real boy, not just a kid somewhere from overseas in a photo that lots of people looked at. And now I don't know what to do."

I gulped down the rest of the lukewarm tea. Nick offered me another from the pot, but I shook my head. "It was never real to me till today. It was remote, from another country. At least the photos were – and I just ignored the other stuff Mr Szili told me. I pretended it wasn't important. It was all about me and Anthony, but now it's about the kids. Was that wrong of me?"

"Can I just check whether I have this right?" He spoke tentatively. "After meeting the boys, you see what Anthony did differently. It's more real than when you thought it was just photos, because you could distance yourself from it then. And because it is more real, you are in doubt about your decision to support him?"

As he spoke, I realised the incident was critical in determining what our relationship was going to be like. I felt a sense of release and relief wash over me. I nodded. "Yes, that's right, though I didn't have it in words in my head."

"Do you feel you have to decide about whether you stay with Anthony and support him, or whether you leave him? And if you leave him, whether you still support him?"

I nodded. I didn't want to say the big D word, not in the priest's house, even though I knew he was realistic about divorce.

"How are you going to make that decision?" I had no clue about how I was going to do that. I wanted someone to tell me what to do, not leave it up to me.

Suddenly Nick was out of his chair and in the next room, returning with a box. "Hang on a minute!" He scrabbled around and pulled out a double handful of little Lego pieces. "These are for my nephew when he comes to visit. But they might come in handy for our discussion." He dumped them in the centre of the table. "If we ask 'Should I leave Anthony?', then the green pieces are in favour of leaving Anthony, and the red are for staying, and the blue are neutral. We could get a visual of what you are thinking. Does that sound useful?"

I gave him a watery smile. "Can't do any harm," I conceded. "I haven't been able to decide any other way!"

He asked me to speak each idea out loud and to put the Lego pieces where I thought they should go.

"The Church says we are married for better or for worse. This is worse, but it's what I said in my vows." I picked up a red piece and put it to one side.

"I believe in the Church's teachings." Another red.

"My parents think I should leave." That was a green.

"And so does Nellie." Two all.

"I might be able to help him." Red.

"He has hurt people." Three all. We weren't getting anywhere.

'The law will punish him, and so will society. He doesn't need me to add to his punishment." Red.

"I might not be able to help him. He might have gone too far." Green.

This was useless. I looked up at Nick, trying to appeal to his sense of fair play in making me do this. He smiled at me. "Keep going. Maybe consider more than one red or green piece, according to how big you think the point is."

I swept the pieces aside. "This is too hard. I can't think like this. Just tell me what to do, please." The tears came from nowhere and quickly turned into torrents, then into hiccups. I found myself beating my head against the kitchen table, trying to mask emotional pain with the physical. Nick put his hand down on the table so my head banged on it instead of the hard wood.

"Leave me alone, Nick!" I sobbed at him. "Leave me alone to just feel."

"I can't do that. Let us pray instead."

I had been praying in my head, as if saying "Oh God" over and over again was praying, but with Nick there to say the words, it was different. A feeling of calm came over me. I had spent hours on my knees in the church during the past few months, but somehow the words hadn't come and I had hoped God would just work out what I meant to say. But here, in Nick's kitchen, where I had only ever experienced kindness and compassion, I felt I could say the words without Nick's help. I don't know if they were out loud, but they just flowed.

"Heavenly Father, give me the strength to cope with this. Show me the way that You think is the right one for me to take. I am so confused. Whichever way I look, there are reasons that seem compelling. I don't know what is right. I want to follow Your word and be true to the vows I took at my wedding. But is that the path that You expect me to take? Do You expect me to stay beside my husband? Where is the line I have to draw between staying and going? Give me the strength to see the path You have laid out for my life, and the courage to see it through. Amen."

As I lifted my eyes from the table where they had rested on my hand during the prayer, I saw Nick moving his own lips and I knew he was praying for me, too. I felt comforted. It wasn't as though an answer had miraculously appeared before me in smoke, or a vision of the Virgin Mary had appeared telling me what to do. It was a feeling of warmth and love and support, and then it seemed to me that the power to decide had been handed over.

Without Nick saying anything, I knew God would understand if I choose to leave Anthony – that, despite being for better or for worse, God only expected me to abide by a promise that was made in truth and trust, neither of which Anthony had shown me. And that meant that I could leave him with a clear conscience. Knowing that made it easier to stay because I would stay on my terms, not because my religion told me I had to.

I managed a smile at Nick. "Good idea of yours, Nick!"

He smiled back. "Prayer is always a good idea. Leave yourself open to the message of God and you are more likely to hear it clearly."

By now, Anthony would be well and truly home and wondering where I was. I couldn't face going home tonight, and I asked Nick to ring him while I called my parents. I heard Nick on the phone.

"No, Anthony, she isn't coming home tonight. She is staying at her parents' place. I am not discussing the reason, just passing on a message. She will be in touch with you tomorrow." He raised his eyebrows at me as he said this, and I nodded. "Just not tonight. OK? She said there is food in the fridge… oh, you've already found it? Good. OK Anthony, good night."

He looked at me. "He was fine. He wanted to know why, but you heard what I said."

"Thanks Nick." I gave him a hug. He waved goodbye, and I headed off to Mum's.

My two cousins came over and we played Balderdash, which sent me into hysterics. Dad was so good at this game, and he managed to make up the most extraordinary imaginary tales about movie titles; he had us all laughing. It was only in between that I remembered everything, and a chill ran down my spine. They didn't ask what had happened at court, but Dad said he was glad to see me looking happier. I didn't think I was, but maybe I am more of an actress than I think I am.

I slept well in my old bed. But before I drifted off, for no reason that I could discern, something popped into my head. It had been over six weeks since I had my period. Stress played havoc with my cycle.

The next day, I went in to work as though nothing had happened. I pushed the thoughts of the previous day to the back of my mind and turned away from the prospect of what to say to Anthony when I got home. I ignored his mobile messages. He rang about eight times when he got to work. I hadn't thought about how I was going to explain, and I hoped the words just would come out OK.

When I got home after work, I started getting dinner ready. Anthony came in about seven, having worked late for the boss again. He came straight over to me in the kitchen and put his arms around my waist.

"You didn't come to court yesterday. I looked for you. And I missed you so much last night. Is everything alright?"

I looked up at him, craning my neck against his tight hug. "Let's eat, then talk?" He paused, frowned a little, then nodded, and went to have a shower while I dished up.

Over dinner, the conversation was mundane, as though we were both warily avoiding anything important.

"What happened at work today?" he started, twirling spaghetti around his fork.

"Nothing much. I had lunch with Suzie, and learnt about the fast track system they use for special customers. What about you?"

"Same old, same old. I did some website development for the business – offline, so don't get in a panic, OK?" He must have seen my expression. He didn't know that hidden behind my carefully schooled expression was a seething mass of questions. We ate in silence, and I was grateful for having the television on quietly in the background, providing some cover for the lack of conversation.

As we took cups of tea over to the lounge chairs, I went on the attack.

"Anthony, is there anything more you want to tell me about your childhood, the photos, or anything? Now that the court case is so close, I need to understand."

He folded his arms in a gesture I interpreted as angry. "Before that, you could start by telling me why you didn't come to court, and why you didn't come home last night? I was frantic. I kept looking round the court, worrying that something had happened to you. And then I thought you had left me. I had to sit in that court by myself, and you weren't there, and you promised to come. Why weren't you there? What happened last night?"

I hugged the cushion to my chest and couldn't meet his gaze. I'd never noticed what looked like a coffee stain in the centre of the cream-coloured fabric.

"I needed time to myself. The whole court thing really threw me. I thought I'd be OK, but… listen, you know what's going on in your head and what went on in the past. I don't have any idea. I just imagine the worst. You have to let me in if you want me to understand. It's part of the honesty thing." At last, I was able to look up at him. He was sitting across from me, hands now wrapped around the mug.

He shook his head. "There's nothing more I can say. It's like trying to experience something totally outside your understanding. It's alright for you – you have these incredibly supportive parents and your extended family. I have a mad mother, a bad brother, and four different father figures. Three of them abused me physically, sexually, emotionally, or a combination. And as a result of that, I became who I am – frightened of sex, frightened of relationships, and doing what I had to do to feel better. And then you came along – and everything changed, but too late." He banged the cup down on the table. "And now it's too late for us. I've wrecked that, too."

He didn't cry or shout. He just spoke in a conversational tone. If anyone had been watching us from outside, they would have thought we were just passing the time of day. Only the sharp crack of the cup on the table showed his emotions. But the way he spoke, it was almost as though the speech was learnt, part of a play. Perhaps he did learn it. He knew that eventually I would want to hear it.

Silence fell. I wanted to respond, but I couldn't think of anything to say. I hadn't decided whether to mention the children I saw in court, the photos, the emails… it was all too difficult.

"I want to think about it. I'm sleeping in the spare room," I said slowly. It didn't matter what he said, because that was how it was going to be.

He nodded slowly. "We haven't got many nights left. But you have to do what you have to do. Let's leave it till later." With that, he got up and went to bed. I felt guilty, as usual, but held firm and didn't go to bed with him. I felt proud of that.

To my surprise, I slept well. I heard Anthony get up in the morning, but I stayed in bed, waiting till he had left the house before I got up. I was thankful that I had work to go to. I would have gone mad being alone with nothing to do. This way, I could intersperse thinking with routine tasks.

I had lunch with Nellie. She was visible at the café from a good hundred metres away, in a pillar box red dress with black spots, and a little black hat with a veil. Not many people could get away with that, but on Nellie it just looked right. She looked so different when she wore her plain nurse's uniform; I wasn't surprised that the creative side of her splurged in her everyday dress. I told her what had happened. Most of it, anyway.

"So you didn't tackle him about the emails, or the photos of the kids?" Her tone was neutral, and I knew she was not being judgmental.

I shook my head. "It was too hard."

"And what's the next step for you?"

I took a bite of smoked salmon on potato pancake – my favourite dish at this café. I chewed slowly, to put off having to answer. "Well…" I paused. It was as if saying the words made it the truth, and I didn't want to say them, so I went the long way round. "I'm sleeping in the spare room."

Nellie nodded her head. "Go on."

I took another bite while she waited patiently. "And I am going to support him until the case is over."

"That's two tough decisions you have made." She understood.

"But after the case is over… I haven't decided what to do." The words came out in a rush. Sometimes I thought I had decided to walk away, and other times I thought if I had gone this far I should stay. My talk with Nick had shown me how difficult the decision was going to be.

Nellie stretched over the table and took my hand. "I don't think that's quite true. I think you have decided, but you don't want to be committed to that decision, and if you tell people, then you will feel you have to keep to it."

I thought about that for a moment. "No, I truly feel I have not made up my mind. I go over the pros and cons every day, every spare moment, and whenever I think I have decided, the next moment, the other way seems better, fairer."

"Better and fairer for whom?" she was quick to respond. "Because that's the issue, isn't it? On the one hand, are you better off walking away today, now, for your own life and finding a new path? On the other hand, is that a good decision for Anthony?"

I picked up my bag and got out my purse. This was too hard, and I wanted to get back to work. "Let me buy lunch. I'm working now, you know!"

Nellie smiled. "Listen champ, after it's all over, then you can shout me. For the moment, I pay for my own!"

I knew she wouldn't pursue the topic. For a moment I contemplated talking to her about missing that damn period, but it really didn't seem so important. We kissed and hugged goodbye. "Thank you, Nells." She just smiled at me.

Chapter 30

Suzie, Jackie and Josephine – the girls at work – were lively, outgoing and accepting of me, though I was a little older than they were. Over the three weeks with them, I had many days when I could just forget everything and act normally. I sometimes felt guilty that I was leading a double life. No-one at work knew about Anthony.

Josie asked whether I had a boyfriend, and I said I was married, but he was away so much I might as well not be. They all laughed at this, and invited me to a girl's night out.

"Why not?" I thought. It was my last week of temping at the firm. I had taken off my wedding ring to go to work, but it was always in my purse. That day, I left it at home. I told Anthony I was going out with the girls from work.

He looked sad. "It's girls only?" he asked with a lift of his eyebrows.

I nodded firmly. I was less vulnerable now to his unstated pleas for my company. "Girls only. Just Jackie, Josie and Suzie."

"I'm glad you've found some friends there, hon. Enjoy yourself. I'll… be home."

"Don't wait up for me!" I was annoyed to find myself putting a teasing tone in my voice, almost flirtatious, and immediately worried that I was giving him the impression that he could talk me into staying home. But he didn't pursue it, and changed the subject.

I took a sparkly top with me to work and wore my day-into-evening black pants. After work, I changed, put on some makeup – for the first time in months – and fluffed up my hair. I felt fantastic. The four of us primped and posed in front of the mirrors in the office bathroom, laughed hysterically, and took selfies on our mobiles.

We were going first on a coffee crawl, so we caught a tram to Lygon St, where there was an endless selection of cafés and eateries. They wanted me to choose and I selected Brunetti's, an old favourite. We downed a latte and one of the tiny delectable cakes that went so well with coffee. Next we moved on to Cicalata, and an hour later, the Lygon St Café. It's funny how outrageous and revved up you can feel on a caffeine high and good company. We laughed at the silliest little things – a cyclist who nearly ran into a lamppost when a truck roared past and frightened him, a dog that raised its leg and urinated on an advertising sign, fragments of conversation from passersby – the joy of life seemed to be made up of such simple things. I realised I had lost that in the past months. I wanted it back.

After the coffees we didn't really feel like dinner, so we moved on to the jazz clubs. I had never been a clubber, but the others had been and knew where to go. I found the thought of it a bit frightening – I remembered all those warnings about having your drink spiked and people being assaulted, but the club we went to was nothing like that. It was more like a posh hotel, but with music and dancing. There was plenty of room at tables scattered around the venue, though as Josie said we were very early (it was about 10 pm and I felt it was past my bedtime).

We started off sitting and having a drink, but gradually guys came round and asked for a dance, and within about twenty minutes we were all dancing. The music was 80s rather than current, so it was vaguely able to be danced to. My partner was an old-fashioned looking man. I was relieved that someone asked me and would have danced with anyone. Gary was an accountant. Admittedly, he dressed like one (his shirt had been ironed with creases, and his tie was a thing of beauty) and he spouted at length about unromantic things like balance of trade and the government's interest rate policy. But I was not there for romance, so I was happy to listen to his monologue on the financial status of the country.

When the dance was over, we returned to the tables and waited for the next round of music. Gary had obviously found my responses to the balance of trade discussion unsatisfactory because he went off to another table. Suzie's guy, Johnno, pulled up a chair and seemed keen to monopolise her. We had agreed to watch out for each other, so we made sure not to leave them alone until we got a glare from Suzie and took the hint. They moved off to the bar and left Jackie, Josie and me at the table.

A tall, slim man approached tentatively and asked me to dance. He introduced himself as Shep, short for Shepherd. His first name was Brian, but he said he only answered to Shep. We danced and talked, and I told him nothing about me but listened to everything about him.

I learnt a lot during the last waltz. Shep was a mechanic, had his own business, employed half a dozen young guys, some apprentices, and had a middle-aged lady with a heart condition as a receptionist. None of this was very interesting, but I found him sexy and exciting. I hadn't counted on that. I had come out for a girl's night, but I didn't mean to end up feeling quite interested in another man. I tried not to give off signals to Shep, but as the music wound down, he moved his face towards mine and went to kiss me. I turned my face away, so he kissed my cheek rather than my lips.

"Oh," he sounded disappointed. "I was enjoying our dance, and I kind of got the feeling you were, too."

"I was, Shep. Thank you. But it's a bit early to think of kissing. I'm sorry."

"No, that's fine. I actually appreciate knowing where I stand. I've been to this club before, and usually the ladies expect me to kiss them. I'm glad to meet someone who doesn't!"

I smiled, and we walked back to the table.

"Can we dance again later?" he asked.

I nodded. 'I'd like that. Thanks Shep." He smiled and walked away. Jackie nudged me, and Josie made a face at me as if to say, "Good on ya!" I just smiled and shook my head. "I'm married, remember! This is just a bit of fun!"

"Yeah, yeah." Jackie and Josie elbowed each other and pretended to agree.

I didn't dance with Shep again. The girls encouraged me and I wanted to, but I felt I was deceiving Anthony, and I was the one who had stressed trust and truth in the relationship. The girls thought I was crazy. But as we were on our way out, Suzie pressed a piece of paper into my hand. In almost illegible scrawl, 'Shep' was written with a mobile number. Now I had it, just in case. I tucked it into the zip compartment of my purse.

I couldn't recall having such a fun evening for years – since before I'd met Anthony, at any rate. I wondered why we hadn't gone out more often – but then we were content with each other's company most of the time.

I was sad to say goodbye to the girls, but they were confident that before long the firm would find a position for me. They and I could see how well suited we were for each other. Workplaces are funny like that. Sometimes you can tell the moment you walk in whether it will be a place you can be happy.

I caught the last train home. It was a bit intimidating – a few drunk guys, one possibly on drugs, but they weren't aggressive. My car was sitting all by itself under the single working street light at the station. I turned the radio up loud, then regretted it. The song they were playing was 'Stand By Your Man.' I only heard a few lines before I switched it over, but the song stuck in my head. *"He'll have good times doing things you don't understand"* and *"Tell the world you love him."* Tammy Wynette was right. I didn't understand. But did I not have a duty to show the world I loved him, to stand by him?

Anthony was waiting up for me. He opened the door as I had my key in the lock and kissed my cheek. "Did you have a good time?" he asked anxiously.

"It was fun – more than I expected. What did you do?" I pushed aside the feelings of guilt.

"Stayed home. Not much choice, really. Nothing on TV. Watched some soccer."

"You shouldn't have waited up for me." I had half expected it, but I wished he hadn't. Then I could have slipped into bed thinking about how Shep had seemed to really like me. There was another twinge of guilt, and I contemplated telling Anthony.

"Where did you go? Tell me all about it and I'll make tea." He pottered around in the kitchen while I went to the bedroom to take off my glitter t-shirt and pull on an old one.

"Well, we went on a coffee crawl in Carlton, and then on to a tame sort of jazz club," I called out from the bedroom. "Old time music and stuff. It was nice."

"A nightclub? In Carlton? That's like where all the gangland murders are! You sure it was safe?" He appeared at the bedroom door as I was wiping off makeup with a tissue.

"Perfectly. Here I am as proof." I emerged and took the cup he offered. "I've drunk so much coffee tonight I am sure I won't be sleeping much. You go to bed, and I'll wait up a bit until I feel tired." Neither of us mentioned I was sleeping in the spare room.

"OK, hon." He came over and kissed me again. His cheek was all bristly – by the end of the day it was always ready for a second shave.

I thought having to shave under the arms was bad; I can't imagine having to shave one's chin every day.

Now I was home, my fears seemed imaginary. I had made a monster in my mind out of a man who was just misguided. I heard him in the shower and I wondered for a split second whether I should just slide into our bed and be waiting for him. Then I remembered the photos hidden in the Fonts file, and that I had never asked him about them. It was all topsy-turvy again. I went into the spare room and shut the door.

I tossed and turned that night. Visions of Shep, children at the swimming pool, our wedding day and my parents all presented themselves in various combinations. Sometimes the horrible photo of Anthony in the paper appeared before my eyes. Most of the time I was sure I was awake and these were just thoughts; other times, I thought they were nightmares. But by morning, I was fast asleep and didn't hear Anthony leave for work. It was the weekend and I was sad to finish my temp job, but he was working as many days as he could – partly for the money, partly to keep busy.

It was after 9 am when I got up. I packed the laptop in its bag and set off to visit my parents. I wanted one last chance to discuss things with them. I pulled up in the driveway and saw Dad in the vegetable garden at the back.

Instead of going in the door, I went down the drive and opened the gate. Dad didn't hear me and I watched him for a few moments. He was leaning on his favourite shovel, looking out at the vegetables. There was something indefinably older about him. Maybe it was his drooping shoulders, or his head hanging slightly. There were some wrinkles I didn't recall seeing before. He didn't have the soldier-straight back and the determined look that I remembered. I wondered if his distress over my situation had caused this. Despite the times I got angry about their interference, I knew my parents loved me deeply and only wanted things to go right for me.

"Hey, Dad!" I called to him and he swung round, his face lighting up with a smile.

He came towards me, holding his arms out. "Little one! How good to see you!" I loved his hugs. You were never in doubt of how much he cared for you when you got one of those hugs. "Let's go in – your mother's inside."

He speared the spade into the garden bed, and as we walked toward the back door he pointed out the progress of the cauliflowers, broccoli and sprouts. "I have a lot of trouble with that white cabbage moth, you know. I sit here and try to catch them, but they move too quickly for me. They can really ruin my cabbages."

I smiled. "But your veggies always taste wonderful, Dad. I must have some lessons in how you do it." We linked arms.

"You never showed any interest in gardens before! I tried to get you to help me weeding, but you knew best and pulled out all the carrots." I laughed, remembering his distress at his baby carrots being uprooted before they were even an inch long. It became a family folklore story repeated to visitors for years.

Mum was baking as usual on a Saturday morning, and the smell of fresh butter biscuits filled the kitchen. She had seen me arrive, and the tea was already on the table. When we had our steaming cups and a biscuit, they both looked at me expectantly.

"*Cica*, there is a different feel about you. Something has changed. What's going on?"

It was difficult to start, but eventually I told them that Nellie and I had discovered some new photos, and I had decided I was going to take them to the police. I saw them exchange glances, and Dad offered to come with me to the police station. I thought about it. I wanted so much to be independent, but doing this alone was tough. I agreed. "But I don't want you to say anything, Dad. Just be there with me, OK?"

He went to have a shower and make himself respectable. Mum smiled at me, then got up to clear the table. "This must have been a hard decision, pet. But whatever happens, you know we will be here for you."

I blinked away tears. My family was a real blessing, and Nellie. You don't know who your friends are until you are in a tough spot. Then you find out how shallow most people are. When the going gets tough, they certainly disappear.

Chapter 31

I drove to the police station. I had no idea if Sergeant Price worked on a Saturday, but luck favoured me – he was there and available. I introduced him to Dad, and then we went to a small interview room along with another constable. I brought my laptop with me.

"How can I help you, Mrs Grey?" He indicated seats on the far side of the table, and he and another man in plain clothes sat opposite. We refused an offer of coffee. I just wanted to get this over.

"I have a dilemma, and I thought I should ask your advice." Dad put his hand on my shoulder; he could see I was nervous.

"Is it to do with Mr Grey's case?" He frowned at me. "It's just that I might have to caution you before you say anything, if it's relevant to the case. Is it?"

"I have no idea. It sounds awful. Why do you need to caution me? I haven't done anything wrong! Maybe I'd better not say anything." I started to panic and went to stand up. Dad murmured something in Hungarian and pulled my sleeve so that I came back to my seat.

My calmness deserted me. I had been thinking about this for so long and now it seemed like I would not be able to say anything.

"The caution is just to preserve your legal rights, and ours. I will tape the interview. I don't want to frighten you, but I don't know what you are going to say, and I think it's important that we do this right. Is that OK?"

I looked at Dad and he nodded. He was certainly obeying my instructions not to say anything. In turn, I nodded at Sergeant Price.

His sidekick left the room and moments later wheeled in a machine and plugged it in. "Are you OK to start?" They had pens and paper in front of them, and the other man was writing busily. I felt guilty before we'd even started. Sergeant Price raised his eyebrows at me, and I nodded.

"This is a taped interview between Erica Grey and Sergeant Alexander Price on Saturday 3rd October. Mrs Grey, do you agree the time now is 11.03 by my watch?"

"Yes." Just like the first time, it seemed an unnecessary amount of detail.

Sergeant Price went on. "Also present are…"

The other man spoke. "Senior Constable Dennis Prior."

Sergeant Price continued. "And Jozsef Binzer, the father of Mrs Grey. Mrs Grey, you are not obliged to say anything, but anything you do say may be used in evidence. Do you understand?"

Remembering my previous interviews, I spoke out loud. "Yes."

"Mrs Grey, you are not under arrest and are free to leave at any time. Do you understand that?" Again I agreed.

"How can I help you today, Mrs Grey?" He had such sympathetic eyes, and he inspired confidence. I am sure all the bad guys he interviewed also fell into the pools of blue he fixed on them.

"A few weeks ago, I was playing on my computer, and I found myself looking for a particular font that I liked, but it wasn't there. I knew there was a folder on the hard drive called Fonts." I stopped, getting to the hard part.

"Please go on, Mrs Grey. Take your time."

I swallowed. "OK. I found the Fonts folder and opened it." He nodded. "In there was a folder I didn't recognise. I clicked on it, but it asked for a password. I thought that was a bit strange, but I tried the usual passwords that we use, and one of them opened it. The first thing I saw was a file called 'Photos'."

Both men sat up, alert the moment I mentioned photos. "What did you do next?"

"I looked at the titles. They were called things like "BareBabies" and "Babies for U" and "xxxlittlies." I opened one, and it was like the photos you showed me from Anthony's computer. I don't know where they are coming from and I don't know what to do about it. But because it can't be Anthony, I thought you ought to know."

There was silence for a moment before Sergeant Price spoke. "Has Anthony had access to your computer? Or any computer?"

"My computer is usually in my car. I have a little memory stick to access the internet but I haven't even told Anthony that I have it." I didn't mention the mobile phone – they were detectives; let them detect.

"Can I see the photos you are talking about?"

"I brought my laptop so I should be able to show you." I opened the computer and there was silence in the room while it booted up. Once I put in my password, Sergeant Price held out his hand.

"Can I do this now? I'd like to swing the computer round so that the camera can catch what I am doing." I didn't speak, just pushed it over.

Sergeant Price pushed the computer around so the screen was facing the camera in the recording machine, and clicked on the first of the photos. He nodded. "These look to have come from the same source." He swung it around to Constable Prior, who continued to open the photos while Sergeant Price went on. "How long ago did you find these?"

I found myself in tears, though I had no conscious wish to cry. Dad produced a hanky, and I mopped myself up. "About two weeks ago."

"These are dated from about a month ago." It was the first time Constable Prior had spoken since the start of the interview.

"May we try to source these?" Sergeant Price spoke quietly, and I got a fright. Somehow my mind had drifted in a split second back to Anthony's arrest, and I had forgotten for a moment where I was.

"Of course. What should I do? Just leave these as they are?"

"Yes, please leave these and we can monitor it. Do you object to that?"

"That's good. Then I don't have to even check it. I can just pretend it doesn't exist."

"Our computer experts might have more luck tracing the sender this time. Is that all you wanted to say?"

I felt the pit of my stomach sinking. Had he detected my fear that it was Anthony asking for the photos? Surely not. Should I tell him Anthony had internet access for a couple of days? No, this was enough. But I must have hesitated too long.

"Mrs Grey? Are you sure there is nothing else?"

I managed a smile. "No, nothing." He looked at me long and hard, but I held his gaze, though I found myself moistening my lips.

"Then thank you for coming in. Interview terminated at 11.25." He pressed buttons, and the machine whirred and then replayed the first few seconds of the interview. It was horrible seeing myself on the screen in bright colour. Sergeant Price opened the three plastic DVD cases and as the machine spat out the discs, he put them into the covers.

"Here is your copy of the interview in case you should need it. I'll let you know how we go." He turned his notepad to a fresh page. I wanted to look and see what he had written, but I didn't dare.

Dad and I held hands as we left the station. "Thanks for coming, Dad. I was glad you were there." He squeezed my hand. "Can you look after the DVD? I don't want Anthony to find it by accident."

As we drove home, I breathed a long sigh. I felt much better. This thing had been weighing on my mind. Now it was done, and the outcome was out of my hands. I had already decided not to tell Anthony.

The final stages of the legal process were looming. There was to be a hearing where the psychologist and priest talked to the judge, and Anthony could say something if he wanted to. It was the last chance to change his plea. He was still prepared to plead guilty to everything. Then the judge would tell us when to come back for the sentence.

Nothing happened for a week or so. I checked my mobile constantly, waiting for Sergeant Price to ring or leave a message, but there was nothing. I often thought about my visit to the police station and wondered if I should phone them, but I didn't really want to know the answer. I had no idea of the outcome of the investigation or what was happening. But at least they had not come and arrested Anthony. I was surprised I didn't feel guilty every time I looked at him.

The agency offered me more work in a bank, and I took it for a couple of weeks, refusing a longer term contract because of the case. It was not as pleasant as the insurance company, but kept me from being in the house all day. Mostly I was stuck in the back room doing paperwork that should have been done months ago – mindless, which suited me.

By the end of the two weeks, I had to concede that I might be pregnant. We had made love over two months ago, just the once, but I was not on the pill, and he had not worn a condom. The chances were low, very low – but nevertheless, I shouldn't ignore the possibility. The irony of even the chance of pregnancy, having been trying without success, overwhelmed me. But I put it aside for consideration later. It was too hard a topic to take on board just at present. Hopefully, I was worried about nothing. But it hung around at the back of my mind. Anthony and I had hardly been speaking. He was working long hours, doing the extra stuff for his boss, and I was at the bank all day and tired when I got home. We had dinner, then watched a bit of TV and went to bed. We didn't discuss the case. There was so much to say, but it was too late to say it.

It was Anthony's suggestion that we went away for the weekend before the court appearance. I didn't really want to, but it seemed petty and mean to refuse. He wanted to go back to Sorrento, but the memory of that was spoilt for me by my swimming experience. I suggested we fly to Mildura and hire a car.

It was quickly arranged. We spent Friday evening at a hotel. The room only had a king-sized bed. I was already lying there when he joined me, freshly showered and shaved. We lay with our arms linked, watching the blinking lights of the town from the full-length windows. The curtains were open, casting an electric glow over the room.

He pulled me closer and turned on his side. "Hon, can I talk to you?" I knew there was no choice, so I nodded and looked into his eyes. All I saw there was expanded pupils. Nothing hidden, no instant revelations. He cleared his throat. "You know that in a few days I might be locked up? If the judge decides to send me to jail, Mr Szili said that at the next court date they will take me away then and there. I'm scared stiff. I haven't known how to talk about it. I want to talk about it, but it sends cold shivers down my spine just at the thought of it. But if it happens, what about you? How will you manage?"

I shifted onto my back, but turned my face so I could look at him. "Of course I'll manage. I can't imagine what it will be like. I don't want to think about it. I'm just as worried about you. What it was like?" Now I swung my body to match his.

He shut his eyes, lips pressed tightly together. "I'm really scared of going back. Really. It was horrible. I think the worst thing was the humiliation. There was always someone telling you what to do, ordering you to stand here, stand there, do this, do that. Call everyone 'Sir' or 'Ma'am'. There were searches all the time, and questions, and everything was taken off me like I couldn't be trusted with it. They even gave me a foam cup with water in case I used a plastic cup to cut myself. I mean, how can you possibly cut yourself with a plastic cup?" I shrugged my shoulders. It seemed foreign to me.

"And apart from not be able to go anywhere, you were always being watched. You weren't a person, just a number. They didn't even think of you as someone with a career and a family. It was just that you were to be locked up, and that was it. They weren't mean or nasty, just formal. I suppose most people they had there were dead beats, no hopers."

I sat up and smoothed his hair back from his forehead.

He paused for a few moments. 'It stank. Everywhere I went, it stank – of sweat, urine, vomit and stale air. It's the smell that haunts me most. The walls were sort of grey cement. There was graffiti, scribbled and carved all over the cell. There was a single bed just big enough to fit on, and two grey blankets, rough ones and a coarse sheet. The pillow was rock hard."

I knew how he liked a comfortable bed. He would have hated that.

"They gave me a single cell, and there was a shower and toilet, but no screen or curtain, so the guards could look in at you any time. And the toilet was stainless steel, no lid, and it stank. I mean, it was like having the toilet right there in your bedroom. Until you brought in things for me, I had nothing but a Bible and the Rules and Regulations to read." He picked up the glass of water from the bedside table and drank it all.

"You had a TV, didn't you?"

"Yes, a tiny one up in the corner, but the guards chose the channel. You couldn't pick what you wanted. And they turned it off at ten o'clock, and the lights went out. I couldn't sleep, and there was nothing to do. I nearly went nuts. I banged on the door and begged for something to read, or something to do, but they refused to give me anything."

"But you were allowed out of the cell?"

"Only for a couple of hours each day. They didn't let me talk to anyone. They thought I might get beaten up. I think most people got to talk to other prisoners, but not me. I can't tell you how glad I was to get those things when you brought them in."

I felt strangely removed from this ordeal as he described it. I remembered that at the time I was frantic to get him released, and I believed everything could be sorted out. Now I was hearing about it months afterwards and it didn't upset me as much as I expected.

"You were in remand, though. Is it the same in the real jail?"

"I think so. I don't know. Maybe there might be more time out of the cell, I think. But it was so impersonal, like you didn't deserve any consideration because you were a bad person, and I hadn't even been convicted. I expected them to treat people more like humans. I just don't know if I could cope locked up for, well, years."

"They have programs though, like education, and there are some industries you can work in, I think. It was in the brochure I got. I mean, they don't put people away for years and just leave them sitting in a little cell? Surely people would go mad that way?"

"Maybe they don't care. Why should they? If it isn't one person, it would be another. It doesn't make any difference to them who is in each cell. But at least you'll come to visit, and I'll be able to imagine what you are doing and where you are going. And you'll write to me, like you did when I was locked up." He looked down at me, eyes wide. "You will come, won't you? Please? And write?"

"Of course." I lay on my back to avoid looking at him. "Why even ask? I've supported you this far, haven't I?"

He nodded without speaking. "It's a hard thing to ask of anyone, though. I do appreciate it, hon." We lay together again. His arm was behind my head, and we nestled comfortably together. Eventually we fell asleep.

I woke in the night and looked at Anthony. His brow was wrinkled as though he was frowning in his sleep, and as I watched, his body twitched and he gave a little groan. I wondered if it was a dream or a nightmare. Luckily, before I could become too maudlin thinking about it, he emitted a long and extremely smelly fart. I climbed out of bed and walked to the window while the smell dissipated.

The weekend away was a good idea. Despite the tension of knowing the case was imminent, we managed to laugh a bit and enjoy ourselves. We flew back early Monday morning and went straight to see Mr Szili one last time. How relieved I would be never have to sit in those chairs again, waiting for the bad news, which always seemed to accompany such visits.

"Mr Grey, you understand that if the judge is contemplating jailing you, then you will be remanded into custody from the court on Wednesday?"

Anthony was wearing his glazed "I'm not listening" expression. Mr Szili must have been familiar with it.

I answered for him. "Yes, we understand that." But it was as though I hadn't spoken. He directed his speech to Anthony.

"Mr Grey, you do understand? You'll stay in custody, and be brought back for the sentencing on the date the judge sets. I'm not sure where they'll put you for the week or so, but you start your sentence on that date."

Anthony sat with his head bowed and didn't reply. I patted his hand. "If the judge is considering not jailing him, then does that mean he could come home like he has in the past?" I wasn't really hopeful of this happening, but until there was certainty I kept a little window of hope in my mind.

Mr Szili nodded his head. "But in all honesty, Mrs Grey, it is highly likely that Mr Grey will be jailed. The prosecution has made it clear from the start that they will ask for a substantial sentence. We will argue that there are no prior convictions, and of course offer character evidence."

"Does that mean the psychologist? And the priest?"

Mr Szili nodded. "I have asked them to be there again on Wednesday, and if the judge seems to be considering our case, then I might also call on you Mrs Grey, so please be prepared."

I was dreading the thought of being called. Just the memory of the few minutes on the witness stand at the bail hearing was enough for me, but of course, I would do it if necessary.

"What would I have to say?" I wished he would tell me for sure whether I had to speak in court.

"Mostly about your relationship, your marriage, how you have found Anthony's character in the time you have known him." I nodded and bit my lip. It sounded easy, but the atmosphere in court was so intimidating, and having to face Julia again...

"Will the other side ask me anything?" It was best to know.

"Not likely, Mrs Grey. They are more inclined to allow the judge to give whatever weight he feels to your evidence. And the evidence of a wife is usually not worth that much – so unless things look pretty grim, I probably won't call you." I exhaled with relief.

"Should we pack an overnight bag or something? What will he be allowed to bring in with him, if the judge does remand him?"

Mr Szili looked at me, I thought with pity, as though it was a silly question. "Nothing, Mrs Grey. The State will provide everything. His clothes will be kept safely and he will be given prison clothing. You will be notified about picking up his belongings once things have been processed."

Anthony and I looked at each other. His eyes dropped before mine. Suddenly, it became more real. It was crunch time.

Like the last few days of a holiday, the rest of the time flew. On Monday night, we ate at an expensive fish restaurant. Tuesday I cooked Anthony's favourite meal of spaghetti bolognaise. I put lots of garlic in the sauce, which in retrospect might not have been a good idea since he would be breathing it over the court officials the next day. It was washed down with a bottle of red wine and Lindt chocolate.

There was a poignancy as we prepared for bed. As he neatly folded the clothes he had been wearing, we exchanged a glance. I think we both realised that he might not need them again for years. I had prepared his suit and tie. Everything had been dry cleaned – not that it made any difference, I suppose. The judge wouldn't change the sentence just because Anthony looked neat. Anthony opened the wardrobe to put his jumper on the shelf and stood with his back to me. I saw how stiff his shoulders were, and realised he was holding them rigidly to try to avoid crying.

We lay awake most of the night, taking turns to reassure each other that it would be OK and that we could deal with things when we knew what we were facing. He said he loved me. We told each other that, no matter what, we would both survive.

Every time I started to drift off, he stirred and pulled me closer. I heard him snore a couple of times – gentle, peaceful snores – but I don't think they lasted long, and he was awake again.

At about midnight I got up and made us some hot chocolate with a dash of whisky. Anthony thanked me, but said I could have left out the chocolate and the milk.

It was one of those nights when nothing worked to send you to sleep. The red numbers on the digital clock glowed brightly; cats fought outside; the street lamp flickered from a faulty globe and cast an eerie glow through the light window shade.

Anthony asked me many times, "Will you be OK?" and I said, "Of course, will you?"

We got up in turns to use the toilet about three times. Anthony put his bedside light on and tried to read, but soon gave up.

At about 5 am, I drifted into a light sleep lying next to Anthony, my hand in his.

Chapter 32

Eventually, it was daylight. It was eleven months and twelve days since the raid, which had started this whole saga. I could barely remember life before. At other moments, it was as though I was living in a dream. My counsellor had said this was post-traumatic stress disorder. I felt it was more a reaction to something incomprehensible.

Anthony looked sombre as he dressed in his grey suit, white shirt and shiny black shoes. He threw a small tantrum about fixing his tie just as he wanted it, and I helped him to neaten the knot. He shaved carefully and used plenty of deodorant and breath freshener. I wore a black skirt and jacket, which I usually kept for formal work occasions. He kissed me and I didn't draw back. The morning was full of last times.

His mother drove us in. Anthony sat in the front seat while I climbed into the back. My parents weren't coming, neither was Nellie. I didn't want anyone there. Leila had been very good about not intruding on us in the past few weeks, and I thought it was only fair to give her some time with her son. I didn't listen to her unending monologue, and Anthony only gave monosyllabic replies.

She dropped us at the court and went to park the car. There were no reporters outside – it was only half past seven. Anthony had to surrender to bail, so we parted at the court entrance with a brief kiss. There was nothing more to say or do. It was surreal to think it might be the last time we could kiss for months, if not years.

Leila met me in the foyer of the court and we sat in silence. She took my hand. I wanted to pull away from her, but I didn't. We had nothing to say to each other. I was glad she didn't ask me my intentions regarding our marriage. I didn't dream of telling her I might be pregnant. If it had happened before all this, I would have been ecstatic. Now it was a nuisance. I didn't care.

The court foyer became busier. Lost-looking civilians came in and asked where to go for jury service, police officers wandered in and out with papers and folders. After an interminable time, Mr Szili bustled up and greeted us, and said we could wait in the court. He told us Anthony's case was third on the list, but that "the other two matters should not take long." I thought how ironic it was to call these life-changing events 'matters' when it obviously didn't 'matter' at all to those people who were paid to be there.

I looked out for the woman who had come with the boys the last time, and was glad she wasn't there. I had decided on a story in case – that my friend had asked me to 'cover' the case for her and make a report. I hoped it would not be needed.

We went through the security procedures and up the escalators to the court. The light airiness of the galleries contrasted with the vision I had in my mind of the cells where Anthony would be waiting. He was somewhere below in the bowels of the court complex, waiting.

I paid no attention at all to the cases that were on first. They were quick, just as Mr Szili had said they'd be. The Magistrate took an adjournment after the first two cases. I felt frustrated. I just wanted the whole thing over and done with. The fifteen minutes dragged, but finally we all assembled again. I wondered if they'd told Anthony what was happening, or whether he was just sitting in a cell.

When the clerk called "the matter of Anthony Grey," I suddenly became alert. Heat flushed through my body and I broke into a sweat, heart galloping. I pushed aside the sudden feeling of needing to go to the toilet.

The courtroom door was pushed open and Julia Obermeyer strode to the table, opened her briefcase and extracted a file. It was about four centimetres thick, and I wondered what all the papers were about.

Anthony was then led in by two security guards. My stomach churned. Visions flashed through my head of our meeting, courtship, wedding, and the happy times in our house. I saw the fish swimming in their bowl, the blue and white coffee mugs, the meals shared on the balcony. Anthony, tousled from a shower. Making coffee, cooking a barbeque. But a memory of the photos brought me back to the present.

The prosecution went first. Julia Obermeyer talked at length about how evil Anthony was and how he deserved everything that society could throw at him. She talked about the safety and innocence of children, and how people in his position had betrayed their trust. She said that the more people bought these photos, the more children are abused to create them. I thought of the boys I had met. She made the things Anthony did sound like something only a depraved and callous monster did. And I was afraid the judge was paying attention to her, more than he would to Mr Szili. I didn't want to look at the judge, but he was higher up than anyone else and everyone had their gaze fixed on him. His face gave nothing away.

Then our barrister was on his feet, looking impressive in his black gown. The clerk called the psychologist, and he went to the witness stand, looking impressively tall and serious. He talked about the results of some assessment he had conducted on Anthony. I didn't understand half of what he said, but I hung on the words "innocent and naïve." I didn't know the context in which he was using them, but I thought they were important. I hoped the judge was listening.

Next came Father Nick, looking grand in his collar and a dark jacket. He flashed me a smile and a nod as he walked to the witness box. He spoke simply about our attendance at church and the talks he had with Anthony since he'd been arrested. He didn't make any grandiose claims, just said that Anthony was not a bad man.

It all went very fast. My heart was beating violently at the thought that any moment Mr Szili might call my name. But after Father Nick left the witness stand, Mr Szili turned and looked at me, and just shook his head slightly. I assumed that meant he was not going to ask me to say anything, and I felt my body sink in the not-very-comfortable seats. I was relieved at not having to get up and stand in the witness box. I might have crumpled into a heap.

When Mr Szili had finished, the judge gazed over the courtroom, shuffled some papers, laid the tips of his fingers together and asked Anthony to stand. I found my fingernails digging into the palms of my hands and all my muscles seemed frozen. I couldn't even turn to look at Anthony, only stare straight ahead and try not to cry.

"Mr Grey, you have pleaded guilty to the offences with which you have been charged. Society does not tolerate offences against children, and rightly so. You have betrayed the trust of young people in your care in the most callous manner. You have abused young children from all around the world, many of whom will never be identified and given the help to which they are entitled.

"I will give consideration to the matters your counsel has put before me regarding your background, previous good character and your prospects for rehabilitation. Sentencing will be in two weeks. In the meantime, you are remanded into custody."

I felt nothing at the words. We had known this was likely. Now I turned and looked at Anthony. He was pale and sweating, and I could see damp patches under his arms, which had spread further than could be hidden by his jacket. I caught his eye, nodded and somehow gave a smile and a wave. He nodded grimly back, and was taken away by the guards who had been sitting next to him. As he disappeared behind the door, I wondered what was going to happen to him. Would this be different from the last time? Now he was convicted and awaiting sentence, not just an 'innocent until proven guilty' casualty of the system.

Leila turned to me and clung, sobbing loudly. It was embarrassing. I wanted to stay anonymous, but this public display was letting everyone know I was closely associated with the case. I tried to detach from her, but she hung on.

The clerk called the next case and Mr Szili came to my rescue, taking Leila's arm and prying her away. "Let's go into the conference room," he said quietly, "so the court can continue."

As we made our way to the little room, I wondered what the judge did at lunch, and after work, and whether his job ever bothered him. Did he sit and read the paper over a three-course meal at the club, or have a sandwich in his office and look at the court documents? When did he read the reports Mr Szili had provided? Did he read them at all? What did he have in his mind when he calculated a sentence? Maybe he sat up till late at night over a glass of fine red wine. Did he remember the people who appeared before him? Did he need the paperwork to prompt his memory when he got around to considering the sentence? How did he decide what to give Anthony? I wondered where he went on holidays. Perhaps he went to visit courtrooms around the world and prided himself on the fair and just way our courts dealt with people.

Well, if he was to ask me, I would say he was wrong about our justice system. If you want people to be rehabilitated, you should take into account their family circumstances and try to provide some sort of system so that in the future, everyone feels they have been listened to, not just the victims. I think, since it costs hundreds of thousands of dollars to put someone through the court system and jail, why not dedicate a certain amount of money to that person, to try and make them conform to society's expectations and get better? Say, put the cost of a year in jail into a fund for each prisoner, and use it to support the person to improve and not re-offend.

Finally, I prised Leila away from the court. Mr Szili had told me I could not see Anthony till tomorrow at the earliest. Leila started the drive home, dry-eyed. I sat beside her, my fists clenched into tight balls.

"Leila, can I talk to you about something? Something personal?"

She was driving erratically as usual, weaving in and out of lanes without indicating, so I was grateful she didn't look at me. "Yes, of course. I don't think there are any secrets between us." She swerved into the centre of the road to avoid a parked car and was tooted by the driver behind, who had to brake suddenly.

I hesitated. I had not told Leila any of Anthony's revelations about his early childhood. It had been so hard for him to tell me – how much harder would it be for Leila? But getting some more details from her would be another little piece of jigsaw.

I took a deep breath. "Anthony told me about the difficult childhood he had. I wanted to say I'm sorry about it. Things must have been awful."

She pulled up at a red light, and glared at a cyclist who had stopped next to the car. "What do you mean? Anthony didn't have a difficult childhood. He didn't get on with his stepfather, but what child does? His brother was difficult, though, I admit that."

"I wasn't talking about those things. I meant about his father and Sam. And the violence to you. It must have been awful."

This time she did turn to face me, brow wrinkled. The light was still red. "I don't know what you are talking about. Anthony has never met his father. He doesn't even know who he is. I never put the name on the birth certificate, and he has never asked me. It was not the man Anthony grew up with."

I was puzzled, and didn't respond while I tried to figure this out. Maybe Anthony had been talking about one of his stepfathers.

The light turned green and Leila accelerated jerkily, barely missing the cyclist in his marked lane. "What has Anthony told you about the family? What do you mean? Tell me!" As her voice got louder, she accelerated more.

I was confused and needed time. "Nothing, Leila, nothing. I must have got it mixed up. Sorry."

"Look, his father left when he found out I was pregnant. I never saw him again. I lived with Rob for most of Anthony's life. Rob and I separated when Anthony was about fifteen. There were no other men around when he was a child. What did he say? I have the right to know."

"Nothing, Leila. We talked such a lot, and I can't remember it all. It was all so confusing. Don't worry, Leila, it's nothing."

She kept at me for a bit, but eventually I turned the radio up louder and she stopped. The beat of the music made it hard to think, which was fine by me. Leila's total repudiation of Anthony's stories left me in a bind. I felt anger starting to rise.

Turning my mind away from what Leila had said, I reviewed the last moments at court, when Anthony had been led out. My mind was filled with images of where he would be. Strangely enough, I worried about what he would eat and whether they fed them lunch. Or maybe he wouldn't get anything to eat until he was in prison tonight. Stupid thoughts. I guessed he would stay in a lockup at the court, and after they finished for the day, everyone in custody would be taken somewhere. I couldn't imagine they would take each person separately as their case finished. The logistics of the custody system was not something I had given any thought to before, but now I wondered – prisoners, guards, transport, food... it all had to be worked out by someone. Later, I found out that they had taken him to the Melbourne Assessment Prison for two nights, and then straight to Barwon Prison.

When we reached home, at first Leila offered to come in, then pressured me to let her in, but I refused. Now was the time to regroup and look at my own options. I felt calm and quite strong, though when I opened the front door and realised that it was only me, and I was alone, my heart started racing, and my hands were shaky. There was bitter sweetness at the sight of two blue striped bowls and mugs in the kitchen sink. Tomorrow, there would only be one. But I had been gearing myself for this moment for months, and while on one hand I was anxious, I also felt something else. Eventually, I recognised it as relief. There was at last some finality to my situation.

Chapter 33

Picking up my car keys, I headed straight out again. First stop was the supermarket. Now that I had nothing further I could do for Anthony, I had to consider myself.

I only bought one item; a little packet which held two pregnancy tests. How difficult it was in the supermarket to even pick them up! I cruised up and down the aisle a couple of times before I swooped on a packet and went to the self-check-out, in case the shop assistant wondered why I was buying a test.

I read the instructions once I got home. I hated having to do urine tests. I could never aim into the cup or bottle. Men had such an advantage in that situation. But it didn't seem to matter with this test, as long as you hit the spot with enough liquid.

"No time like the present!" In the silence, the words rolled off my tongue and echoed through the kitchen. There was no-one in the house except me, but I still shut the toilet door for privacy. Then I set the test aside on the bathroom bench and made a cup of tea. The packet said to leave the test long enough, but not too long. Fussy!

I picked up the cup and cradled it in my hands. All very well to try and be glib and careless about the result, but here, alone, the burden of the decision I might face overtook me and I felt the familiar, dreaded weight on my chest, the beating of my heart and the shaking of my whole body.

This journey had been taken hand in hand with my religion. It was my stalwart companion, the rock on which I based my life. In fact, over the past few months it had become more and more important, increasingly seeming to be a certainty in the shifting ground under my feet. Whenever things seemed too complicated, I thought of Father Nick, kind, non-judgmental Nick, who could balance demands and desires – if not without pain, then at least with calm serenity. Two nights ago, when I had conceded the near certainty of a growing baby, I faced the biggest religious challenge of my life. Now I relived it, there, alone in my kitchen.

As I dashed my hand across my face to wipe the tears, I spoke to God out loud. The words flowed simply and easily. "For heaven's sake, Almighty God, make this test negative. It has to be. You can't possibly put an obstacle so great in front of me – not now, not until I'm ready for it. We only had sex once, and You know how much we wanted a baby. You aren't a cruel God, You wouldn't give me a baby now, not when its father is in prison, surely. When I am stronger, when I understand more what You want from me, then I can cope, but not now, not when I have to give all my energy to Anthony. Why else did you put us together?

"God, I know this life isn't fair, but don't You think I have enough burdens for one woman? I'm not Mary, nowhere near saintly enough. If I am pregnant, if I have a baby growing, Heavenly Father, I can't have it. You tell us to love our enemies – but what if my enemy is my own husband, the man I promised to stay with, love and cherish through sickness and health, for good and for bad, as long as we both should live? How do I reconcile the enemy I married and the vows I took? If I fulfil my promise to You and Anthony, how can I possibly bring an innocent child into the world?

And yet, if I give birth to this scrap of humanity, how can I stay with a man who abuses children? I can remove the baby, I know that, it's easy these days. But will such a decision condemn me to eternal damnation? Never did I think I would even consider for a moment aborting a life. It's murder, I've always believed that. But God, I can't possibly have husband and baby, too. Not in these circumstances…"

Perhaps I was in a trance, because the cup dropped from my hands, spilt over the table and dripped onto my lap. It was no longer hot.

Mopping up the spilt tea brought me back to reality. I pushed away anger, not being sure whether I was directing it to God, Anthony, or myself. Anthony and I had discussed a family many times. The spare room was to be the nursery, and Anthony had wanted to work part time and be a father to the child. We had even tossed a few names around, and despite my dread, I smiled at the memory. I favoured Alex after my grandfather Alexi, and it was suitable for a boy or a girl – but he wanted a flamboyant, badly spelt name like 'Kaaylah' or 'Krist-Yan.' But as the months went on, with no pregnancy, our hopes had faded. Now they were back, just when I longed to be without hope.

What if I leave Anthony? Then I could keep the child and pretend its father was dead. If I valued our marriage vows more than Anthony did, then surely I had the right to decide. But who had the right to decide about the value of vows? God would judge that in His own good time.

I didn't want to talk to Nellie. I couldn't talk to Father Nick. I certainly didn't intend to tell my parents, and I abhorred the thought of termination. I hoped desperately that the test was negative.

I sat there longer than the minutes required for the test, then padded back to the bathroom. Without allowing my eyes to fall down to the test, I studied myself in the mirror. Some grey hairs had sprung up where there were none previously. My skin looked drawn, and heavy bags sat under my eyes. No oil painting, that's for sure. I tried smiling at myself, but it just looked like a grimace.

Not able to wait any longer, my eyes slid down to the bench.

Two lines. Positive.

Pregnant, with his baby. My plea echoed around the room – *no... no... no...*

Test in hand, I walked numbly back to the kitchen. From time to time I looked at it, willing it to be different. "It isn't always right!" I tried to comfort myself. "I know lots of people who have a positive test but are not pregnant!" Of course, I couldn't think of any. Maybe I should go to the doctor, to be sure – but not my own doctor; one at a clinic, who doesn't know me. I didn't want my doctor to know, to judge.

I wrapped the test up and threw it in the bin. I knew exactly when I conceived, as we'd only had sex once recently. How ironic. I trudged back to the bathroom and looked in the full-length mirror, hauling up my top to reveal my stomach. I was pudgy, but I couldn't see any signs of a developing baby. Surely that meant there was nothing there.

I took a tablet and went to bed, but the chemicals were overridden by my thoughts, which churned incessantly through the night.

My faith could not give me the answer. Whatever my decision, I had to live with the consequences, in this life and the next. I didn't want to believe in eternal damnation if I terminated the pregnancy. God, in his all-seeing wisdom, must have understood that it was my duty to devote myself to Anthony. If I divided my loyalties, neither baby nor husband would get the energy they needed. But underlying this was a secret dread – if this is a sickness in Anthony, might this child also carry it? Might I give birth to a child who would ultimately carry on injuring and betraying children? If this is the case, I wouldn't know for years, maybe in my own lifetime, that I was exposing more children to trauma, however unwittingly.

And how do I explain to the child that his or her father was in prison, that society had judged him to be bad enough to remove him from contact with the outside world, to take away privileges and to punish me for marrying him? The child might be old enough to understand by the time Anthony was released. Could Anthony legally live in the same house as a child, even if it was his own? I tossed and turned, pummeled the pillow, and turned it over so the side that was wet with tears was underneath.

Finally, I sat up in bed and heaped the pillows behind me. Underneath these thoughts lay the one I hadn't been able to voice. It was time to be brutally honest with myself.

If Anthony could not be cured of this sickness, then how could I ever be sure that he was not looking at our child in the same way as he had those others? Easy to brush this thought aside and say he wouldn't, he couldn't, but what if he did? How would I know? And the answer had to be that I could never know. He had successfully hidden this from me the entire time we had known each other. I couldn't read him any better now, and who knew what he would learn in prison.

Should I leave him? Write a 'Dear John' letter and tell him it's best if we separate and live our own lives? Part of me wanted desperately to do that, and the only thing hauling me back was the certainty that we met, we loved, we married because it was God's Will. Who was I to override that with selfish human desires? To take the easy path, just because it's easy? Think of the love we had before all this. Remember the warmth in his eyes, the touch of his hand, the way he cherished me throughout our courtship.

Put aside the falseness and the lies – the family history, which was, according to Leila, totally made up. But in the years I had known him, I just had not seen this side to him, so surely it is a small part of him, a tiny part of his character. The rest is fine, upstanding, honest.

Honest! Was he honest with himself, let alone with me? He refused to talk about it. If he really loved me, wouldn't he want to explain himself? Why would he lie about everything? Surely the only reason was to keep my love for him, to allow us to have a future?

How can I make two momentous decisions in this state of mind? I almost screamed with frustration and agony.

I must have slept, because I woke up at seven, already feeling worn out. Amazingly, I found my mind had made itself up while I slept. I would stay with Anthony and try to heal him. And if I was pregnant, I would have a termination. I don't know how I came to change my mind on abortion, having been against it my whole life, but in the morning, it seemed so obvious.

Even though it could condemn me to eternal damnation, it was a risk I had to take. But I hoped a God of Love could not be so cruel. A God of Love would hold me in His arms and comfort me for having to take such a decision. A God of Love would forgive.

Chapter 34

Several days later, I met Nellie at our usual café. She pushed coffee towards me. "Now what's happened?"

My face must have reflected that there was news. In answer, I silently took the remaining test in the packet from my bag and placed it on the table.

"Oh." Our eyes met. "You've already done a test?"

I nodded, still holding her gaze.

"And now you want to discuss what to do?" Nellie tapped the teaspoon on the table.

"How do you know it was positive?"

"Because, my dear girl, there isn't an issue if it's negative!"

We glared at each other, and then I relaxed. My mind was obviously not as clear as I thought. "You're right, of course!"

"Then we had better go and do this test and see. How many weeks do you think you might be?"

"We only had sex once, and it was nine weeks ago."

Her eyes narrowed as she started calculating. "Not that you're counting! OK then. Off we go to the Ladies."

We weaved our way through the tables. People looked at us, but I didn't care, I think because my path was clear. I knew what the test result would be, and I knew my course of action.

The toilets were empty, and we waited in silence for the test to develop. When the time was up, Nellie picked it up and examined the blue lines carefully. "Hmm. Positive. You seem very calm about it. I expected you to be totally in tatters."

"I've already had time to think about it. To be honest, compared to everything else that has happened this year, it somehow doesn't seem a big deal. It happens to people every day. Pregnancy, that is. Pedophilia in the family, no."

"But it will grow into a big deal if you keep it!" Her dry sense of humour brought a smile in me.

The bathroom door was pushed open by a mother with a small child, so Nellie buried the test in the bin under some paper towels, and we left. We wound our way back to the table. We could be more private at a busy café table, where the chatter of people meant no-one listened to anyone.

"We were trying to get pregnant before all this, but I haven't told Anthony, and I won't. If all this hadn't happened, I would have been ecstatic. But now…" I buried my head in the froth of the coffee, licking the edges of the mug.

"A baby is a life-changing thing, my pet! Right at this moment, it might not seem that way, but babies do grow and become real people. If you have an abortion, there are consequences, both physical and mental, and sometimes very long-lasting. I know you think you have come to a decision, but later, even years later, the guilt can really hit you."

"But Nellie, getting rid of it is easy and then it would be just as though it had never happened. It's only one little sperm wriggling up to an egg, after all, and lots of things could happen along the way in the pregnancy. I might miscarry, and that would be worse.

It shouldn't have happened in the first place. The chances of conception were so low that I never even thought it possible. And if I had an abortion, I never have to think about it again."

"It might seem like you would never have to think about it again, but that isn't always the case."

"I have prepared for this conversation for about two weeks, ever since I suspected I might be pregnant. I have decided to have an abortion as soon as possible, and preferably within the next week. I want you to book me in somewhere. Will you do that?"

Nell seemed indecisive. She screwed up her face and bit her lip, looking away so I couldn't see the full extent of her displeasure. At least I think it was displeasure, though she wasn't Catholic, and it shouldn't matter to her.

"I can, of course. Why don't you discuss it with a family planning counsellor? I know a great girl at the hospital. It's such a final decision to make so quickly."

Nodding, I smiled at her. After months of being buffeted in the hands of the law, at least this was a choice that was totally in my control.

"I know it's final. That's why I like it. Come on, if I'm OK with it, why can't you just accept it and go along with me?"

She played with the coffee spoon as though trying to avoid answering me. "As a nurse, I've treated heaps of people who have abortions. Sometimes they end up in hospital, wishing they hadn't. It changes their life in ways they don't anticipate, and it's a decision you can't re-call. Once it's done, it's done. Look at that child there." She pointed at a nearby table where a woman sat with a child on her lap – maybe the child was about two years old, though I'm not an expert judge. The pretty, dark curly-headed baby was spooning a baby chino into her mouth, leaving streaks of chocolate on her cheeks. She was adorable.

Nell stared at the baby. "Imagine she never existed because of your decision."

I patted her hand, in the first role reversal since this whole thing had started. "I know that, Nell. But the decision is made. There wouldn't be a baby if it had been terminated, so no-one would know what the child would be like. Look Nell, it could be disabled, or damaged, or have the intellect of a pea – but I will just never know! I don't want this baby. I've thought about it. I've prayed about it. But in the end, I can't carry it knowing that it might turn out like Anthony. And even if I have it and it's fine, doesn't have any problems, at some stage I will have to explain to it about its father. That just isn't an option for me. What would I say? How could I explain how it came to be conceived when I knew damn well that its father got off on child porn? So come on, let's make the call!" I was relieved and I could see Nell didn't have the faintest idea why.

"What about if I make it for a week's time, just to give you some space to think?"

"Nope. Tomorrow sounds good, or the next day. If you won't, Nell, then I will do it myself. It's not a problem, but I thought I could count on your support, that you would be there with me."

She half smiled and shook her head. "Don't worry, I'll see you through it. I haven't seen you looking this energetic for ages. What about having a chat with Father Nick?"

I started to lose my cool, just a little. "Stop it! I am fine with this decision, really. Look, maybe it's better if I do it myself. I don't want you to be uncomfortable."

It was a mean trick. Underneath, I knew this would make her retreat and help me. Emotional blackmail. She looked at me sternly from under her eyebrows, and without any more argument booked me in to a clinic three days later.

I had told Mum that Anthony would be sentenced in two weeks and that he was in custody. She wanted me to come round but I stayed away, fearing that she might detect something about me and become curious. I had examined my stomach time after time in the mirror and could not detect any sign of a bulge, but still… mothers sometimes have an instinct. I told her I wanted to go away for a couple of nights with Nell and hoped she didn't check.

The next day, I didn't go to church. Instead, I tidied the house, blasting music while I vacuumed and mopped, then watched mindless television till I was too tired to stay awake and fell into a disturbed sleep in the armchair.

Nell picked me up at seven in the morning, and we went straight to the clinic near the city. After the interview and paperwork, I was operated on straight away – a simple procedure they told me, the sort of thing that might be done for many reasons, not just for pregnancy.

When I came to, I was in recovery. I felt no pain, no regrets. While I was eating a sandwich and drinking coffee, I tried to feel bad about what I had done, but I couldn't. In a way, I wanted to feel guilty, to regret my decision. But I didn't.

When Nellie dropped me at home after the termination, abortion, whatever you want to call it, she wanted to come in. "Please let me stay with you and get dinner. I'd feel happier if you had someone with you." She helped me to a chair; I was feeling exhausted.

"No thanks. I'm going to have some instant noodles and go to bed. Honestly, that's all I feel like."

She insisted on preparing them, but left me sipping the chicken stock and sucking up pads of hardish noodles. I was angry with her for leaving, even though I had insisted.

Chapter 35

I hadn't been allowed to visit Anthony for the first two days. Then I needed a little more recovery time after the 'procedure', so it was some days later before I made arrangements to see him. I felt stronger physically, and sometimes checked my feelings, waiting to feel the guilt, but there was nothing. It seemed like my God of Love had excised away that moral value which I had held so dear.

When I finally visited Anthony, I felt stronger than at any time in the past year, both emotionally and physically. The day following the procedure I had been a little tired, and there was a small amount of bleeding, but on the whole it was as I told Nellie – just as though it had never been. Now I felt energetic and, in a strange sort of way, hopeful.

Barwon Prison was a nightmare, a place of sadness and anger. It was another humiliation getting through the security process to get in to the prison. As Anthony wasn't yet a sentenced prisoner, I was only allowed 'box visits' where we sat separated by a window and talked with a pane of glass and mesh between us. There isn't much you can say in that situation. There was emptiness behind his eyes that spoke to me of withdrawal from the real world. He asked the right questions and responded to my enquiries, but everything between us was artificial. Some of the time, we just sat and looked at each other. I was afraid for him, despite the mixed feelings I held about our relationship. I hoped it would be better when we were allowed to visit normally.

He didn't comment on my appearance, so I didn't have to lie about being ill. I am sure it never even crossed his mind that a potential offspring had been created, then terminated. I don't think he had considered anyone except himself, and I certainly didn't blame him for that. I asked him to tell me more about Sam and that incident in the tent, but he just said, "Not now. Not ever. I've said all I'm going to say about that."

The remaining days till sentence passed in a haze. I got up, did the shopping, cooked meals, ate little of them, and called around to my parents' place. Mum and Dad fussed over me the night before the last court process.

"Let your dad come in with you, pet," Mum suggested for the umpteenth time as she dished up cauliflower in cheese sauce, with home-made gnocchi – lots of carbs, but that never worried Mum. "You shouldn't have to do this alone."

Dad looked at me over his half glasses and nodded, lips pursed. I knew he would come like a shot if I just gave him the nod. But just as Mum made the offer, I suddenly worked out what I was feeling. It was shame. I didn't want anyone to see I was associated with the case, even those closest to me who knew all the details.

All at once, I saw what a hypocrite I was. On the one hand, I was visiting Anthony and playing the supportive wife. On the other, I was taking extraordinary measures not to be seen as part of the case. If I was being honest, I would proudly stand up and announce myself to the media as his wife, and face the condemnation of people who didn't understand. What a coward I was, and a coward I would continue to be.

I shook my head. "It's better for me to do this by myself. I know you don't agree with me supporting Anthony, so it's hypocritical if you come." That was a hurtful thing to say, and I felt a rush of regret. It was me who was the real hypocrite. I got up and hugged Dad. "I'm sorry, I didn't mean that to sound like it did. It's only…"

"It's alright, pet. We understand." Dad returned my hug, then picked up his fork and stuck it in the cauliflower. "My favourite dish! Thank you, my love."

He beamed at Mum and the love I saw in his face sent my heart plunging. I would never have that sort of relationship with Anthony, and I never had. There was a bond of mutual respect and love between my parents that I now realised Anthony and I did not share. But I comforted myself with the thought that they had been together for decades, and in their maturity they could look back rather than forward. I knew the relationship between Anthony and I would never be like this. But every partnership is different.

If the truth be told, it would only sap my energy to look after them if they came to court. And it would make me far more obvious. I had learnt so much about the law in the past months, and if they didn't know what was happening, then I knew my dad would hiss questions at me.

After dinner I went home, giving each of my parents an extra long hug and a whispered 'thank you'.

The next day, I caught the train into town. It was anonymous. I did not want to share a car with Leila. I hoped that this day would bring me peace of mind, the end of the road.

I reached the court at 9 am, wanting to avoid the press and any members of the public. After I had gone through the x-ray and electronic doorway, I checked the day's listing. It jumped out at me in black and white. "For sentence: Anthony Grey, Court 13." I looked around for that woman, the one with the boys, but there was no-one in the court foyer. I breathed a silent thank you.

I had to sit outside Court 13 in the corridor till about twenty minutes to ten. The door wasn't even unlocked. Then lawyers started wheeling in suitcases of documents and bundles of papers. Some were in gowns, some in suits. They weren't with our case, so they must have been on later. They greeted each other in a friendly manner, exchanged incomprehensible legal jargon, such as, "Any movement from your man?" and, "Thought about the plea bargain, Micky?" They ignored me, though. Maybe they were on opposite sides in court, but they acted like they were part of some secret society outside.

I had thought I might be able to see Anthony beforehand, but the policeman on the door said it was not allowed.

Mr Szili and Mr Gurney arrived. It wasn't strictly necessary to have a barrister today, but it was part of the package. They greeted me kindly and we went inside, one on either side of me as though I might need support. Sergeant Price and Julia Obermeyer were already there – I hadn't seen them come in.

Anthony's case was the first to be called. I wanted to look around to see if there were any strangers in court listening like I had that other time, but I just kept looking at the front. I was aware of two reporters sitting with little notebooks, and I thought there was a sketch artist behind them, but it was too challenging to turn around. I didn't need to – there was a sixth sense I had developed which screamed out at me, "Reporters! Reporters!"

I heard the door at the back of the court open, and knew that they were bringing Anthony in from wherever he had been held. A quick glance showed him standing between two prison officers, but he didn't look at me.

The judge came in, and we all stood until we were told to be seated. No-one had much to say except the judge. I listened to him, but I don't remember much of it. He started with a description of the offences and Anthony's history, and my mind wandered in and out as he droned on. After that, I only remember some phrases – "Society abhors this type of crime" and "I do not believe that you did not know what you were doing," and "I am mindful that the psychiatrist said you had very little empathy for your victims."

Mr Szili had estimated that five years was a likely round figure. He explained the judge gave a high and a low figure – the high being the maximum prison term and the low being the more likely release date if there were no problems.

Once the judge had started, I didn't think he would ever finish. Why oh why does he have to go on and on? Why can't he just give the sentence and then do the lecture? Finally, he sounded as though he was winding up, and my heart started thumping faster. I couldn't turn and look at Anthony, even though it would have only taken a slight movement of my head.

"Please stand up, Mr Grey." He waited while Anthony used the support from the railing to help him stand. "I have given consideration to everything your barrister had to say. I accept that your childhood was somewhat disturbing, and that events you experienced as a child and as a young man may have caused you to develop particular personality traits. But nevertheless I am not confident that you will not re-offend.

"I consider that an appropriate sentence is one which reflects society's views and which will allow you time to realise how wrong your actions were, and the effect that they had on the victims. Therefore, I am sentencing you to six years in prison, with a minimum of four years and eight months. You will be a registered sex offender for life." He nodded his head towards the guards, and they stood up.

I swallowed hard. Tears filled my eyes, but I blinked them away quickly because the reporters might notice. However, like everyone, I turned to look at Anthony. In the past two weeks, he had lost weight, especially in the face. This seemed to accentuate his facial hair, which had started growing already, even though he must have shaved in the morning. He looked fierce and, more than at any other time, he looked guilty. Our eyes caught, and I tried to smile at him.

He nodded, but the guards were already unlocking the door at the back and he was ushered out of my sight.

I let everyone else leave the courtroom. Leila bolted as soon as possible without speaking to me, but my feet seemed leaden. The benches on either side of me were being filled with other people, friends and relatives involved in the next case.

It was time to go. I couldn't do anything more for Anthony. The words of the judge kept echoing in my mind. *"Sentencing you to six years in prison. Sentencing you to six years in prison. Sentencing you…"* I unclenched my hands and stood up.

As I left, Sergeant Price was shaking Julia's hand. He saw me and came over.

"Mrs Grey. I am sorry." He was considerate, for a policeman whose job it was to arrest people.

"It's tough. But I am relieved it's over. Thank you for what you have done." A thought struck me. "Sergeant, you never contacted me after I came to your office. Were you able to track the photos?"

He looked at me, holding my gaze, and I felt my heart sink. There was a moment of silence. "Do you really want to know, Mrs Grey?" he asked softly.

I shut my eyes tightly, maybe for a second, maybe for a minute. When I opened them, he was still there, eyebrow raised, fixing me with a gaze.

"Do I, Sergeant Price?"

He gave a tiny shake of his head, and I detected pity in his gaze. Then he turned on his heel and walked away. My good intentions vanished, and the demons jumped on my back and made me dance with rage. Betrayed again. The Sergeant had all but told me the photos were acquired by Anthony. Maybe he would lay charges, maybe he wouldn't. Suddenly, I didn't care.

I left the court and walked up to Flagstaff Gardens, where I boarded a tourist circle tram and went round and round the route till mid-afternoon, gazing out the window and listening to the tinny recording playing over the loudspeaker.

That evening, I walked along the beach until it was completely dark, then I sat on the sea wall and listened to the rhythm of the waves. The tide was going out, and I pictured it picking up all my pain and sorrow, washing it out to sea where it mingled with the vast oceans, diluting the emotions until there was nothing left. The next morning, when the tide rolled in, it would bring for me a new beginning.

I think the good in Anthony outweighed the bad. I think he made many mistakes, and that these resulted from his upbringing, his genes, his character, the people he met, of everything over the past thirty-odd years. He would be changed forever by the experience of prison. So will I.

But I have to acknowledge that his actions also changed the lives of children and their families. And that is the balancing act I need to think about over the next few years. God alone knows how much easier it would be for me to walk away – on impulse, that is certainly what I would do. But it was not a decision I could make when we were in the throes of the case. Now I had six years to contemplate what to do.

I went home, picked up the phone, and rang Shep's number.

Epilogue

I sat in the hot sun, contentedly watching the children from the beach chair. They played on the sand, darting in and out of the water in their little swimming togs and squealing with delight. They had built a large but lopsided castle, complete with a moat.

Three-year-old Constance busily decorated the construction with shells and seaweed, while older brother Adam dug frantically in the wet sand near the water to divert the oncoming wave from knocking over their creation.

Out of the corner of my eye, I saw another child, maybe seven or eight years old, watching them. The same age my first baby would have been. She had a sense of serenity and stillness, perhaps of envy. She had curly fair hair, and wore a blue waisted dress with a sash tied into a bow. But when I looked again, she wasn't there.

On the chair next to me, Shep snoozed, a can of beer loosely held in one hand.

The tears dried on my cheeks.

Acknowledgements

I would like to thank all those friends and relatives who patiently read and commented on sections of the manuscript, along with the Boroondara and Surrey Hills Writers groups.

I would also like to make special mention of Blaise, from Busybird Publishing, who is sadly missed by the Busybird fraternity.

About the Author

Rosemary is a commerce teacher and school counsellor. She has taught in Canada and England, and worked as an au paire in Germany. (Her pre-employment German lessons resulted in one phrase committed to memory – "Mein auto ist kaput!")

In past iterations of her life, she has been an avid singer, director and performer. She enjoys gardening, knitting, bike riding, and of course writing and reading. Rose has travelled widely, including through Antarctica, Iceland, Greenland, Alaska and North Korea.

For several happy decades she and her husband Peter sang, travelled and taught singing, until Peter's untimely death in 2002. Although this is the first book Rose has published, she has four more in the pipeline.